Irrational Numbers

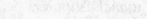

Irrational Numbers

GEORGE ALEC EFFINGER

DOUBLEDAY & COMPANY, INC.

GARDEN CITY, NEW YORK

1976

All of the characters in this book
are fictitious, and any resemblance
to actual person, living or dead,
is purely coincidental.

"LYDECTES: ON THE NATURE OF SPORT"—© 1975 by Ultimate Publishing Co.,
Inc.
"AND US, TOO, I GUESS"—© 1973 by George Alec Effinger, originally appeared
in *Chains of the Sea*, edited by Robert Silverberg
"25 CRUNCH SPLIT RIGHT ON TWO"—© 1975 by Mercury Press, Inc., originally
appeared in *The Magazine of Fantasy and Science Fiction*, April 1975
"HARD TIMES"—© 1973 by Ultimate Publishing Co., originally appeared in
Amazing Science Fiction, March 1973
"AT THE BRAN FOUNDRY"—© 1973 by Robert Silverberg, originally appeared
in *New Dimensions 3*
"CURTAINS"—© 1974 by Mercury Press, Inc., originally appeared in *The
Magazine of Fantasy and Science Fiction*, August 1974
"HOW IT FELT"—© 1974 by Terry Carr, originally appeared in *Universe 5*
"BITING DOWN HARD ON TRUTH"—© 1974 by Damon Knight, originally ap-
peared in *Orbit 15*

Library of Congress Cataloging in Publication Data

Effinger, George Alec.
  Irrational numbers.

  I. Title.
PZ4.E27Ir   [PS3555.F4] 813'.5'4
ISBN 0-385-11189-4
Library of Congress Catalog Card Number 75-14818

For the Morristown Whites, especially Dr. Mary Lou White and Mickey, Stan, and Peggy. Fine Americans, all of them.

Contents

Introduction

By

ROBERT SILVERBERG

The essential thing to keep in mind about science fiction as it is usually published in the United States is that it is called "category fiction" by publishers. Among the other categories of category fiction are detective stories, nurse novels, gothics, westerns, spy-thrillers, and *macho* adventure stories; there also used to be such things as World War One battle-ace fiction, baseball stories, and ranch romances, but they vanished long ago. The point about category fiction is that it is supposed to be a predictable commodity—by definition, categories are rigid containers for the thing contained—that will not disturb, baffle, discommode, or otherwise annoy the customer, for annoyed customers tend not to come back to the newsstands in proper Pavlovian style to purchase more of the same.

Category fiction is to real fiction as singing commercials are to symphonies. It is pre-packaged, schematized, formularized, so-many-beats-to-a-measure stuff. The difference may not be as great as that which distinguishes the lightning rod from the lightning, to borrow a figure from Mark Twain, but it might be useful, in understanding these things, to consider Clemenceau's aphorism that military justice is justice in the same sense that military music is music. We are dealing, when we deal with category fiction, in hyphenated entities, tricked out with funny hats, waxed mustaches, stagey accents, and other paraphernalia of stereotyperie.

Science fiction is one species of category fiction, yes. Publishers distribute it with little tag-lines on the jacket that say such things as "Doubleday Science Fiction," or they ornament their product with cute infinity-symbols or atomic-nucleus symbols to indicate its sciency content, or they wrap it in gaudy red, yellow and blue pictures of ferocious robots and soaring spaceships, or they do all three, for the sake of notifying the reader that what is being offered for sale belongs to the s-f category and not any other. But this does not necessarily mean that the reader who reaches by conditioned reflex for that familiar package is going to get the ray-guns and rocket-ships he's looking for. The habitual buyer of nurse novels is going to get a nurse novel, every time out, full of irresistible doctors and patients with menacing aneurysms. But the habitual buyer of science fiction is likely to get almost anything whenever he puts his cash down on the counter.

He might get, for example, a book by George Alec Effinger.

Science fiction is a troublemaker among fictional categories, for, like the class of all classes, it is a category with pretensions toward containing infinities, and a container for infinities is apt to be a lumpy, troublesome thing, constantly undergoing severe stress around its boundaries as odd objects break loose within and head outward on would-be hyperbolic orbits. Probably this is annoying to publishers, who are accustomed to the orderly and reliable cost-accounting phenomena of the other categories and would like science fiction sales to follow the easily computable curves that make for profit without undue risk. Very likely it is annoying to many readers, too. I suspect that most readers of nurse novels or gothics pay very little heed to the author's name on the jacket; so long as Nurse Chalmers' uniform is starched or the light is shining in the attic of that sinister purple mansion, they can be sure they'll be getting what they want. But the science-fiction reader who buys the package on the basis of the yellow-eyed robot on the cover may be in trouble if he's after the likes of Asimov and gets Ballard, if he wants Larry Niven and gets Tom Disch, if he's hankering for Simak and gets Ellison. They all write science fiction, sure, and they usually all get packaged the same way; but what's in the package tends to be a highly individual product.

Like the stories of George Alec Effinger.

Effinger has never claimed, at least not within my hearing, to be a science-fiction writer. You ask Asimov what kind of fiction he writes and he'll answer unhesitatingly and unblushingly, "Science fiction." You ask Poul Anderson and he'll say the same. So will Silverberg. You ask Effinger and he might say that he writes nurse novels, or bubble-gum cards, or mainstream fiction, or he might say simply that he writes stories, or he might try to deny that he writes fiction at all. I don't know. He isn't a predictable commodity. He's not terribly likely to identify what he writes as science fiction, though—not because he'd be ashamed of being a science-fiction writer, particularly, but because he isn't entirely sure that what he writes ought to be classed in the same category as what Asimov and Anderson and Silverberg write, and what they write is by general consensus agreed to be science fiction.

On the other hand, one of Effinger's first published stories, "Trouble Follows," appeared in June 1971 in a paperback anthology called *Clarion*, drawn from the work of the students at the first Clarion Writers' Workshop in Fantasy and Science Fiction. The words "science fiction" appear eight times on the jacket of that book. (Which, incidentally, contains Effinger's next two published stories as well.) Over the next year or two, Effinger's work was published in such vehicles as *New Dimensions, Universe, Orbit, Analog,* and *Fantasy & Science Fiction.* All of these publications were explicitly labeled somewhere on their bodies as "science fiction," all of them were packaged to look the way science fiction usually looks, and all are generally considered by readers of science fiction to be science fiction. If George Alec Effinger's stories are published in such places, they must be science fiction, right?

More evidence. I first met Effinger, then a beardless youth of 20 or so, in Milford, Pennsylvania, eight or ten years ago. I was there to attend something known as the Milford Science Fiction Writers' Conference, or words to that effect. So was he. He hadn't yet published anything, but he wanted to be a writer. Why would a fledgling writer attend a science-fiction writers' conference, if not to learn something about the writing of science fiction?

In 1972 the aforesaid Effinger's first novel was published—*What Entropy Means to Me.* I have a copy of the first (and only) (and quite rare) edition before me at the moment. It says, down near the bottom of the jacket, "Doubleday Science Fiction." When you open the book, you encounter jacket copy that begins, "An allegorical fantasy with many parallels for today." An allegorical fantasy is not quite the same thing as a science-fiction novel, but if you get as far as page 14 of the book you will discover that the story takes place on a planet of another galaxy, to which the parents of the characters had come from our world. Stories that take place on extraterrestrial worlds are normally classed correctly as science fiction. (If you get as far as page 14, you will almost certainly proceed to read the remaining 177 pages of that delicious novel, and you will observe that what you have read is in fact an allegorical fantasy, closer in spirit to the works of James Branch Cabell than to those of Robert A. Heinlein. But it does take place on another planet.)

Effinger's second novel, *Relatives*, published by Harper & Row in 1973, is identified on its jacket merely as "a novel by Geo. Alec Effinger." The biographical squib on the jacket flap informs us that the author "has had stories published in science-fiction magazines," and the copyright page declares that portions of the book were previously published in *Fantasy & Science Fiction*, and the publishers did advertise the book in the science-fiction magazines under the heading, "New Books for S-F Fans," but there is actually nothing about the package to lead the casual bookstore browser to think he is being offered science fiction. The novel takes place on our planet, but in a society quite different from our own, one in which the course of twentieth-century history has been altogether unlike the events you and I have heard about. The parallel-world theme is universally accepted by authorities on science fiction as legitimate science fiction.

Effinger has also published one collection of short stories prior to the book you now hold: *Mixed Feelings* (1974), also from Harper & Row and also packaged simply as a book of uncategorized fiction, labeled, "Stories by George Alec Effinger." The only place the words "science fiction" appear on the jacket is in the flap copy, where readers are informed, "George Alec Effinger is a young writer of extraordinary talents with a firmly established reputation in the science-fiction field," and then are told, "Effinger does not write traditional science fiction. . . ." The stories in *Mixed Feelings* all appeared originally in science-fiction publications; so did the stories in *Irrational Numbers*, and the first story "Lydectes" is a science-fiction story by my definitions, and probably by yours.

What are we to make of all this? Effinger is a writer (young, slender, bearded, saturnine, a Capricorn) who hangs out with science-fiction writers, is frequently seen at science-fiction conventions and workshops, and submits nearly all of his manuscripts to science-fiction publications. He has published two serious, ambitious novels, one of which was packaged as science fiction but really wasn't, the other of which was science fiction but wasn't packaged that way. He has published two books of short stories, one bearing the s-f label, one without it. By most reasonable definitions he is a science-fiction writer, but is what he writes science fiction, and, if not, what is the casual reader, looking for a good rousing tale of adventure in the nether galaxies, going to think of it?

I have no slick answers. I think Effinger is a science-fiction writer some of the time. I think he's a surrealist, a Dadaist, a lot of the time, the sort of person who'll pose for a jacket photo holding a bowling trophy instead of a Hugo, or who'll give all the characters in a short story the names of famous baseball players of the 1950's without explaining what he's up to. What he is, more or less, is a writer of stories who uses the material of science fiction, the thematic accretion inherited from Verne and Wells and Gernsback and Kuttner and Sturgeon and Asimov and Bradbury and Clarke and everybody else along the way, uses all those robots and spaceships and time machines for his own playful purposes.

He writes a kind of category fiction, that is. But he can't be categorized except in that loose cop-out category, the class of writers who don't fit into their category.

Category-fiction writers who insist on messing with the boundaries of their category usually get into trouble. They upset and confuse the great herd of readers who form the commercial hard core of the category's support; their books don't sell as well as those by the people who stick by the established rules; eventually they can't even get published. A writer who insists on bucking that system will probably be destroyed, on one level or another. Some of the greatest science-fiction writers live in quite astonishing poverty, or divert their best energies into non-literary work, because their attempts to transform category fiction into individual idiosyncratic fiction have met with such disaster. A few, like Ray Bradbury or Kurt Vonnegut, somehow get away with producing the uncategorizable; they slip safely through the boundary membrane and cavort freely in the airy spaces beyond. Most, though, fail in the attempt, fall back, and are ground up in the machinery. I like to think that George Alec Effinger will not be among the casualties. He shows, already, distinct signs of survival. He will never be of much value to those who read by conditioned reflex, those who want the energy-eating robot running amok on the cover to be part of the cast of characters inside, but, if we are lucky, he'll continue to delight and amaze and surprise those of us who hope always to find new wine in the old bottles.

Which is not to say that Effinger won't do stories about energy-eating robots who run amok. His cast of mind is such that his very next story could be about a super-Godzilla of a robot who nibbles the World Trade Center's north tower free at the base and tosses it toward Philadelphia. It'll be a story full of thrills and chills, and he'll say so, too, right in the opening paragraph, delivering a neat little come-on to drag the rubes in. Effinger's material includes all the standard schlock furniture of contemporary pop culture; what he makes out of it is something more than schlock, however, something more than pop. There once was an old man in Los Angeles named Simon Rodia who built a kind of Taj Mahal out of broken soda bottles and bits of castoff tile, and Effinger is doing something of the same thing, at times, with his ballplayers and mad scientists and sinister computers. His purposes as writer tend not to be congruent with most people's purposes as reader; but that's their problem, at the moment. I hope it won't become his. I have the feeling it won't.

—Robert Silverberg

Irrational Numbers

Lydectes:
On the Nature of Sport

(Office of His Democratic Dignity,
The Representative of North America

To the Representative of Europe, greetings:

Dear Chuck:

Enclosed you'll find a rough translation of that ms. one of my boys brought back from some planet or other, let me see . . . yeah, the star was Wolf 359, the planet was B. I don't remember authorizing that job. Was it one of our joint ventures? Anyway, my team reported finding extensive ruins of some kind of honest and true civilization, but no living things at all. Too bad. Especially if the damn computer's evaluations can be trusted. I don't know about that machine. TECT was a great idea, I guess, and it's a nice plaything for my boys, but I can do without the second-guessing. I mean, after all, if you're going to be an autocrat, you ought to be a real autocrat. TECT takes a little of the fun out of it, if you know what I mean. I suppose you do.

This ms. I'm talking about has my boys all excited. We held on to it for I don't know how long before TECT worried a clue out of it. Now my team says it has the ms. all figured out, and what I'm sending you is the official-for-now version. If anything changes in the next few weeks, I'll let you know. What's fair is fair, I always say, and you never know when I might want something you have. You can't say I don't lay them right out on the table, can you?

Regards to Cindy.

Best, Tom)

At the conclusion of the comedy, the actors removed their masks and waited for their due. We applauded and shouted praises, particularly for Melos, whom we all understood to be consumed with a strange fever, a symptom of his advanced age perhaps, or a curse from him who strikes from afar. Nevertheless, it was commonly agreed that Melos had given a performance worthy of the daughters of Memory themselves, and we in the amphitheater felt privileged to be allowed to observe. After a time, though, my companion and I decided to leave our seats and walk slowly back toward the center of the city, where we maintain our modest dwelling, even though I am king of this proud land.

"King Herodes," said Dimenes, my friend, "why is it that a man like Melos performs, even though he is ravaged by illness, and stands to gain nothing but an ephemeral sort of fame?"

"That is difficult to answer, Dimenes," I said. "As we walk along these mist-shined streets, perhaps you can help me unravel that mystery."

"I doubt that indeed," said Dimenes. "I cannot believe that such as I can be of aid to a philosopher king."

I laughed. Before we had even left the grounds of the theater, my companion and I were joined by several young men of the city, among them Polytarsus, son of Proctis; Baion of Memnaris; Lactymion, son of Irion; Stabo of Herra; and others.

(Okay, Chuck, does this look the least bit familiar to you? The names are different, and the subject is new, but doesn't it kind of ring a bell? Think, Chuck. Remember Mr. Martinez? Philosophy 101A? Sophomore year? We had to read that Plato, and we made all those dumb remarks in class, and he was going to report us to the dean. I always wondered what happened to Mr. Martinez. Now that, as it happens, I'm the sole authority on this continent, I guess I could look up old Mr. Martinez and make him nervous. But that's beside the point.

This ms. was discovered in a sealed container made of titanium alloy. Along with the ms. was a map, a candle, and a bundle of stuff that apparently was some kind of offering—flowers or fruit or something like that. Now, the important thing to note, and I'm sure you will, is that the map I mentioned was of the Earth. The cylindrical

*titanium container was found in what looked like a ruined temple.
My boys dated the contents. They are over five thousand years old.
What was a map of the Earth doing on Wolf 359, Planet B, five
thousand years ago? Aha. I've piqued your curiosity.*)

"Greetings, King Herodes," said Lactymion, son of Irion. His
manner was open and friendly, in a way that has endeared him to all
the most influential men of our city. He dispensed with the false hu-
mility and deference with which a king in other lands is often treated,
for I had made it clear in the early part of my reign that I considered
myself to be an administrator only, with no special claim to personal
honor. I am pleased that my company is sought more for intellectual
discussion than for the selfish seeking of favors.

"Good evening to you, fair Lactymion," I said. "Has your father accompanied you? It would indeed be a shame if he missed Melos'
grand performance."

"I am afraid that my ancient father will see few festivals to come.
He is confined to his bed, on the orders of the physicians."

"I am truly sorry to hear that."

"We were just speaking about Melos," said my friend Dimenes. "I
asked King Herodes why an old man like Melos would exert himself
so, when it is common knowledge throughout our city that he is near
the grave himself, and that the best thing for it would be a regimen of
complete rest and quiet."

"Perhaps," said Stabo of Herra, a crude fellow and a bore, "he had
to put on the mask and phallus one last time. There is no accounting
for the follies of the senile." The remainder of our party ignored the
words of Stabo.

(*We have guys like this Stabo today, and they're governing billions
of people, not that I'd mention any names. Stabo was just born in
the wrong place in the wrong time, I guess. Just goes to show you,
Chuck. Remind me to tell you what Denny was up to this morning.*

*My boys asked TECT, of course, about the similarity between this
King Herodes and our own good old Plato. Well, seeing as how
TECT is the repository of everything there is to know, final and
ultimate synthesizer of all knowledge, TECT came up with a
pretty outrageous answer. TECT has a way of doing that. Did you*

know that one of my boys asked TECT "What is God?" a couple of months ago? Can you imagine what the answer was? No, you can't. One long, I mean huge chemical formula. A structural formula that runs on in very fine print for 3,370 computer printout pages. You can guess how this excited my team. They're busy right now, building one. A God, that is. They divided that, uh, ungodly formula into pieces, wherever they decided one chunk could be joined to another with a simple peptide bond (You do remember peptide bonds, don't you? Mrs. Assad, Chem 110B.). It appears that God is a ketone. That's funny. I always thought a ketone was a kind of wall paint. Or Pennsylvania, the Ketone State. Ha ha. My boys tell me that the formula is, let me see—I'm checking my notes here—an asymmetric hydrocarbon. That means that if you made a mirror image of the formula, the two wouldn't be "super-imposable." That's why I can't give you a copy of the formula; my team tells me that if there were the slightest error, typographical or otherwise, there would be no telling what you'd build. Pandemonium, in the truest sense. And who needs three Gods? Two will be quite sufficient.)

"It may be of value," said a young member of our party, as we turned the corner of the Panta and strolled across the neutral square before the thieves' quarter, "to examine the nature of all entertainments, to see what they have in common that so drives men to participate, as much as it drives such as us to observe."

"A very fine idea," I said, peering at the young man who had just spoken. Dimenes saw my perplexed expression, I suppose, for he made an introduction.

"My king," said my old friend, "this lad is Lydectes, son of Auguron, leader of the Logic party in Carbba. You may recall how this young man's father aided you during your long war against the Suprina's bandits."

"Ah, yes," I said. I was somewhat amazed, for I had last seen this same Lydectes wrapped in a blanket, held in his mother's arms. "It has been a long time, indeed, but I am glad that our ways have crossed. I suggest that we follow your idea. Does anyone have an objection?"

There was silence from our group, and the only sounds were the gentle slapping noises of our leather sandals upon the slick surface of the paving stones.

"Then let us begin with a definition."

(Sometimes he sounds a little like you, no offense. How you ended up ruling Europe, I'll never know. You and me and Denny ought to trade continents, you know that? You'd be happy in Asia, sitting around and making obscure but philosophic-sounding pronouncements. And I'd love to move my stuff to Majorca. But that would leave Denny here, wouldn't it? Gee, I'd hate to see what he'd do with his sneakiness and my resources. He's bad enough already. And besides, I don't know what Ed and Nelson would say.

Which brings up an interesting thought. Remember when we eliminated the sixth Representative? Everybody except Stan thought it was a great idea: consolidating forces, reducing duplication of effort, etc. Well, maybe it's time for a little more consolidating. I could consolidate Nelson, down in South America. And you could consolidate Ed in Africa. That would give us a lot more bargaining power with Denny, wouldn't it? Think it over.)

"Indeed," said Lydectes, that admirable youth, "give us a definition of sport, a broad definition that entails every sort of entertainment, and we will see if we can find fault. Perhaps in that way we will arrive at a meaningful approximation of what sport means to us, and what proper place it has in the affairs of men."

Once more Stabo of Herra spoke up. "I have an idea," he said, though he had few listeners. "Let us find an inexpensive leaf house."

(At this point, you are probably wondering just what a leaf house is. I did, too, and I asked my boys. After sifting all the material from this Planet B, they came up with a probable answer. That's all I ever get from them, probable answers. Even with TECT's infallible brain; my boys feel a little threatened by that machine, you see, so they always hedge TECT's decrees with some nebulous preface of their own. Do you have the same trouble? Anyway, apparently there was this ancient sculpture or something, I don't really care, and one of my top men said it showed (1) a young man; (2) what appeared to be a pile of leaves; and (3) what appeared to be either a

serving maiden on her hands and knees or a German shepherd.
That's just what he said, I swear. Now you understand how Denny
can keep hinting at taking over, if I got guys in the upper echelons
that can't tell serving maidens from big brown dogs. The point is,
I guess, that this guy Stabo is trying to get them all to find some
cheap bar or whorehouse. I kind of like this guy Stabo.)

"I should think," said Lactymion, "that an adequate definition of
sport, in the manner in which you wish to use the term—that is,
including all entertainments that free men enjoy—would be that set
of occupations that men follow that cannot in their successful performance provide profit, either spiritually or monetarily."

"That is indeed a good beginning," said I. "But under so broad a
roof, would you not be inclined to shelter many things that otherwise
you would shun?"

"How so?" asked the son of Irion.

"By this I mean such ills and misfortunes that befall a man against
his will, and gain him nothing but sorrow."

"For instance, disease and accident," said Polytarsus.

"Yes," I said.

"I, for one, agree completely with the fair Lactymion," said Stabo.
"And, considering the matter closed, I plead that we take up again
my earlier suggestion."

"Well, then," said Lactymion, frowning and studying his strongly
shod feet as we walked along, "I shall have to amend my definition.
Sport is therefore those activities that men follow of their own will,
wholeheartedly, and from which they derive pleasure but no other
gains."

"Ah, better," said the ill-mannered Stabo. "Much better, indeed,
do you not agree, King Herodes?"

(*Hey, Chuck, I think I ought to remind you, before you get the*
idea—like I did—to go out there to Planet B and play Alexander the
Great beside their wine-dark sea. They're all dead, remember? Sure,
you remember. And anyway, Chuck, we need you here. We need
you to stand between me and Denny.

One of the interesting things about this ms. and the objects that
were found with it is that map of Earth. It was pretty accurate, con-

*sidering that it was made five thousand years ago, when our ances-
tors' idea of the universe was rather primitive, to say the least. The
only discrepancy seems to be a gigantic island in the Pacific Ocean
where there isn't anything today except Indonesia and water. There
was a curious symbol drawn in the middle of this island.* TECT *says
it's probably a mythical land, like Lemuria or something.*)

"And what of those athletes or thespians who perform their talents
at public gatherings, and who thereby receive great outpourings of
gold and silver from the admiring throngs?" asked young Lydectes.

"Indeed," said I. "Would you consider that to be sport?"

"No," said fair Lactymion.

"But there are those who perform with every bit as much skill and
taste in other situations, and do not receive a single valius of gold in
return. Do you consider what these men achieve to be sport?"

Lactymion thought for a moment before he replied. "Yes," he said
at last, "in that situation I would."

"Then," I said, as we began the difficult ascent of the Gaetan hill,
"your entire argument depends on the matter of remuneration. But,
for the sake of the discussion, if the men in the latter circumstance,
exercising their so-called sport for the purest of motives, happen by accident or fate to be rewarded, as by, perhaps, a wealthy and appreci-
ative stranger chancing upon them, would their activity cease to be
sport at that point?"

"I realize that my definition was hasty," said Lactymion. "I beg
that you demonstrate to me my error." Only one man laughed
derisively at this point, and that was Stabo of Herra.

(*It gets interesting here. I don't particularly care about these
bickerings—I mean, do you think even fair Lactymion of the swift
foot remembered any of it after he got home? Not if they had serving maidens bent over all around the place. Or even German
shepherds—but we, even we, can sometimes pick up on something
if we're paying attention. Pay attention.*)

"Let us begin simply, then," I said. The others in our party fell
silent, allowing the discourse to proceed. "If, by discussing the moral
values of sport, whether it be for pay or for the elevation of the soul
alone, we permit ourselves to fall into the argumentative trap of

defining good and bad, we shall learn nothing. Let us leave all that aside, except for a single point that I shall mention."

"That is an admirable suggestion," said Lydectes with a smile. "Many a time have my teachers begun to unravel that knot of good and evil, and never yet have they loosened the first strand."

"Just so," said I. "But will you not agree that to emulate the gods is a thing of virtue?"

"I will grant that," said deep-browed Lactymion.

"And I," said my friend Dimenes.

"If we're going on to the House of Sycon," said Stabo, "we must turn aside at this road."

"And have not every one of us seen the gods at their recreation, many times?" I asked.

"Full often," said Lydectes.

"Each morning, before their silver temples, upon the plain of Bry," said Lactymion.

"Until our visit by the gods," I said, "our learned men thought that they had an accurate picture of the condition of the universe, and of our creation as a race, and of the creation of our world and its sun, and of our entire system's place in the cosmos, is that not so?"

"Certainly," said my friend Dimenes, whose place in these dialogues is second to none.

"I do not understand what our scientists have to do with the question of sport, either as game or drama or whatever," said Baion of Memnaris, who had not spoken before.

"You shall presently see, I have no fear," said Lydectes.

"I thank you," I said to that youth, "but if that is the case, the honor for such a discovery shall be shared equally among all of us." At this point, Stabo of Herra left our group, and his part in the conversation is no more.

(*I'll miss him.*)

"Our scientists once believed that men evolved from lower animals," said Lactymion.

"Yes," said Baion, "that is so. My tutor described that theory to me, before my parents banished him."

"It is all common knowledge," I said. "In our library, you may read of this hypothesis, which was known as evolution. Indeed, the theory had a lot of evidence in its support, and for quite some time all learned men in all nations accepted it without question."

"It is perhaps a mistake to accept any matter so completely," said Polytarsus.

"Ah," said Baion, "but that is the way with learned men." We all shared a pleasant laugh.

"Nevertheless, gentlemen, it was taught, and I am sure that as king of this blessed land I will not be held a miscreant for repeating what our forefathers believed to be true—"

"No, no," cried Dimenes.

"Then listen," I said. "Men were thought to have an ancestor that was not a man, some creature that was in many respects very manlike, but not fully entitled to the nobility of humanity."

"There is a certain attraction to a theory along those lines," said fair Lactymion. "It implies that this almost-man achieved his humanity by other means than mere accident of birth. As though his humanity were bestowed as a reward for conscientious effort."

"Not precisely," I said. "But, to continue. Before this postulated creature, there was a stupendously long line of animals leading down through ever simpler beasts, down through animals without backbones and animals that dwelt in the sea, animals that resembled the starfish that raid our oyster beds and animals we cannot even see with our unaided eyes. All creatures, then, were cousin to some primary, impossibly simple animal."

At this time we had reached the crest of the Gaetan hill, where our city's builders had made a small covered place for the benefit of travelers such as ourselves. Though this covered area is now in ruins, we stopped briefly to refresh ourselves and to admire the evening.

(*You are no doubt aware that Denny is preparing even now to stab us both in the back. You know that you and I have always been friends. That's why I'm sending this to you. I know you have little academic interest in this kind of thing, but TECT's analysis and our own political uncertainty in regard to Denny makes this King Herodes' meanderings of more than casual interest. I hope you're taking notes.*)

"It is a very beautiful night," said Dimenes, as he says almost every night.

"Let me ask a question, then," said I.

"Please," said Polytarsus. "And I hope you will continue your tale."

"I shall do both," I said. "A person who appreciates beauty, as our companion Dimenes appreciates the loveliness of this night, is partaking of that beauty in both an active way and a passive way. A person who thus relates to an activity or an object is in a unique position, and cannot be adequately described without reference to that activity or object. Now, as we beforehand put these activities and objects together under the term sport, how does this define the term art?"

"I should think that art is an extreme of that which we were calling sport," said Lydectes quickly. "It is an unfortunate extreme, and in our city is overused by those with pretentions to special sensitivity."

"Perhaps so," I said. "And the word entertainment? For surely, one may be entertained by a work of art or the exercise of sport."

Lydectes spoke again. "Entertainment is the opposite extreme, standing in precisely the same relation to sport as art, but in a negative sense. Art and entertainment are both corruptions of what we meant by the pure sense of sport."

"Now we are getting closer to a definition," said fair Lactymion.

"If you will do me the favor of keeping that idea in mind," I said, "I will go forth with my history of the discomfort of our scientists."

"Yes, yes!" cried the company.

"Well, then, our scientists had the scheme charted farther back than there were living things to record. It was commonly believed that at one time our world was covered by a great and lifeless ocean, filled with chemicals washed from the sterile rocks that gave it limits. These chemicals and elements floated in prehistoric currents for many millions of years, forming combinations and breaking down again countless times, until, by accident, the very building blocks of life came into existence. By the mere fortunate contiguity of certain lengths of chemicals, the first crude living thing was spawned. And in their ignorant vanity, our scientists believed this."

"It is astounding to hear," said Lactymion.

(You know, Chuck, governing a billion people is not the unmixed joy I might have imagined in my childhood. I wanted to go to the ball game this afternoon but, no, I had to stay and get this out for you. Technically this report is still secret. For you, Chuck, I personally, the Representative of North America, solitary dictator of

the wealthiest continent in this part of the world, ha ha, had to okay this drivel. In any other time, I would have been there to throw out the first ball. When I was a kid, I used to watch the games on television and I always wondered who that was, sitting there in those special seats by the dugout. I could have been there today. Instead, I'm still watching on television. Anyway, the Yankees are losing, I don't suppose that means much to you. I mean, I could kill every single person on the entire continent, I have that power. All I have to do is say, "Shoot them" and they're dead, but I can't make the ball game on time. I just want you to appreciate it.)

We left the shadowed ruins on the top of the Gaetan hill and walked slowly toward my small villa. "I recall the day the gods arrived," I said.

"As do I," said Dimenes. "It is something I will carry to my grave, the sight of those fiery silver spears slowly burning toward us from the heavens."

"We all remember that day," I said. "Although you, Lydectes, and perhaps some of you others were very young. It was the day our scientists lost their superb confidence. Those of our people who were called into the gods' silver temples, they who became prophets and oracles, who seem mad to our eyes and our ears but are merely washed with the inconceivable aura of the gods, have given certain bits of knowledge to our scientists. The gods claim that they are not gods themselves, but rather merely another race of men. Although we worship them, as is their due, they claim that there are gods higher than even they."

"Yes," said Baion, "what you say is true, King Herodes, but it is something that I cannot understand, although I have tried ceaselessly."

"I must admit the same failure," said I. "Our scientists could well cling to the idea that we all arose from some primal bath of accidental chemicals, if we were the only race of men among the stars. But to think that the same incredible happenstance should occur twice, why, the odds against that are too great even to consider."

"And the gods of the silver temples claim that there are likely dozens, hundreds of other worlds like ours, all with men like us," said Lydectes.

"Could they have all risen from unplanned accidents, in the same way?" I asked.

"It does not seem likely," said Polytarsus.

"No," I said. "The more races of men that are discovered by the gods, the more they are caused to believe that something greater developed them all. The chances of coincidence diminish into near non-existence. So our scientists were at last convinced, by the evidence given by the prophets who had visited within the silver flame temples of our gods. And the carefully wrought theories had to be abandoned."

"How does this aid our discussion of sport, then?" asked Lactymion.

"If there is a greater god above our gods, an ultimate God, then whatever this God does or desires or thinks must be right, as there is nothing superior to dispute it. Do you not agree?"

"Yes," said Lactymion, "I will grant you that."

"Then, with all the wisdom available to their lesser minds, our gods emulate this greater God to the best of their ability. Is that not so?"

"Again, I cannot find fault with your statement."

"And further, we in our poor way emulate our gods."

"Yes," said Polytarsus, "although at our level our behavior must only little resemble the ways of that greatest God."

"Of course," I said, "but that does not matter. Where we fall away from the emulation of our gods, we enter into sin. Thus, there are those who seek to gain by their imitation of the gods from the sky. They believe there is money or fame to be had in this way, rather than the peace and contentment of the soul, which ought to be their primary concern. In this way, such things as entertainment and art were created."

"I believe I see your point," said the brilliant Lydectes. "Then sport is the faithful emulation of the gods, in whatever form, for the purposes of worship and attuning of the spirit closer to that greatest God of which our gods speak."

"Yes," I said, as we reached the door of my small house. Dimenes opened the gate and invited the others in. We sat in the courtyard and continued our discussion, while the slaves went among my guests and attended to their various needs and wants. "It is for this reason that, along with the consistent but evidently false ideas of the scientists, we have abandoned the foot race, both the short- and the long-distance, the vaulting with the pole, the hurling of the javelin, and

other contests, in favor of the games of the gods: chiefly, the underhand throwing of the small white ball, the hitting with a stick of
the ball having been thrown, the catching of the ball having been hit,
the overhand throwing of the ball having been caught, meanwhile the
hitter of the ball attempting to complete a circuit of stations whose
significance has been lost in the extremities of time and space, and
which our prophets cannot explain. In all these things the men participate with grim faces, and the women run about, laughing. In these
ways we imitate our gods. In these ways we come closer to the
greatest God about whom our gods teach us. Thus, sport is a gateway
to worship and wisdom."

"And now," said Lydectes gratefully, "we have well disposed of
that topic."

"And I must bid you all a good night," said I, and I retired to my
chamber.

(*Well, that's all of it. According to the test samples, the civilization
on Planet B was destroyed about twenty-five hundred years ago.
This ms. and the curious map were made about five thousand years
ago. TECT says, if you can accept this, that an advanced civilization from our "Lemuria" visited Planet B five millennia ago;
Planet B at that time had a culture approximating the pre-Golden
Age Greek society. Our Lemurian cousins so influenced the Planet
B folk that the latter began the long dusty trail toward technical
civilization, copying the style and manner of the Lemurians. That
island culture on our own world then knocked itself out of existence and disappeared from our histories. In the meantime, Planet
B developed interstellar travel and visited us twenty-five hundred
years ago, influencing our pre-Golden Age Greeks (Are you following this?). That's why King Herodes seems so much like Plato. Actually, Plato was copying him. Now, this isn't so unlikely, except
that TECT also says that there is tangential evidence that the
Lemurian culture of five thousand years ago was begun by another,
even more ancient visitation from Planet B seventy-five hundred
years ago. It gets better. This previous Planet B culture seems to
have been instigated by an even earlier visit from an Earth civilization centralized in what TECT is pleased to call "Atlantis,"
which left Earth over ten thousand years ago. So our history and
that of Planet B have been ping-ponging back and forth across the*

vast interstellar reaches at five-thousand-year intervals. We had a prehistoric culture that went out there, inspired the Planet B people, came back, and destroyed itself. They took twenty-five centuries to develop, came here, inspired a prehistoric culture, went home, and destroyed itself. And so on. TECT must have a lot of fun coming up with things like this.

We haven't had the nerve to ask whose civilization came first. That's scheduled for next Thursday. But the interesting thing to note is that Planet B is now without any people to inspire. They really wiped themselves out, this last time. That doesn't especially sadden me, other than to realize that if we bomb ourselves, or more precisely, if Denny bombs us all, back to the Stone Age, we can't expect any big brothers from Planet B to nudge us along this time. But how many generations are there in five thousand years? You see, it doesn't pay to get worked up over it all.

Nevertheless, the timing seems to be about right. We ought to be blotting ourselves out soon, according to TECT. You'll realize that you and I ought to be hearing from Denny in just about . . . twenty minutes from . . . now. Either gentle taps at our chamber doors or loud, bright goings-on in the atmosphere. But that's Denny, right? Too bad, because I have to go to the john, and that would be a really terrible way to die. I mean, sitting there, reading Sports Illustrated, *with your pants down around your ankles. How much sympathy are you going to get like that? What could you say to God (either of them)? "Gee, God, I was just sitting there, minding my own business . . ." It would never work. Well, we'll see. Catch you when the dust settles.*

P.S.: *By the way, in case we have to start chipping axes out of rock, do you know what flint looks like? Just thought I'd ask.*

Say hello to Cindy for me again, and write soon.

Yours despotically,

Tom)

AND US, TOO, I GUESS

It was certainly a *quiet* cataclysm.

I remember very well how I reacted in its early days. Of course, it was by no means my first disaster; I had graduated from a good school where I received the best practical training, and afterward I had found a job with a well-known metropolitan research team. In the following months, during which I worked with some of the sharpest minds on the East Coast, I witnessed a small but decisive catastrophe. It ruined at least three lives, in addition to dissolving the research team and forever discouraging financial support in my own chosen field.

I was not deterred. It was necessary for me at that point to choose another field. No sooner had I re-educated myself and gathered the essential literature and equipment for my first solo experiments than the world at large was struck by a singular and devastating disaster. Again my work had to be postponed. I weathered the disturbance easily, but millions of people in the United States alone were permanently affected. My own assistant, Wagner of the hunched back, disappeared with my only set of keys, and I was forced for the third time to set out afresh.

I sought counsel from one of my former associates, Dr. Johnson. I felt that it would be foolish to continue entirely on my own, especially now that hardly anyone else could be at all useful. So I moved into Dr. Johnson's spacious apartments, and together we planned a good scientific project with plenty of chemicals and glassware, leaving the matter of goals and hypotheses for later. This partnership required that I leave my own headquarters in New York and begin a residence in Cleveland, a city that I had always thought of as primarily for Ukrainians, hoodlums, and other nontechnical types. After a short time I grew more comfortable there, and our work began to lose the ugly dilettante aspects that new laboratories always seem to harbor.

Of course, with my luck, that's precisely when the cataclysm occurred. Or to be more exact, when we (the scientific community) first began to acknowledge its existence, with whatever private misgivings. Not yet fully recovered from many superior twentieth-century disasters, the world was already beset by another. This one was not manmade; no, the proud scientific community could not take the slightest credit for it. Perhaps, I have come to think, perhaps that is the reason it took us all so many years to accept the truth. If only we had been granted a small part, a tiny creative task in the grand scheme of things, then the world and its inhabitants could have perished overnight without causing us an instant's regret.

But it's no use second-guessing the cosmos. Some ten years after my last meeting with Dr. Johnson I arrived by plane in Cleveland. My first impression of the area was unfavorable. Before I had even reacquired my luggage I had decided that it would be impossible to breathe the Ohio air. The temperature in mid-July was ninety-four degrees, and it was an hour and a half past midnight. The humidity was a Devonian 92 per cent. I felt as if I had been squeezed from the plane into a huge stewpot at the simmer. My white labcoat seemed too heavy to carry, let alone wear. My legs and arms were unbearably weary, and if I had not seen Dr. Johnson waiting for me at the gate, I might well have climbed back on the plane and gone home.

"Well, hello there, Dr. Davis," said Dr. Johnson, shaking my hand firmly.

"Hello, Dr. Johnson," I said. "It's nice of you to meet me."

"Not at all. Hot enough for you?"

I looked closely at my old friend. The Dr. Johnson I had known in my youth would never have permitted himself such a cliché. I had an inkling that I'd have to suffer more than merely the climate.

"Is it like this all the time?" I asked, forcing myself to proceed through the entire weather routine.

"No," said Dr. Johnson, pleased at my acquiescence, "sometimes it rains as well!" We both laughed briefly and walked in silence to his car. The parking lots were nearly deserted; the world's previous disasters could not yet be forgotten, and life continued on a much more distracted plane than I preferred.

Dr. Johnson had chosen a lovely old home in the Garden District.

The former owners, like so many mere landlords, had been "incapacitated" by the catastrophe of the midseventies. So many of the old mansions along St. Charles Avenue had been deserted and taken over by the scientific community, alone among the city's residents still able to appreciate the neighborhood's charms. The two of us could barely fill a single chamber with our possessions, but we found ourselves masters of two dozen rooms. For the first time in my life I had a dormitory room of my own, plus a reading room, an office, two private baths, a private parlor for whatever visitors I might entertain, and a strange little closet-sized room at the end of a long corridor. There were no windows in this room and but the one door, and there was no clue as to what purpose the previous owners might have put it. Dr. Johnson suggested jokingly that I use it for a chapel, and at the time the idea was exquisitely foolish.

The entire back of the house, shaded by arching palm trees and great, leafy shrubs I could not identify, was given over to our laboratories. The city of Cleveland was ours, as far as acquiring matériel was concerned; our only limits were placed by the other members of the scientific community with whom we competed. But the house was already admirably furnished. What appeared to be an old pantry had been converted into the main lab. Dr. Johnson had set it up along the lines we had learned both in school and during our mutual, ill-fated project of a decade before. One wall had been covered with pine plank shelves, which supported hundreds upon hundreds of little bottles of chemicals, all in alphabetical order. Their tiny red-and-white labels were peculiarly comforting. Along the opposite wall were cages of small animals, their marble eyes following us about in our splendid pursuits. Could they know what part they were to play in our work? No, of course not. But as Dr. Johnson could not avoid the effects of the earlier disaster, now speaking in annoyingly trite phrases, so, too, have I felt the most unclean anthropomorphic urges. It was not sympathy I knew for the unlucky beasts we kept, but it was another fell emotion with matching symptoms.

We worked long hours, feeling certain that some day we would find a method and an object. But none of that was important; it was the joy of pipettes and gram atoms that maintained us. Indeed, we did not recognize the hoped-for stimulus when it came. Surrounded by cataclysm, we labored blithely on.

One morning I came down from my rooms to find Dr. Johnson

hard at work, although it was not yet noon. He had fed the fish in the tanks, had thrown some decomposing material into the terrariums, and was beginning to examine the wood shavings in the rodents' cages. He turned to me as I entered. His broad smile and the crackling freshness of his lab coat were all the reward I ever needed.

"Good morning, Dr. Davis," he said. "Your mollies have all kicked the bucket."

Yes, it was the beginning of a pleasantly restrained disaster.

*   *   *

Paul Moran searched his pockets for the house keys. "Come *on*, already," said Linda, his wife. It was very late, well after midnight, and her habitual mistrust of the city overruled any desire to placate Paul. At last he found the keychain and handed it to her; she took it nervously, glancing up and down the street to see if anyone lurked in the shadowed doorways.

"Go on, you're safe," said Paul. Then to himself he murmured, "I can't see why anybody'd bother, anyway." For all her insecurity, Linda took foolish chances. She hurried up the tenement steps while Paul unloaded the suitcases from the trunk of the car. He watched her for a few seconds, again thinking that some day a guy was going to be waiting for her inside the foyer. That would teach her, all right. Then maybe she wouldn't be in such a hurry to leave him with all the luggage. Linda opened the front door and disappeared for a moment while she unlocked the inner door. As Paul slammed the trunk lid closed, he heard her voice.

"Paul?" she said. He did not answer. "Paul? Are you all right?"

"What's the matter now?"

"The light in here's burned out. It's dark inside, I can't see."

Paul swore under his breath. "What do you want me to do about it?"

"Wait a minute," she said, her voice shaking audibly. "I'll come down and help you."

"Hallelujah," said Paul angrily. He waited on the sidewalk beside the suitcases. Linda stuck her head out of the front door, peering up and down the street once more. "It seems to be okay," said Paul cynically. "I mean, you only have to come about thirty feet, you know."

"I just want to be sure, that's all," she said harshly. "One day you're going to run out of luck, you're going to walk down some dark street not paying any attention, and you're going to end up with a Saturday-night Special stuck in your back. Knowing you, you'd wind up getting your head blown off."

Paul didn't react the way she expected. She forgot that he'd heard all of this several times before. He just bent over and picked up two of the three suitcases. "Don't be so smug," he said at last. "I mean, where would that leave you?"

Linda had never considered that aspect before. She just stared at him. He smiled coldly and shoved the third suitcase toward her with his foot. Then he turned and carried his suitcases up the stairs to the door, never once looking around to see if she followed. Linda stood on the sidewalk for a short time, glaring angrily at his back, ignoring for the moment her nervousness on the night-shaded street. She started to shout something after him but stopped abruptly. Finally she just picked up the heavy bag and hurried up the stairs.

The Morans' apartment was on the fourth floor of the building. The light was out in the ground floor foyer, and the first flight of stairs was hidden in a vague darkness. Paul considered how the city forced an unhealthy fear on its populace; passing beyond the inner door, Paul paused before he began climbing the stairs, suddenly feeling vulnerable and too much like an easy target. He readily granted what that notion implied: someone to take a sight on that target, waiting, quietly hiding in a second-floor ambush. Often the stairwell smelled of urine and vomit. More than once the Morans had returned home at night to find drunks and vagrants passed out on the narrow landings between floors.

Linda walked up the stairs behind Paul. She hated the building, but Paul insisted that they couldn't afford to move. As he struggled up the stairs with the luggage, Paul could hear her loud sighs. Tonight, fortunately for their ragged tempers, there were no foul-smelling bodies to block their way. At their door at last, he dropped the suitcases heavily; his deep, rapid breathing was intended to let Linda know that he hadn't enjoyed carrying the luggage. She was unlocking the door, but turned to look at her husband.

"All right," she said, "I'm proud of you for carrying those things up here. If it wasn't for you, we'd have to leave them out on the sidewalk all night. I think you're wonderful." She gave him a spiteful frown and finished opening the door.

"You know something, Linda?" said Paul, throwing the suitcases over the threshold into the kitchen of their apartment. "You know what? I think you're crazy. I think you're about the most frightened person I've ever known. It's almost sick, how scared you are all the time. It's not normal."

"Shut up, Paul," she said wearily. "It's time to go to sleep. We'll talk about my mental illness in the morning."

"That's just it, for God's sake. You're even too scared to talk about it. You're too scared to go on a trip out of the city, because the junkies will rob the apartment while you're gone. You're too scared to drive with me because I'll wrap the car around a telephone pole. You're too scared to stay here alone because some strange person will mug you. You're too scared to stay here with me because *I* might mug you."

"Have you ever listened to yourself?" asked Linda, already in the bedroom undressing for bed, leaving the suitcases where they had fallen in the other room. "You want to talk about sick, you just listen to the crazy stuff that runs out of your own mouth."

"You're scared that I'm telling the truth, isn't that right?"

She peered around the doorway; Paul was lying on the couch, his shoes making grimy trails on the slipcover. "You want to know what I'm really afraid of, Paul?" she said. "I'm terrified that some day you *will* tell the truth. I mean, I can guess all the shady things you do behind my back. But I'm just scared that the true story will make my imagination look like a Disney movie, rated G. See, honey, I still love you. I give you the benefit of the doubt."

Paul didn't answer. He just sat up, clenching his fists angrily, composing several variations of his natural reply. But he wouldn't give her the satisfaction of making him shout at her. She smiled again, with even less affection, and disappeared into the bedroom. She continued undressing; at last he heard her turn down the bedspread and plump her pillow. Then he heard the creak of the bed's springs and the click of the light switch. He sat on the couch for a while. In his furious, illogical mood he didn't want to follow her too soon. That would be a sign of weakness.

When he did decide to go to bed, about ten minutes later, he went into the bedroom and turned on the lights. Linda groaned sleepily, and Paul just sighed loudly.

"You're getting good at heaving those heavy breaths," said Linda, propping her head with one hand.

Paul hung his shirt in the closet. Without turning he answered her.

"My God, look who's complaining. The original martyr. What's the matter, does the light bother you? Don't try to tell me you were asleep already."

"You going to work tomorrow?" she asked.

"Of course I'm going to work," he said loudly. "Somebody has to around here. Just because you're having a baby doesn't make you the Great American Princess, you know."

"Because it's late. You'll never get up."

"You let *me* worry about that. I don't mind getting out of this house." After he finished undressing he went into the far corner of the bedroom, where two large tanks sat, their pumps humming, aerators bubbling, green lights shining and casting soft reflections on the dingy walls of the room. He switched off the green lamps first, then stooped down to check the equipment.

One tank was a normal, large aquarium, holding fifty gallons. This was placed on a stand against the short wall, beneath a window that opened out on the street four stories below. The other arrangement was a group of three smaller tanks connected step fashion, situated against one of the longer walls, opposite the bed. A ten-gallon tank was on a platform about chest-level; a second was set against it about two feet lower, and a third rested on the floor. Water pumped up from the bottom tank caused the top aquarium to overflow into the second, which emptied into the lowest one, and so on in a cycle. This was Paul's breeding apparatus. Young fish born in the top tank were swept over the edge and into the second tank, thus protected from their cannibalistic parents, which were prevented from following by a strip of netting across the waterfall's lip. The babies eventually were swept again into the bottom tank when they came to the water's surface in search of food. Then the bottom tank was sealed off, so a later brood of babies from the top tank would have the middle area without competition from the original fry.

"Feed them and come to bed already," said Linda. "God, you worry more over those fish than you do about me." Paul said nothing; Linda sighed. "Well, I knew that already. I mean, you worry more about them than you do about yourself, and *that's* crazy."

"My mollies are dead," said Paul quietly.

"That happens," said Linda, turning impatiently to face the other direction. "Mollies are not such a terrific long-term investment. So scoop out the dead ones and flush them down the toilet."

"Linda," said Paul softly, tensely, "they're *all* dead."

"All of them? For God's sake, you can't even be trusted with some fish. What kind of care did you take of them? I mean, God, what kind of trouble is a lousy fish?"

"They were all right Friday night when we left."

She turned to gaze at him, completely without sympathy. "You let all those fish die. First you move in that ridiculous tank and spend I don't know how much to fill it full of fish. Then you pay a hundred dollars for filters and pumps and all the junk the guy in the store said you needed. Then you build that ugly waterfall thing. And when you're all done, you let your fish die. You like looking at just the water and the green light? What's the matter, the fish get in the way?"

"They don't even look like they've been sick," said Paul. "No fungus or nothing. And it's silly to think the ones in the big tank would catch something from the mollies in the breeding tank."

"You left the heaters on too high. You boiled your own fish."

"The thermometers say eighty-one degrees. Perfect."

"You starved them."

"Don't be stupid," said Paul sourly.

Linda gave him a mocking laugh. "Me? I'm not the one who killed all your fish."

"I had two broods in the step tanks, plus the breeding stock. I had over a hundred mollies in the big tank. Not a single one of them's still alive."

"It must look pretty sick, with all those dead fish floating around on the top of the water. Well, you don't need that pump noise no more. Turn it all off and go to sleep."

Paul stood slowly. He felt completely helpless. Linda was right, he *did* look foolish. There was nothing he could do to stop her gloating over his misfortune. If only he could just explain the thing to her without looking like a total idiot. But he had no idea why all the fish had died; in the morning he would test the water for acidity and salt content. Even so, he could only go to the store and buy more mollies. He didn't look forward to what Linda would say then.

*   *   *

It was a Sunday morning when Dr. Johnson gave me the bad news about my poor mollies. Of all the tropical specimens in our community tank, the mollies were my favorites. There was something about them that attracted me—the cherry barbs were far too ferocious; the black-lace angels too prim; the upside-down catfish, though comical, were still too gross. But the mollies held a simple charm. Flat, stark black they were, darting like scraps of shadow somehow let loose in the water. The males were so aggressively sexual that I always had to laugh. The poor exhausted females would try such maneuvers as hiding behind the plastic clamshell bubbler, but it never did any good. And the constant production of live young mollies appealed to my scientific senses—here was the Mystery of Life in miniature.

Except that now I had the Mystery of Death on my hands. I scooped out the bloated bodies of my former pets and examined them hurriedly. No white spots of ich, none of the telltale symptoms of velvet. I couldn't bear to look at them for long, and ran downstairs to the unoccupied servants' quarters to flush the mollies down the loo. The toilet water swirled and roared, and the fish were swept along, tails pointing down toward their porcelain necropolis. I have to admit that I shuddered to see them go, imagining that in their dead, sodden movements I could recognize a sad farewell gesture.

The death of my mollies had upset me more than I had thought. I felt a sudden and very intense attack of anthropomorphism, and I hurried back to the lab. There was only one thing to do, and that was replace the fish as soon as possible, and forever after pretend that nothing had happened.

"Did you see them off all right?" asked kindly Dr. Johnson when I returned.

"Yes, indeed. Thank you."

"Why, you're as pale as a ghost," he said, with his customary concern. I started violently. Apparently my coworker noticed, and apologized. "I'm sorry," he said. "I suppose I'll have to guard my tongue for a few days. I had no idea those mere fish meant so much to you."

"How could you know?" I said bitterly, immediately regretting my tone. "*You* care for nothing but those cold glass test tubes of yours."

"I'm sorry you feel that way," said Dr. Johnson, not taking offense. He must truly have understood the extent of my grief, and deep inside I was grateful for that. "Have I never shown you my own pets?" he asked.

"No, you have not."

"Then I must, tonight. They can be seen to best advantage after the moon has risen. It is nearly full, isn't it?" I only nodded, wondering what strange hobby he had adopted and had successfully kept hidden from me.

"It is a strange thing," I said, feeling suddenly philosophic, a mood I had rarely entertained since achieving adulthood. "I fail to understand how we, as members of the scientific community, can still be so upset by death. I mean, inasmuch as we are privy to so many of nature's quixotic secrets. Should we not, therefore, be more apt to accept death as just another universal constant, to be calculated and assessed, with no more emotional weight than, say, Boyle's Law?"

"For me, at least, that *is* true," said Dr. Johnson with a faraway look in his eyes. "I cannot fear death. I am not repelled by its concrete signs. It is so common a phenomenon and, as you say, so universal that I tend to overlook it as I do the nightly progression of the stars. Death, where is thy sting?"

"The sting of Death is dying," I said quietly. Somehow I had to shake this illogical humor, in which I forced human traits on objects inanimate or even incorporeal. I had to change the subject. "What do you think of the Indians' chances this year?" I asked.

"Haven't followed them since 1954."

"It's very interesting lately," I said nervously. "With most of the country's athletes still suffering from the old disasters, the ball clubs have signed many well-known scientists to play."

Dr. Johnson turned to look at me thoughtfully. "I wonder," he said, and then fell silent again.

"Did you like the Indians?" I asked sadly.

"They died like flies in the midseventies. I saw a bunch of dead Indians in Arizona. Just lying around, stacked like cordwood. It's not true what they say about dead Indians vis-à-vis good ones. You have to learn which generalities you can trust."

And there we were, talking about death again. This new catastrophe, of which the death of the mollies was the first indication, was a lot more drawn out than the usual. Almost as if it wanted to inflict every last bit of mental torture before it began the physical.

I will cease calling my phrases "anthropomorphic." From now on I think I'll just say "romantic." Nowadays, who cares?

*   *   *

The morning after the loss of his fish, Paul arrived at the factory at nine o'clock sharp. His foreman met him in the coatroom. Paul nodded and hung his jacket in his locker. The sight of Kibling waiting by the bank of dark green lockers annoyed Paul. The foreman couldn't wait for five minutes while Paul punched in. The company had to drain every penny's worth of work out of its employees.

The Jennings Manufacturing Corporation paid Paul three and a half dollars an hour to do meaningless tasks. At least, the succession of chores never seemed to him to have any connection. Today, more concerned with the mollies' mysterious accident, he was in no mood to be bullied by his employers.

"Morning, Moran," said Kibling. "Here, I got a job for you."

"You know something, Gary?" said Paul, grinning so Kibling might think that he was only joking. "You know, you *always* got a job for me. It never fails. I come in on time every morning, and every morning you sure as sunshine got some dumb-ass job for me."

Kibling did not think that Paul was joking. Kibling just sucked his teeth for a few seconds. "Any time, Moran," he said at last. "Any time you don't want the job, well, we got enough guys waiting outside."

"I wasn't serious, Gary," said Paul. "It's like a game. I never know what I'm supposed to do from one day to another."

"Try to think of that as an extra."

"Great. What's today? Front panels again?"

Kibling shook his head. "No, you didn't do too good on them last time. You're going to do the oven this morning. Get these plates done by lunch and I'll put you on subassembly for the afternoon."

Paul frowned, and took the small, odd-shaped pieces of alloy steel from the foreman. The oven was the worst of Paul's several chores. Kibling must have understood that; Paul only got the assignment once or twice a month. He had to toss three or four of the metal sheets into a small but fiery furnace. Every ninety seconds he reached into that glowing pit with a long-handled shovel and flipped them. He let them bake according to a standard schedule; when he removed them he put them aside to cool, dipped them in a strong-smelling chemical bath, knocked the coating of ash off as best he could, and sent the package on to Quality Control. Then he began all over, pitching another three or four sheets into the kiln.

The job gave him a lot of time to think. That was by far the worst part. Every word that Linda had spoken the night before came back to him, and he was infuriated all over again. He remembered his own replies without pleasure. While he waited for the steel pieces to cook, he thought up better answers. He knew what he'd say to her tonight if she started that same argument.

After Linda, he thought about his fish. By lunchtime he had stopped worrying about them. The situation didn't allow that; there was nothing to be gained by regretting the waste. Black mollies were cheap enough. Wholesale, he could get a good pair of them for about a quarter. Ten females, three or four good, strong males, and he'd have all the dead fish replaced in six to eight weeks. No, it was just the surprise of seeing them all dead that had upset him the night before. He couldn't summon up the same emotion now, twelve hours later. And, no doubt, Linda would try to run the matter into the ground when he came home. He changed his mind: Rather than fight, he'd have to ignore her.

Paul decided to get the new mollies after work. Then he wouldn't have to go straight home, and when he did he'd have something to occupy him. Even cleaning four tanks and changing the water was better than hearing Linda's new problems. Paul watched the clock all afternoon, and punched out on the timeclock precisely at five. The subway was uncomfortably crowded with rush-hour commuters, but Paul just closed his eyes and disregarded them. They were all a little like Linda, in their pushing and shrieking. If they were quieter, more subtly insistent, then they might have infuriated him. But Paul had a great deal of practice in shutting irritations out of his mind.

The Fish Store was not just a neighborhood pet shop. It had no large front windows filled with romping puppies to lure the sentimental passerby. The store dealt only in aquariums, equipment suited to the needs of the fish-raising hobbyist, and the fish themselves. In the past couple of months Paul had become well known in the establishment, so that the proprietor had offered to buy Paul's growing supply of mollies. Paul had agreed to accept payment lower than the store paid to its regular distributor. But now, with the demise of all of Paul's salable goods plus the breeding stock, he was back in the role of customer. No longer did he *belong*, in the sense of being a fellow breeder, a colleague in the small field of tropical-fish raising. Now he was just a man with eighty gallons of bubbling water and no fish.

"Mr. Moran!" said Moss, the store's night manager. "Haven't seen you in a couple of weeks. Have you thought about our offer?"

Paul nodded glumly. "Yeah," he said, "but the deal will have to wait. I had some kind of accident or something. I was away for the weekend, and last night when I got home every molly I had was dead."

Moss looked surprised. "You had quite a few, I know. It sounds like you had some kind of plague."

"I doubt it. The fish were in four separate tanks, one big one and the step breeder. I can't figure it out. There wasn't enough time for them all to catch sick and die."

"No," said Moss thoughtfully, "I didn't really mean that. It would have to be a mechanical failure, or a sudden change in pH or temperature."

"That was what I figured, too," said Paul, "but I checked all that as carefully as I could. The pH was perfect, the salt was as high as it's supposed to be, the temperature was right on eighty-one, where it's always been. Even if the pump had quit, there wasn't enough time for the water to go bad. I know there *wasn't* a mechanical failure."

"Have you ever had a pandemic infection before?" asked Moss.

"Huh?"

"You know, something gets in and kills a few fish. Then in a couple of weeks they're *all* dead."

"No," said Paul, discouraged that the expert in the store wasn't being more helpful. "Anyway, you'd have to be pretty careless to let something like that happen."

"A lot of people are that careless," said Moss. "We build our profits on them."

"This was just over the weekend," said Paul impatiently.

"I don't know, then," said Moss. "So what do you want, more breeding stock?"

"Yeah. I guess I'll just have to start from scratch." Paul followed Moss toward the back of the store, where the walls were lined with scores of small tanks, each containing a different variety of tropical fish. When they got to the three tanks of black mollies, Moss stopped abruptly and stared. Every molly in the store was dead. "You ought to keep a closer watch on your tanks," said Paul. "That sure won't impress a new customer."

"I just started work about fifteen minutes ago," said Moss. "Let me see if any of the day staff knows anything about this." Moss went back to the front of the store to question the young man who worked behind the cash register. Paul stayed behind and examined the tanks of dead mollies. There was something chilling about them, beyond the mere coincidence. Whenever a single fish had died in Paul's tank, he scooped it out with the long-handled net and ran with it to the toilet, where he flushed the limp, dead thing out of his life. But the sight of so many fish lying on the bottom or floating upside-down forced the idea of death into his consciousness.

While Moss was checking with his employee, Paul tried to see if the store's mollies resembled his own dead fish. The common diseases to which mollies were susceptible were obvious to the knowledgeable observer. Mollies are small fish, smaller than goldfish but larger than guppies. Mollies come in many varieties and many colors, but the most popular strain is the pure black. The black molly is a dramatic addition to a community tank; the jet-black color is an exciting contrast to the sometimes luminescent hues of other tropical fish, and mollies can be bred to develop fantastic fin and tail forms. They are usually hardy fish, prolific breeders in captivity, and thus make ideal pets for both the specialist and the casual hobbyist.

The most hazardous illness is ich, a parasitical disease that shows up as small white specks against the pure black body. The disease is extremely contagious, and a tankful of mollies can be wiped out in a matter of days if no steps are taken to check it. Its presence generally means that the water doesn't contain enough salt, as mollies like their water a little brinier than most other tropicals. Without the salt, their protective coating of slimy film is easily penetrated. But there was no sign of this disease, either on Paul's dead fish or on the store's. Looking closer, he could see no symptom of mollie velvet or any other sickness with which he was familiar.

"Mr. Moran?" said Moss. Paul turned around, startled. "I asked some of the day staff, and they knew that the mollies had died. Miele said they were already dead when he first checked them this morning. But as you can see, there aren't any traces of disease. The tanks were left for me to examine, but I don't think I'll have any more success diagnosing ours than you had with yours."

"They *are* a lot like my mollies," said Paul tonelessly.

"Yes, of course," said Moss, watching Paul uneasily, unwilling to agree that there might be some connection. "Of course, you purchased your original stock from us, but I don't think we can be held responsible."

"It's certainly comforting to know that it isn't just the little people who can be careless." Moss frowned but did not answer. Paul shook his head, turned, and left the store.

The ride home was as crowded as the ride to the fish store had been. But, he told himself, now he had the rather sad consolation that Linda wouldn't be able to mock him for buying several dollars' worth of new mollies. Right after supper he could go into the bedroom and begin the arduous job of cleaning and sterilizing the tanks.

The meal with his wife passed silently, tensely. Linda had made spaghetti again, finding time in her long, lonely day only to boil water and warm a jar of commercial sauce. Paul was very angry; he came home to spaghetti at least three times a week. As soon as he finished eating, Paul left the table and disappeared into the bedroom. Half an hour later, Linda came in to see what he was doing.

"You taking all those sickening fish out of the tank now?" she asked.

Paul turned around slowly and regarded her for several seconds. "You want me to leave them here for you to look at?" he said quietly.

"Oh, don't be like that," she said, tossing a dish towel over her shoulder. "Just don't drop any on the rug. And watch that you don't splash that filthy water around my bedroom. Are you going to get rid of those tanks now?"

Paul turned back to his work. "Naw," he muttered. "Going to get some more."

"Huh?"

"I said I'm going to order some new mollies."

"So they can die off, too, and waste more money?"

Paul scooped the last of the dead mollies from the large fifty-gallon tank. He picked up the pot that held the others and carried it into the kitchen. As he passed Linda she backed away, a disgusted expression on her face. "Listen," he said, dumping the fish into the garbage bag, "I went to the fish place after work. All of *their* mollies died last weekend, too. And I bought mine from them, so it can't be my fault. Your trouble is you're too quick to make me look like a fool. I'm not as dumb as you think I am."

Linda went back to the sinkful of dishes. "Just take that garbage downstairs before you do anything else. Use some common sense, for heaven's sake."

That night, when the large tank and the step breeder stood empty and clean, after the filters and air lines had been washed and sterilized, Paul decided to order some breeding stock from a supplier in Connecticut. Paul wrote a letter, asking the price for ten females and four males. Several days later he received a reply, and the situation took a stranger shape. The letter said, "We here at G & G appreciate your interest, but regret to say that your order cannot be filled at this time. Our entire stock of *Mollienisia sphenops* perished early this week, and we have been unable to receive replacements from our usual sources. I would normally suggest that you try our competitors, but curiously they have all experienced the same misfortune.

"Hoping to be of more service in the future, I remain,

Very truly yours,

Walter G. Gretne

G & G Aquarium Supply."

Paul was confused. It was as if somebody was making it hard for him to refill his tanks. Linda would say that they were trying to tell him something. But Linda only believed in fate or God when something bad happened to someone she knew. He decided not to mention the letter at all and, in fact, to seem to forget all about mollies until he could locate a source of healthy fish.

The next day, Sunday, he ignored Linda's pointed questions about all the expensive equipment going to waste in the bedroom. He didn't want to think about it. It was his weekend, and he wanted to relax. The Sunday paper was split up all over the house. Paul had the baseball news with him in the bathroom. The remaining sections were divided among the other rooms, and Linda had the television section with her in the bedroom. When Paul finished with the sports, he stuck his head around the corner of the bedroom. "You got the movie section in here?"

Linda lay on the bed, the tiny portable television next to her. She was listening to an old Alan Ladd film while she read the paper. "Yeah," she said, "but I'm going to look at it next. You can have the TV section."

"I don't want the TV section," he said impatiently.

"There's something in it that might interest you." She pulled the first and last pages off the section, further separating the newspaper. She handed the sheet to Paul. "Something about your stupid fish," she said.

Paul searched the pages for the article she meant. At last he found it, a small piece several lines long, stuck in as a filler at the foot of a column. It said, rather tersely, that "scientists" had noted that no members of the species *Mollienisia sphenops* could be found alive in the United States, or even at their natural breeding grounds in the waters around Yucatan and Guatemala. The paper said that the "scientists" were puzzled.

* * *

The next few days were among the most bewildering of my somewhat eventful life. The situation certainly appeared simple enough on the surface: My mollies had died, I had to get new ones, and I had difficulty locating healthy specimens in Cleveland. At first Dr. Johnson took little more than amused interest in my problem. You must remember that at this time we had no idea of the magnitude of the circumstances; we were ignorantly working away on our mice and rabbits, frogs and flies. We gave no thought for anything more serious than the weekly party with our colleagues or our lapsed subscriptions to various scientific journals. Often we went down to watch the sun set over the river or rise over the lake, while around us the universe prepared its next terrible blow.

The day after the mollies died, Monday, I was busy all afternoon helping Dr. Johnson construct a towering, brittle webwork of glassware. It was supported by heavy black iron stands at critical points. Flasks were the major component, a strong, optimistic theme that was typical of my friend. Connecting them were dozens and dozens of long glass arteries. Where some members of the scientific community in Cleveland would, I'm sure, have been satisfied to remain with the straight, purely functional tubes, Dr. Johnson did not hesitate to introduce long, delicate bends or even rude petcocks. The levels at which the flasks stood were pleasingly random, another nontechnical touch that made Dr. Johnson's creations superior to those of his contemporaries. Certain obscure, baroquely contorted pieces of glassware punctuated the whole structure, adding definite statements of progress and enterprise among the soothing chords. As a minor helper to the construction, I could only watch with amazement and respect as Dr. Johnson added one faultless detail after another.

By evening the thing was completed. Dr. Johnson ceremoniously made each of us a champagne cocktail, and we toasted his new work.

Then I snapped the switch, killing the lights in the auxiliary lab; meanwhile Dr. Johnson had moved to his new *parvum opus*. He connected a plug from a strange piece of apparatus to a long extension cord. A bright blue spark began to flick among the towers and tiny catwalks of glass. The eerie light cast hideous shadows in the room, and I was seized with a new, almost unpleasant awe for Dr. Johnson and his creative faculties. But no sooner had I begun to creep forward for a better view than he turned the lights back on in the room. "Enough," he said, waving his hand impatiently. "It does not work."

"It's beautiful!" I said, dismayed by the fury of his passion.

"It is not," he said. "It is clumsy. Lopsided, unbalanced. Tomorrow I will destroy it."

"You can't, my friend," I said, genuinely horrified. "You're too critical of your achievements."

He studied me for a few seconds, his expression contorted by emotions I fear I shall never experience. "What can you know of an artist's pain?" he asked. He was right, of course; in the morning I helped him destroy it.

His problems, his creative agonizing helped me to forget my own meager troubles. Monday sped by with the assembling of his glass masterpiece, and Tuesday saw only its slow, tedious dismantling. I was greatly fatigued that night, as it was I who had to climb high to loosen flasks and tubes and Fleischer retorts. Dr. Johnson preferred to stand by and direct me; I did not think he was remiss in not helping me more actively. I recognized that he was, in his peculiar way, a genius; people of that caliber are entitled to a few eccentricities.

So, then, it was Wednesday before I was able to get around to calling at the few remaining pet stores in the Cleveland area. I tried one on Melpomene Street first of all, because that store had always given us a good deal on shredded lettuce and dead mice (food for various laboratory animals). Old Miss Fry told me tearfully that all *her* black mollies had died Sunday, too. I remarked on the sad coincidence, and how cheap it seemed of nature merely to duplicate her efforts in our separate aquariums. Miss Fry looked at me blankly, not comprehending my *romantic* notion, and I explained that I thought that possibly "something was going around." She laughed, and I tried another store. This one, on Terpsichore Street, not far from Miss Fry's, had abominable quality fish but very nice "extras." I had spent a good deal of our budget on such things as marbles, painted glass bridges for the catfish to rest under, bubbling skin divers, bubbling sunken wrecks, bubbling treasure chests, and bubbling mermaids. I had even purchased as a joke a couple of dozen plastic fish; these had thin, almost invisible strings with weights tied to the ends. I buried the weights in the sand of one aquarium, and the fish hung suspended, always at one place. Though they never moved, I don't believe Dr. Johnson ever noticed that they weren't real fish. He didn't take to my pets as much as I; I think he even resented the amount of money I spent to keep them happy.

Anyway, I was told in the second shop that all their mollies had died the previous Sunday. I felt a peculiar thrill of fear. I had often felt that thrill before, and so it was not particularly interesting now. But I thought that Dr. Johnson at least, and possibly the entire scientific community, might be intrigued by this gloomy turn of events. There might even be a project worth pursuing by some crewcut statistician.

I followed St. Charles farther toward the downtown area, hitting all the pet shops I knew. In each, the story was the same: Every black molly in Cleveland had died spontaneously, sometime Sunday afternoon. I was becoming increasingly tired as well as fascinated by the latent horror of the situation. I decided to try one last place, a dirty establishment in the Quarter. I rarely had occasion to travel into that neighborhood, because its residents were some of the more lunatic of the city's population, all entirely overcome by the old disaster of several years ago. But I had little choice now; my scientific curiosity, sluggish to arouse at best, was now at last piqued and would not allow me to halt before some slight explanation might be had. I thought immediately of a virus, but dismissed the idea as unworthy.

I entered the sordid little shop unenthusiastically. The owner, one M. de Crout, hurried to meet me at the door.

"Have you any mollies?" I asked, wasting little time.

"No, they're all dead," he said, turning to retrace his steps to the back of the store and his small television.

I took the St. Charles streetcar home and told Dr. Johnson all about my day's adventure. As I foresaw, he was deeply concerned. From that time on he assumed control of the investigation, leaving me with a good deal of time to practice my own glassware sculpture. I had at last built something that I felt approached his own triumph of

Monday, when he burst into the room, his face flushed and his lab coat torn at one shoulder. He appeared not to notice.

"I have news!" he cried.

"Look at this," I said.

"Never mind, we don't have time for such as that. Every molly in the city has been accounted for, and they're all dead. Every molly in the country is dead as well; I have proof." Here he waved a sheaf of telegrams. Each one was a molly count of a particular segment of the United States. Dr. Johnson had organized the fact-finding operation well. His efficient handling of the matter made me see him in a new light; he was, beyond doubt, my superior in such things. "Further," he said, his voice rising to unaccustomed levels of pitch and volume, "there is not to be found a single living molly in all of the coastal waters of the Yucatan or Guatemala, or the Gulf of Mexico, or Florida, their natural breeding grounds."

I stared at him. The thing was monstrous. "What do you make of it?" I asked.

"What else?" he asked, throwing the papers at me impatiently. I laughed with delight. "The species is done for," he said, pacing agitatedly. "I believe that an entire variety of animal life has become extinct, within the unbelievably short time span of a single day."

"Do you know what you suggest?" I said, with the necessary scientific skepticism.

"Yes," he said tiredly. "The world will think me mad, but I have done my duty."

"You mean—"

"I have informed the newspapers."

Then he *was* serious. I considered the problem for a moment. Before I could begin to sort my thoughts, I got the old familiar tingle: disaster! I smelled a disaster brewing, but it was too early to dig up more facts. I would have to wait.

"Sorry, old friend," he said, jerking me from my reveries with a slap on the shoulder. "I know those little buggers meant the world to you. You'll just have to get on without them. Switch your allegiance, as it were. Why not guppies, eh? Or something else altogether. Get out of the fish line." I could see that he was right. I said nothing though, letting him feel sorry for me. I turned and took up my sculpture where I had stopped.

An hour later he came running into the room all over again. This time I truthfully saw tears on his cheeks, the only time I have known him to weep alone. "They're dead!" he whispered hoarsely. "All of them! Dead!"

"I know," I said with some irritation.

"No, you don't understand," he said, grabbing the sleeve of my lab coat. "My beautiful pets! They're all dead!"

Well, now, I remember thinking that at last I'd get to see his pets, which he preserved so carefully guarded from the view of the world at large. Even *I* had never seen them; I did not know so much as what they were, except dead. Now my instinctive tingle let me know: A new and perilous phase was beginning.

*   *   *

There was a great movie on at eleven-thirty. The paper gave it only two stars; Paul had seen the film in a theater when it first came out, and remembered that it was much better than that. The movie was one of Philip Gatelin's last, and Linda had never been one of his fans. She wanted to watch one of the talk shows. But finally she sighed loudly, admitting defeat and accepting the lesser comforts of martyrdom. Paul changed the channel; the news was still on.

"Move that over, will you?" said Linda, pushing the small television set toward her husband. "Maybe I'll just go to sleep."

"Why don't you do that?" asked Paul. "At least shut up."

"Shut up yourself, I want to hear the weather."

Before the local weather report, however, they had to watch a filmed interview prepared by the network. This spot, near the end of the newscast, was usually reserved for the day's absurd happenings, or quick glimpses of the nation's crazier citizens. It was obviously in this spirit that the network newsman had been sent on his assignment.

"Hello," he said, "this is Bob Dunne, NBC News in Romisch, Iowa. I'm standing outside the Pany Institute of Wentell Agricultural College. With me is Dr. Kyril Levy, head of the institute and an expert in pharmacological botany. Dr. Levy has made a rather startling discovery but, like many of his scientific predecessors, he's having a difficult time convincing his colleagues. But I'll let him describe his findings himself. Dr. Levy, just what is happening here in peaceful Romisch?"

Levy was short and gaunt, middle-aged, his hair thinning prematurely, his stooped shoulders accentuated by the rumpled white lab coat he wore. He took a deep breath and began. "It's not just here in Romisch, Bob. That's the point of the whole matter. No, we're all faced with the same problem, every one of us here in the United States and abroad."

Dunne didn't get any information at all with his first question. He tried again. "Could you summarize that problem for our viewers?"

"Certainly, Bob. My primary experiments here at the institute concern the applications of dexterity equivalencies in the production of larger-yield money crops. For my purposes, I've been using a certain type of fungus. The experiments are general enough so that the results may be extended to include most other common money crops; the fungus has the added advantage of economy of cultivating area and growing season. The fungus, called by its Latin name, *Polyporus gugliemii,* is a pinkish-white, leathery growth that is found only on the trunks and limbs of a particular kind of Spanish catalpa.

"My experiments were coming along well, and last week I had reached what I estimated to be the midpoint of the program. So you can imagine how disappointed I was when I learned that every single *gugliemii* had died in the space of eighteen hours."

Dunne regained the initiative, looking into the camera with an amused but patient expression. He was humoring the scientist for the sake of a few laughs. "I can imagine that would be a horrible sight," he said.

"Yes, indeed," said Levy. "When they die, their stalks go limp. The weight of the huge caps bends them over. *Gugliemii* are very bright orange on the underside, you know, with dark brown speckles. Well, it was just awful. All those poor orange corpses staring at me."

"And did you try to replace them?"

"Of course. I called one of my colleagues in Wachnough immediately. I had introduced him to the *gugliemii* at last year's convention. Anyway, he said that all of his had died under the same inexplicable circumstances."

"Admittedly," said Dunne, "the fate of Dr. Levy's mushrooms has little personal meaning for the average man in the street. But what makes the mystery unusual, if only from a specialist's point of view, is the fact that apparently every one of those mushrooms in the world is now dead. Dr. Levy has done extensive research in the short time since his own mushrooms died and has been unable to find any. So check your Spanish catalpas. If you find a pinkish-white thing growing there, let Dr. Levy know. If not, well, maybe the world will have to get along without the *Poly—*"

"*Polyporus gugliemii.*"

"Thank you, Dr. Levy," said Dunne, with an indulgent laugh. "This is Bob Dunne, NBC News, Wentell College, Romisch, Iowa."

Back with the local station, the announcer made a rude remark and introduced the weatherman. Paul watched the set silently, thinking. Linda had said nothing during the filmed interview, probably wondering why the network had invested so much money in such a dumb story. Who would miss a lousy mushroom? It was probably poisonous anyway.

"I know how he feels," said Paul.

"Huh? What do you mean?"

"I said, I know how he feels. That guy in Iowa. All his mushrooms died."

Linda turned around and propped herself on one elbow. "You don't know what you're talking about," she said. "He's a scientist. His mushrooms meant something. Maybe he was working on something important. Your cruddy fish weren't important."

"Not to you, they weren't," said Paul coldly.

"You're doggone right, they weren't. They all dying may be the best thing that ever happened to you. Maybe you'll open your eyes. Now you can get into something useful, if you're smart."

"It's scary," said Paul, once more grateful to be able to shut his wife's words out of his mind. "First, all the mollies in the world die. All at once. Then these mushrooms."

"They both start with *m*," said Linda.

"What does that mean?"

"Maybe Morans are next." She laughed at herself and turned around again to go to sleep.

Paul stared at her back. "I wouldn't joke about it," he said thoughtfully.

Several days passed in their usual unfulfilling way. Paul thought no more about the scientist's fungi; he remembered the mollies every time he saw the abandoned tanks in the bedroom. Once or twice a day he would realize, as though for the first time, that he'd never see a molly again. Eventually he grew bored and sold the step breeder, the large tank, and all the equipment back to The Fish Store. Linda laughed and said, "I told you so."

Paul's life was so carefully regulated that he never examined the events of the week more closely. His job continued the same, day after day; he thought the same things at the same times, admitting his frustration but lacking the imagination to battle it. His relationship with Linda, though not ideal, at least had the virtue of being constant. He could look forward to years of the same, never a misstep from her, never a fall from the peculiar grace they had arranged. And, too, he would be faithful. He had enough inclination to the contrary—surely no one could fault him for looking at other women—but his minor existence sapped whatever energy he might have had. He just couldn't be bothered.

Days and weeks later, toward the middle of September, an article in the newspaper caught his attention and brought back the short-lived feeling of fear. Paul welcomed it; even a change to impersonal terror would be a relief from the flat monotony he had built with Linda.

The article reviewed a speech given by Dr. Bertram Waters of Ivy University. Speaking before a meeting of the American Plasmonics Society, Dr. Waters revealed the results of a month-long survey conducted by himself with the aid of the North American Biological Research Association. Although biology was not Dr. Waters' own field, and although his audience had come hoping to hear of his recent work in the area of applied plasmonics, his lecture caused a great deal of excitement.

"We are right this minute caught in the midst of an unimaginable catastrophe," said Dr. Waters. "Even as we sit here the forces of nature, those immutable ordinances by which we shape our lives, conspire to spell our doom. But because the calamity is a slow one, because it operates on a large scale, striking down victims in isolated places around the globe, we may be inclined to dismiss its effects on ourselves as negligible. That would be a suicidal error.

"A few weeks ago, every member of the species *Mollienisia sphenops* was killed by some unknown agent, no matter where in the world the fish might have been. This event caused some little comment but was quickly forgotten, except by breeders of tropical fish. A short time later, every specimen of the fungus *Polyporus gugliemii* was noted to have perished. Since then, with the aid of NABRA, I have made a list of other species that have become extinct, suddenly and with no apparent—let me amend that: no *rational*—reason. Yes, there are other species. This list has been prepared carefully; all the extensive resources of NABRA have been employed to check it thoroughly, and I have every confidence in its accuracy. There are twelve other species, eight members of the plant kingdom, four of the animal kingdom, which no one here will ever see alive in nature again. Most of them, of course, will hardly be missed by the common man. Three of the four animals, for instance, were insects, tiny creatures barely distinguishable except by an expert.

"But that is not the point. One of the plants was noted by a botanist in Switzerland to have gone out of existence several years ago, 'seemingly overnight.' Other researchers have remarked on similar occurrences, some of which are still being investigated and may eventually be added to the list. What does this mean? Here is my theory, one that is highly speculative and will prove highly unpopular. Some of you will brand me a mad romantic, or worse. Nevertheless, in my opinion this is what the evidence points to.

"Who knows how many separate species of animal and plant life are on the Earth today? The total must run into the trillions. The catalogued varieties alone are far too numerous for any man to comprehend. If only one species disappeared each day, beginning with the birth of Christ, no, the appearance of thinking man, no, even more, *the creation of the world*—it is possible that we would scarcely have noticed the difference. So many unclassified insects, bacteria, microbes, sea creatures exist that man can hardly hope even to name them all.

"I think that whatever put us here, all of us, man and animal and plant alike, is calling us home. One by one. The black mollies have been called. And the *gugliemii* fungus. And the *echai* fly. And who knows how many others over the course of aeons? And who knows which will be next? We cannot even know how often this strange selection takes place."

The article went on at greater length, giving the conclusion of Waters' speech and the outraged reaction of his audience. But Paul was oddly contented. Perhaps it was only the idea that there might be, after all, some sort of *plan*, however gruesome and arbitrary it seemed. He looked into the kitchen, where Linda was making supper. Suddenly he felt a surge of affection for her, something that hadn't happened since shortly after their marriage. Paul wondered how long the feeling would last; he figured sadly that it would take more than a few mollies and a fungus to rejuvenate their union.

*   *   *

Disasters, it seems, have been my stock in trade. At least, I have never felt quite as comfortable as I do in the midst of a good, rending cataclysm. So many things fall into place, so much is settled for good or ill; I sometimes pray for more upheavals, if only to clear the air. But a disaster has its full share of negative values, also. If you happen to be idly standing around, you find yourself clutched, scattered, or dragged away.

It's important to keep your wits about you at all times. Even so, it is often impossible to resist the emotional demands of weaker individuals. Thus it was that I found myself dragged away, down the spiral staircases of our St. Charles Avenue mansion and into the hot, sunny yard. Behind the house the spiky, gray-green plants were still bead-strung with drops from the afternoon's shower. The grass in the yard had been left to grow unchecked, and now the rough blades grasped up inside my lab coat, scraping unpleasantly on the bare skin of my legs below my Bermuda shorts.

There was a door set into the back of the house, a small door only five feet high; unlike the remainder of the mansion, the exterior of which was preserved as well as our budgets allowed, the door was a seedy tatter of another era. Its cream-colored paint was faded and dirty, tending now to peel and chip, littering the small flagstone walk with sad tear-flakes of pigment. I had on occasion asked Dr. Johnson what rested behind that anomalous door, but I had never succeeded in getting a straight answer. "It's the sickled grain room," he would reply. If I pushed him some more, he would go on in terrifying clichés about age and death and the fatal vanity of art.

"I know," I said, suddenly comprehending what ought to have been clear long before. "This is where you keep your pets, in whatever form they may take."

Dr. Johnson fiddled with the several locks. I watched the strong muscles of his back shifting beneath the coarse white duck of his lab coat. "They take only the grim forms of corruption," he said. I considered the uncountable ways he might have described the death of his pets, each way a monstrous perversion of literary style. But he had not chosen one of the more readily accessible clichés, after all. Perhaps he was recovering. I could only think that perhaps there was hope for my own *romantic* affliction.

He flung the door open. Standing in the bright glare of the yard, I could see nothing of the chamber beyond. Dr. Johnson entered, ducking his head; I followed, somewhat bored and resigned to offering my condolences. I stood beyond the threshold of the room for some seconds, waiting drowsily for my eyes to grow accustomed to the dimness. My nose rebelled immediately, however; mixed with the ancient, musty smell of a room long sealed away from the common business of a great house was the fetid odor of decay. The room itself was rotting, a spreading abscess devouring an entire corner of the mansion. But more than that, I sensed an overpowering presence of putrefying material, lately and voluntarily introduced by my friend.

Soon I could make out a series of rough-hewn wooden tables set up in rows, each bearing small boxes of damp earth. In these I saw dozens of mushrooms, their thin stalks no longer able to support the weight of their huge, spreading caps. Dr. Johnson picked up one of the boxes and carried it into the daylight. At last, delivered in death into the full glare of the sun, their colors became evident. They were brilliantly hued underneath, though the stalks and the tops of the caps were a sick pinkish-white.

"My pets!" said Dr. Johnson, in an odd, whining voice.

"Remarkably phallic, aren't they?" I asked.

"Dead, all dead."

"That is the way of the world," I said. He stared at me for a few seconds. Then he roused himself, as though struck by some overpowering thought.

"Come, you must help me carry them all out." I shrugged. He was obviously deeply affected and, though he had spared few tears for my mollies, I felt bound to accede to his sudden wishes. Together we brought out the boxes of dead mushrooms, nearly a hundred containers in all. Dr. Johnson placed them against a low brick wall at the very back of the yard. A row of tall banana plants grew along the wall, and in the middle of the line a space had been left for some sort of arbor. The arbor itself had long since disappeared and its place filled by a sapling crepe myrtle purchased recently by my companion. Furiously he ripped the newly planted tree from the ground, casting it carelessly over his shoulder. I ignored his frenzy. Then he began to dig. He seemed to forget my presence, so intent was he; it was just as well, as I had little desire to aid his foolishness. Hours later he had completed his task—a deep grave, lined with flagstones torn from the walk and driveway. His mushrooms (*fungi*, he insisted on calling them; they were fungi, not mushrooms) were safely buried beneath a towering cairn of stones and old wooden milk-crates.

Days passed, and Dr. Johnson's grief did not abate. I mentioned once, casually, while bringing him a tray of broth and junket, that life must go on. He did not take the hint. I suggested he get another sort of pet. He only growled senselessly. He did not appear to want to work at all until he saw, quite by accident, a newscast in which a botanist somewhere in the great Outback of North America described the coincidental demise of his own fungi. Then, later, came Dr. Waters' brilliant thesis. I remember the look on my colleague's face when he read that. He jumped out of bed, wearing the quaint hospital-style lab coat I had fashioned for him (cut out in the back), and ran to our typewriter. He wrote a letter of commiseration to the Iowa botanist, and a letter of admiration to Waters.

"I'm all right, now," he said to me afterward. "It's okay. As long as it's part of some cosmic something or other, I don't mind. In fact, I'm proud. Maybe the government will reimburse me."

How easily his fungi were forgotten; how grateful I was for the divine intervention. Now at last we had our goal and our first true data, all at once. We accepted as a given Dr. Waters' curious hypothesis. Perhaps every day a different species of animal or plant would leave this God-favored world for good and all; what an exciting prospect to research! It made little difference to us, as callous, disinterested members of the scientific community, what those species might be. But we had to know *how often* the phenomenon occurred. Such is the nature of science: What can be measured, what can be classified, named, catalogued, filed, documented, that was all that concerned us. How often did an entire species croak? We spent many sleepless nights debating, not on the length of the period (we agreed that it *must* be once *per diem*), but on the best method of proving it.

While we tackled the riddle from a purely technical, reasoned, dispassionate angle, the popular media began their hateful commercialism. Each day the Cleveland *States-Item* printed a little box on the front page, much as at Christmas a record of Shopping Days Left To is kept. The box was outlined with a heavy black border, and centered within, in small type, was the name of the species that biologists had decided had gone extinct the previous day, with a mawkish photo of one of the things. It's hard to jerk a tear with a picture of a scarce

Australian peat moss; but I'll never forget the day the kaji lemur passed away. Those huge, pleading eyes turned my stomach.

This went on for a while; most days the box was completely empty, meaning that the scientists had been unable to identify which of the innumerable species no longer was. Less frequently, there was some plant or animal I'd never heard of gracing the newspaper's lower left corner. I complained to Dr. Johnson, wishing that we could end the sentimental exploitation of our disaster. He scowled at me. "You're as bad as they are!" he said angrily. "What about the silkworm? What about the inkwell beetle? What about the diamondwort?" I could only shrug my shoulders and smile in embarrassment.

*   *   *

Through a quirk of the city's public transportation system, Paul arrived at work nearly fifteen minutes earlier than usual. It was late September; already the mornings were retaining some of the night's icy chill. It would not be long before Paul would need a stronger incentive to face the winter cold. Still, the autumn sharpness excited him. The slight dash of cool air, the deeper blue of the sky, even the fresh rustling of the fading leaves revived him, forced him to make a realization that his narrow world could still be beautiful. But that annual discovery was too ephemeral; it never lived beyond the second snowfall, when the first already lay crushed and filthy.

Paul waited in the long snaky line by the timeclocks. He stood behind an older woman who was dressed in faded, torn coveralls. The woman carried a copy of the morning paper folded under her arm, her lunchpail in the other hand. Bored, waiting for the slow line to creep by the clock, Paul tried to read the bits of articles revealed by the woman's heavy arm. He saw the bottom part of the first page, the news index, and the weather forecast. Beside that, half concealed by a fold of the woman's knit pullover, was the day's black box. Paul could see that it was not empty; another something had died off the day before, perhaps. If the scientists had been able to decide what had gone extinct, it must have been a fairly common species.

Paul hoped that it was good and dramatic. He felt a little guilty as he stood in the line, straining to see what the paper said. In years gone by he always turned to the obituary section with a thrilling, eager feeling: Who knew what might be there? A beautiful movie star cut down in the prime of her career, an athlete tragically killed in a freak accident, a leader murdered, leaving a nation directionless. Something to make the day special. Something to talk about. "Did you hear? Korpaniev died. In his garage. They found him in the car with the motor running. Maybe suicide."

That was the way it used to be. Now Paul looked first at the little black box. Most mornings it was empty; the experts had not been able to determine just what had gone extinct the day before. Sometimes the box named a flower or a bug; that didn't mean that they had necessarily died within the previous twenty-four hours, of course. It was merely that the scientists had finally noticed their sudden absence. Day after day Paul hoped for something impressive; he was usually disappointed and had to turn to the obits, where celebrities still passed away in the old proportions.

More and more articles appeared in the paper, each taking some shrill position on the question of Dr. Bertram Waters' theory. Of course, most conservative biologists would not believe that the matter really existed. There was no concrete proof, other than the ragged list of suddenly extinguished species. But that was not necessary and sufficient evidence that Waters was right. There could be no such evidence; the whole situation was too theological for serious scientists to argue. But if Waters *happened* to be correct, then the entire rational basis of natural science meant nothing any longer anyway. Paul was content to skim a small portion of the debates and wait anxiously for something *big* to go: bears. What if every bear in the world died? Wouldn't *that* cause a fight?

One article a few days before had argued that the situation was a great deal more serious than anyone had yet imagined. Surely people like Paul and Linda could not be concerned over the extinction of *Cantepus nepifer*, a microscopic animal that lived in bogs and ponds and such. But, the author of the article continued, the *dirans* flatworm, which fed almost exclusively on the *nepifer*, would be in very bad shape. Perhaps the flatworm, too, would be driven to extinction; deprived of its natural food, it would die off before its natural turn.

The idea intrigued Paul. He had never before realized how interdependent these things were. He did not get concerned, however; no, greater scientists than even the author of the article argued that introducing such concepts as a creature's "natural turn" automatically prejudiced the case by making the argument irresponsibly subjective. There was no way to debate the question without resort to scientifically untenable premises. Nevertheless, the controversy raged, and the newspapers and magazines cheerfully served as forums—and continued to list the forever-gone animals and plants, one by one.

Paul adopted a patient, noncommittal attitude. More accurately, he didn't especially care and, like the majority of people with whom he discussed the situation, didn't particularly believe any of it. It was just another wild scientific theory, like the existence of life on other planets, or proof of Noah's Flood in the streaky strata of the Grand Canyon. The scientists were having fun fighting it out, and everyone was getting a scrap of entertainment, but the matter itself would probably be extinct in a few weeks.

The line shuffled ahead. Paul leaned against a bulletin board, empty except for a single poster. The notice showed a decapitated body searching for its head, which rested far away, eyes Xed out, as the bottom dot of an exclamation point that emphasized the words *Carelessness Costs!* "It don't make any difference," thought Paul as he examined the poster wearily. "My mollies led good molly lives. They were as careful as they could be. They honored their mothers and their fathers. It never did *them* any good." The line moved again. Paul arranged the spare thumbtacks on the board into a large F.

"Could I read your paper for a minute?" he said to the woman ahead of him in the line.

She turned around and regarded him blankly for a moment. "What?" she said.

"Could I see your paper?" The woman blinked, then handed the newspaper to him. He nodded his thanks, unfolded the paper, and sought out the black box. The small type inside said *Norassis scotti*. There was a line drawing of a weirdly shaped tubular thing, with regular segments and large nuclear structures. Paul could see that it was some strange microscopic living thing, but whether it was an animal or plant he could not tell. He frowned and folded the newspaper. As an afterthought he reopened it and turned to the sports pages, to check the major-league pennant playoffs. There was no good news there, either, and he returned the paper to the woman.

The day went by slowly. Paul worked on an assembly line during the morning, tightening the same six bolts on voltmeter chassis until lunchtime. In the afternoon he typed out Quality Control tags with lists of the subassemblers' code numbers. Then he went home. As soon as he stepped into the sunlight he forgot all the petty annoyances of the day. His job wasn't serious enough to make him rehearse his irritation after working hours. He showed up at the factory in the morning and stayed long enough to earn his paycheck; beyond that, the job had no existence.

He was glad to get home, nevertheless. He was tired, and he just wanted to watch the news and eat supper. He said hello to Linda (who failed to answer) and went straight into the bedroom. He lay down and switched on the television. The international and national news rarely interested him; the local news had relevance only slightly more often. But after the major items, and just before the sports and the weather report, the news program presented a summary of the day's activity among the scientists.

Linda came into the room. "Can't you hear me? I've called you three times now. If you want to eat, come on. I'm not going to serve you in here."

Paul looked up at her. She was his wife; she was even now carrying their first child, due to be born around the end of December. He knew it was foolish to be sentimental now, after so much bad feeling had grown up between them. Even the baby was a sore spot in their relationship; Linda never missed an opportunity to blame the unwanted pregnancy on his selfish appetites. She was probably frightened and unhappy; he certainly hadn't been doing anything to ease her anxiety. "Sit down for a while," he said. "Watch the news with me."

"The food's getting cold," she said. "I'm going to eat now. Bring the set out with you if you don't want to miss your program."

Paul pulled the television's cord from the wall and followed his wife into the kitchen. He put the set on the table and plugged it in. "We never watch anything together any more," he said, noticing that it was spaghetti for supper.

"Maybe that has something to do with the difference in our tastes. Maybe we're not as compatible as we used to be. Maybe *one* of us is growing and maturing, and the other is content to let his mind rot."

"Have you been paying any attention to how all these animals and things have been dying?" he asked.

Linda paused in her eating to stare at him. "No," she said, "I haven't. I have other things to do."

"It's just that somebody said today how all these tiny dead bugs and plants may hurt us, eventually. I mean, with them gone, the other animals have less to eat."

She gave him a scornful look. "Listen who has the big heart all of a sudden. He can't spare a minute for his own wife's pains, but he's worried sick about a lousy bug. Look, *we* won't have any trouble, and that's all that counts. As long as the A&P doesn't go out of business, we'll be all right."

"Never mind." Paul gave up his conciliatory effort. After all, he had made a decent try; the next move was up to Linda. He ate his supper resentfully and watched the news commentator, who was remarking on the potential danger caused by the sudden gaps appearing in the ecological food chains.

"What few people beside the scientific researchers can grasp," said the newsman, "is the idea that something as negligible as the pond scum in your backyard may be indirectly important to the well-being of your entire family. Though the individual plants that make up the algae layer are so tiny that they're invisible to the naked eye, they play an important role in the natural scheme of things. Besides serving as food for various larger creatures, they serve a critical function by aerating the water, supplying oxygen to the fish. One species of freshwater algae became extinct over three weeks ago, and as a result the entire population of fishes in several lakes in Colorado were nearly wiped out. Fortunately, an alternate species of algae was artificially introduced by a local high school biology class.

"In the random pattern of Dr. Waters' theory, we cannot be sure what particular species of plant or animal will be next. Perhaps one day soon every shoot of *Oryza sativa,* or common rice, will die. It is not difficult to imagine what effect that will have on the nearly two billion people who depend on rice as their daily nourishment. That's certainly food for thought. This is Gil Monahan, Channel 10 News, New York."

"That's what I call yellow journalism," said Linda.

"Why?"

"Because he can't even prove what he's talking about, and the first thing he tries to do is scare the audience. Sure, it would be awful if all the rice in the world died overnight. But what are the odds of that happening?"

Paul got up and scraped the rest of his spaghetti into the garbage. "Yeah, you're right. But that doesn't mean it's wrong to be prepared."

"And maybe an airplane will fall out of the sky and smash you on your way to work tomorrow. Is that going to keep you home?"

Paul grimaced as he unplugged the television and carried it back to the bedroom. "Maybe it will," he said.

* * *

Above and beyond all considerations of mere change and transmutation, the pure panic of a disaster is fun to watch. I could see the symptoms already—my experience in these matters stood me in good stead—and I could hardly contain my excitement. I could tell no one, least of all Dr. Johnson, what I knew and what I could so easily foresee. My very good friend would himself provide many evenings' entertainment, as I observed his placid frame of mind begin to fray around its selvaged border. His screams and hysterical pronouncements of doom were the sweetest music to me, for I understood that if such an unruffleable sort as Dr. Johnson could be reduced to frenzy, the common crowd would soon break loose altogether.

I forgot one detail. The great masses were not as educated as my companion, and were for the most part totally ignorant of the implications of our disaster. Like those poor souls who lived on the very slopes of Vesuvius, they did not comprehend the proximity of death. And, like the survivors of that ancient Pompeiian spectacle who relocated themselves afterward on those same slopes, I don't suppose the masses especially cared. Human beings have carried within themselves the notion of racial superiority so long that it's very difficult for us to imagine a world without people. If a group or a city or even a nation is wiped out, other cities and nations remain to merely cluck tongue. I had no slightest desire to spell out the imminent doom; I wanted only to be around when the idea dawned on them all.

"We should stock up," said Dr. Johnson one morning. "We ought to get a large vehicle and raid a supermarket. Canned goods. We could live out our lives on canned goods if we had to, couldn't we? Meat, especially. What if all the cattle go? No more meat. Cases and cases of ravioli, that's what we need."

"And all the wheat?" I asked. "What if wheat goes tomorrow? Crackers will soon be very scarce. Of course, you can buy those tinned, I suppose, but that soon gets expensive. Particularly if you're thinking about forty years' worth of rations."

"Forget that," said Dr. Johnson irritably. "Never mind wheat. If wheat goes we can get used to cornmeal products. Or rye bread. Rye toast with fresh butter and blackberry jam is one of the grandest things in the world. Surely the laws of chance prohibit the extinction of wheat, corn, and rye within a single lifetime."

"Then stop worrying about the cattle. There's always pork and lamb."

"You're insane!" he cried, and I only laughed gently. "What sort of ivory tower do you live in? Don't you see what's happening? Don't you *care?*"

Of course I saw. And no, I didn't care. Out with the old, in with the new! Great bloody holes were being ripped in the food chains that Mother Nature had so patiently devised over countless millennia. How would the world react? What would devour what? There are always certain special moments in one's life, like the day I awoke to learn that JFK had died. How stunning! What would happen next? How would the powers realign themselves? Now I felt that precise emotion—what would happen next? How would nature realign things? Would the bluepoint oyster find something else to live on, or choose a species-specific suicide by its overspecialized diet? And all Dr. Johnson (and the rest of the scientific community, for the most part) could think of was his own future.

I did not worry about myself. I knew that I could eat just about anything.

The public, which for so many weeks had ignored the increasingly strident warnings of Dr. Waters and his colleagues (us), now began to panic. They had been blind to the problem for so long that now, when they chose to see, the situation was far graver than their meager hope could battle. They reacted in typically bestial fashion. First, religion. Never before had so many prayers wafted heavenward, so much incense or whatever devoteeward, so many anguished moans helpless priestward. None of that worked, and I had little sympathy. In the meantime, with Dr. Johnson's weak-kneed aid, I made a killing by coralling the canned sardine market in Cleveland's Irish Channel. I convinced several local store managers that the seas were dying, the algae were extinct, the kelp and the seaweed, and that soon every fish in the ocean would be floating belly-up to God. I sold cases and cases of hoarded sardines for remarkable profits, which I used to buy up all the pimentos in town. This proved to be a mistake. I digress.

Anyway, after religion the populace turned to politics, recapitulating the discoveries of universal folly they had all made as adolescents. Countries were urged to war to feed their citizens, all busily envisioning themselves starving on the morrow. No one had yet been beset by these hardships, of course; but Dr. Waters' prose was so persuasive that millions of people developed the most delicious sense of verging destruction. Any minute now, any minute and we'll have *nothing to eat.* I loved it.

Dr. Johnson went berserk. Having neither religion nor politics to turn to, having only the cold embrace of science, he imagined himself abandoned in the cosmos. He smashed every little bottle of chemicals we had; their contents drifted powdery to the floor, combining in useless mixtures, which my friend tried to ignite. No success there. Then he thrust his bare arm into a cage of gerbils, bidding the timid beasts to gnaw his flesh. They would not. In an ecstasy of impotent terror he leaped headlong into a half-completed glassware sculpture, only to emerge with cuts over one eye and charming glitters of jeweled glass in his hair and beard.

As he knelt amid the silicate ruin I touched his shoulder. "Have you had quite enough?" I asked.

"I will not see," he said, sobbing.

"Splinters in your eyes? Shards of glass tubing, unpolished by any Bunsen's flame, stabbing into the soft blueness of your irises?"

He only shook his head. I laughed quietly. Dr. Johnson was finally, completely broken. He had had enough, and I did not wish to cause him any further torture. I helped him rise, brushed off his wrinkled lab coat, ran a brotherly hand through his tangled hair to collect what bloody spikes of crystal I could, and urged him upstairs to bed. As we progressed slowly up that felted spiral, I wished that someone could do the same for the whole race of men. That was sadly impossible. I was needed here.

Dr. Johnson fell asleep quickly, thanks partly to the drug I mixed into his milk and Bosco. I left him and returned downstairs, wondering if any more of our abandoned experimental animals had gone extinct since last I checked. On an impulse I threw open all the cages and set them free; hamsters and monkeys and others scampered or limped to the exit. I flung out the double-shuttered doors; the animals trooped past, obviously in some bewilderment. I threw handfuls of lettuce and wood chips onto the gravel walk outside, and they soon got the idea. The next morning I saw only a single serpent, twined in the iron lace that fringed the pillars supporting the upstairs balcony.

Soon Dr. Johnson regained his mental balance. I read to him of other great catastrophes in the world's youth, from the Bible and various works of science fiction. He seemed greatly cheered by these recitals, and began at last to ask me questions of our current situation, as though I had any more answers than he. I lied to him as best I could, and he improved steadily; soon, about the middle of November, he was well enough to accept my suggestion that we go on some sort of vacation. Even the idea of a fishing trip did not frighten him (it was the thought of poor slaughtered beasts that had driven him wacky, I later learned); he was very eager to go out into the world and get his limit while both he and the fish still existed. I nodded sagely. Everything was all right.

*   *   *

On November 5, the sugar maple trees died.

It was the first really remarkable species to become extinct. It was very definitely the big thing that Paul had been waiting for. But when he saw the black box in the paper that evening, his reaction was rather one of anger, as though the power that caused the event had somehow rudely imposed on him.

"Did you see this?" he asked Linda, holding the newspaper out for her to read.

"What now? Something else die off?"

"Yeah, maple trees."

"That's too bad," she said. She didn't really look very concerned; she rested on the bed, spending the final five weeks of her gravidity conserving her energy. "Is that where we get syrup and stuff?"

"I guess so."

"Oh, well, as long as we still have sugar cane, never mind."

Paul tossed the paper onto the bed. "That's not the point," he said irritably. "This thing's turning into a pretty lousy inconvenience. It's got to be the air. Remember when everybody was saying the bad winters were on account of the Russians or the strontium 90 or something? Nobody ever talks about that anymore. I'll bet there was more truth in it than the government ever admitted. I'll bet this whole thing's our punishment for pollution."

Linda switched off the television impatiently. She had watched six hours of daytime game shows, and now the situation-comedy reruns were too much for her. "That's silly," she said. "What are the maple trees being punished for?"

"They always say that God moves in mysterious ways."

"God? Since when, God? And those aren't *mysterious* ways you're talking about. They're childish and stupid."

"I don't know about anything else. I can't explain it. Sometimes it scares me."

"I still don't believe it's happening," said Linda, turning on her side heavily. "I haven't seen anything that's convinced me; I think a lot of supposedly smart people are getting hysterical over nothing."

Paul felt himself being led into the same argument they had had every day for nearly four months. "What more proof do you *want?* For crying out loud, every lousy sugar maple tree in the world just died, all together in one day, and you say nothing strange is happening."

Linda gave him a forced smile, broad and cold and mocking. "How do *I* know every maple tree in the world is dead? Whose word am I taking? How do *they* know? How can you be sure there isn't one left, far away, in Pakistan, maybe?"

Paul sat on the edge of the bed. He reached across his wife's body to turn on the television again. When the picture came on he changed the station, searching for the early-evening news. An ominous scene stopped his hand: A shaky film, shot with a hand-held camera while running down some nameless street, showed huge boiling clouds of smoke rising behind a row of stores. The windows of the shops were all smashed. Broken bottles and crates, overturned shopping carts, automobiles abandoned where they had smashed into walls or telephone poles, and merchandise, looted and thrown away as useless, littered the sidewalk. A figure farther down the street ran into view. The cameraman stopped and tried to focus on the other person, who threw something and ran. The scene jumped wildly, then settled down with the camera staring fixedly at the sky. The picture went black, and almost immediately a newscaster appeared to gloss the events.

"See," said Paul, "*somebody's* taking this awful serious. That's what it's been like out there. That's why I want to get out of the city so bad. People are starting to panic. If you got outside at all you'd see it, too; but you just want to sulk in the apartment. You're not going to be able to save your skin like that. Not next month when there isn't anything left to buy at the A&P."

"That film wasn't from the city," she said, her voice sounding frightened for the first time.

"No," said Paul, "I think that was supposed to be some little New England town. But it'll happen here, sooner or later. The city sort of insulates you against things. You get the idea that anything you want will be around somewhere, nearby. It's all an illusion. Everything we need has to be trucked in. We're more dependent on the outside world than anybody on Earth. If food gets scarce, you can bet there won't be any happy farmers driving their own share over the bridge to feed us. It's happening already out in the country. The small-town stores are being emptied by hoarders."

"Paul," said Linda. He looked at her, but she was staring straight ahead. He hoped that she'd cry but knew that she wouldn't.

"What?"

"We can't go. The baby."

"I think that's a pretty good reason to get out while we can. We've got to find a place to hole up and wait for people to come to their senses."

"That won't work, Paul. It's people doing just that who are making the situation worse."

"So? Two more won't make any difference."

She turned to look at him. "Paul, I don't like this," she whispered.

"Me neither," he said, taking her hand and rubbing it. He was shocked to find her palm hot and clammy with sweat. "I'm supposed to be the protector and all that stuff. Just let me figure it out and we'll be okay. The three or four or five of us." He breathed heavily, then laughed when he saw her sudden smile.

"Just three," she said. "Don't overwork me."

The condition of life was degenerating. The frequent speeches by the scientists, far from making things clear, served only to confuse the already volatile situation. It was commonly accepted that Dr. Waters' warning was true, that certain species of animals and plants were spontaneously dying out. There seemed to be no pathological reason behind the situation, and no one, neither technologist nor clergyman, cared to offer an explanation. People were far too concerned with the effects to care about the reasons.

Paul doubted whether those effects were serious enough to justify the rioting and looting that was taking place more and more each day. Sure, the order of things had been shaken up; important niches in the ecology had been suddenly left vacant. But the cumulative threat to mankind couldn't be very large, nor could whatever danger threatened become real in the near future. In the meantime, the scientific community had plenty of time to avert a general tragedy.

So Paul thought, until the ninth of December, the morning all the dogs were dead. On the way to the subway he saw one of the neighborhood mongrels lying on the sidewalk, its head and front legs falling over the curb. Paul felt a faint distaste and hoped that someone would remove the dog's corpse before he came home. Less than thirty yards away was another dead dog, a German shepherd that belonged to an old Hispanic lady on the block. It always sat in the open window of the woman's apartment, staring at Paul as he walked by. Now it hung over the windowsill, its tongue swollen and protruding, its eyes opened sightlessly to the ground. A few flies hovered and settled on its muzzle. Paul suffered a touch of disgust, then a quick shock of fear. *The dogs!* Even the most stubborn of Waters' opponents would have a moment's alarm now.

Vindication was a poor trade for what the extinction of *Canis familiaris* would do to the teetering popular mind. Unable to understand what was happening, people everywhere were returning to primal instincts. There was no definite way to answer the challenge, though; no one could say just where the danger might arise. It was this helplessness, this failure of logic to advise one on how best to prepare, that destroyed man's thin shell of culture.

The Jennings Manufacturing Corporation was closed when Paul arrived. There were no signs, no explanations; large steel gates were drawn over the doors and locked with heavy chains. Workmen were busily bricking up the windows on the ground floor.

Paul went up to one of the men. "They're not even going to let me go in and clean out my locker?" he said.

The workman didn't turn around. "Nope," he said. "You'll have to wait until things settle down a little."

"Old Man Jennings must be figuring on a pretty long wait."

"Don't you?"

"I just wanted the instant coffee I left inside. You got a dog?"

"Yeah. Why?"

"Was he all right when you left home this morning?"

"I guess so," said the workman, putting down his trowel to gaze curiously at Paul. "I don't know, I didn't see him. Why?"

"He's dead." Paul shoved his hands deep into the pockets of his jacket and started walking back to the subway.

The bricklayer called after him. "Dogs, today? For God's sake, why *dogs?*" Paul shook his head and kept walking. Sooner or later the world was going to be in awfully bad trouble. People needed to keep their emotions out of it. There had to be a sensible way to live in spite of the problem. Paul had seen the situation develop long before most of the rest; it was his long exposure and his uncertainty that held him from running into the street, screaming. Linda, who had tried to ignore the hints of calamity as long as possible, had at last admitted her blindness. Suddenly forced to deal with a nightmare of doubts, she had thrown herself completely into Paul's care, hoping that he knew better what to do. It had been a bitter trial for her; she had always prided herself on her independence and her reasonable outlook. Now it seemed that reason had little survival value. Confronted with a completely illogical environment, she preferred to have someone else assume the responsibilities. She hid from herself the fact that Paul was no better equipped to take over those functions.

"Hey, Linda?" he called, when he got home.

"Paul? Why are you back so soon?"

He went into the bedroom, where Linda was already awake, watching an early women's panel show. "Jennings closed down the plant. I guess he didn't want the riffraff getting in and tearing up his pile of soldering irons. So it looks like I'm out of a job for a while."

"They were talking about how bad things are getting in Asia. This guy was saying that the people are falling back into tribes and all sorts of stuff. He says he can see it happening everywhere, even here. Everybody's predicting the end of the world, but I look out the window and I can't even see anything different."

"You look out now, you'll see a lot of dead dogs."

"Huh? Dogs? What happened?"

"All the dogs died," said Paul. "Like the trees and bugs and germs. Just that now the thing is a lot more obvious. If you think people were rattled before, just wait."

Linda hadn't really accepted the news. "Is it some kind of disease? Why haven't they come up with a shot or a pill or something?"

"And give it to every living thing in the world? No, it looks like all we can do is watch. This isn't something you can beat with a stick."

"Paul, would you lie here with me for a while?"

He was glad to rest. He was very frightened; he knew that there must be a safe course to follow, some way to protect his family and himself. But he didn't know how to find out about it.

* * *

"It has come to the point where I must believe my own truisms," said Dr. Johnson sadly. I had not been paying close attention, and had to ask him to explain. The sun was warm, though the mid-December air was chilly. I sat in our small boat, drowsing with the gently rocking motion, and gratefully deferred to my companion all intellectual activity.

"We're scraping the bottom of the barrel," he said, and I thrilled to the return of the old trite him. "We're really in a pickle now, and there's nothing for it but to muddle through. What guideposts have we? Only those we build ourselves, out of desperation and ignorance. Science, science, why have you forsaken us?"

"That is not strictly so," I said sleepily. "Science has not deserted us at all. Merely transcended. We fail to understand. Our fault, entirely. We're looking for answers in the same dried-up old wells."

"Perhaps," said Dr. Johnson in his customary thoughtful way, "and perhaps not." He was such a comical sight, sitting in the stern of our little rowboat, dressed in his wrinkled white lab-coat and a beat-up old hat stuck with badly made fishing flies. He held his fishing pole stiffly, staring constantly at the point where the line disappeared beneath the slow ripples. I had warned him several times to relax, or suffer cramped muscles later, but he would not listen. He was determined to catch more fish than I, and do it by concentration. I had not even brought my fishing equipment, to make it easier for him.

"There's a chance all these fish will be extinct tomorrow, so you'd better do as well as possible this afternoon," I said jokingly. He nodded grimly. Only two days before we set out into the bayou area surrounding Cleveland, a popular local species of bait worm had died out, and the prices on everything else had immediately skyrocketed. Such is my luck.

The great muddy river, carrying with it the rich effluvia of its mighty journey, rolled at last near its goal; the bayou country, where the river's fresh water mingled with the salty fingers of the sea, was an eerie, lovely, hazardous place. Immense oak trees, all shaggy with Spanish moss still, though their own leaves had long since died, marked the scattered scraps of solid ground. The maple trees, each dead now, looked forlorn among the verdant splendors we had found not thirty miles from our laboratory on St. Charles Avenue. Cleveland itself was being slowly destroyed, as its inhabitants grew more violently frustrated. But here, in the lonely beauty of the virgin marshlands, I could yet pretend that all was well, that some benevolent hand had created our Earth as a bountiful park for man's enjoyment.

"We may never have to work again," said Dr. Johnson, reeling in his line to see how much sourdough he had left. He never used his flies; they were mostly just for atmosphere. "I don't see any reason to expect this perplexing situation—"

"Disaster," I said cheerfully.

"Yes, disaster, you're right. Anyway, I see no cause to believe that it will end suddenly."

"Other than the fact that it began suddenly as well."

Dr. Johnson grasped his fishing pole awkwardly, up at arm's length, while he swung the line pendulum-fashion. Finally, with an inept jerk of the wrist, he loosed the weighted string into the water. He had not accurately co-ordinated his jerk with the line's arc, and the hook and sinker splashed into the green stuff that lapped against the side of the boat. Dr. Johnson smiled happily. "You're wrong again," he said. "There's no way of telling when these species began biting the dust. Who knows? Perhaps this is the explanation for the rather abrupt demise of the dinosaurs. It wouldn't have taken much to alter fatally their unstable environment. Just a minor food plant becoming extinct overnight. That would decimate the herbivores; the carnivores would soon follow in the familiar domino theory."

"You've got it all figured out, haven't you?" I said. He only nodded, a simple-minded grin on his face.

"I think I may go back to college and delve into German literature," he said later, while he let the various aquatic creatures feast on his sourdough.

"Which college?" I asked skeptically, aware that institutions were tumbling by the wayside all over the world.

"I don't know. I don't suppose the more established universities are having as much difficulty as the less exclusive."

"Sure they are," I said. "They're targets. Besides, you're only seeking sanctuary. You've lost the real drive, the sincere passion for knowledge to which you devoted yourself in your youth."

"Times have changed." He redoughed his hook; I could only make scornful sounds, which he ignored.

He had some points, of course. Things were different now, and no amount of prayer could make them back into what they had been. Football, for instance, had had to make great allowances for the insanity of the fans. The crowds shrunk from week to week, until only a dozen or so spectators turned out for the eleventh game of the season, between the Browns and the Rams. After that the remainder of the schedule was suspended. It was a shame, too, because at that time it looked like the Browns had great Super Bowl chances.

The Detroit Lions had begun the season with a publicity stunt. Readers of the one still-operating newspaper in the Motor City were asked to suggest an alternate nickname for the team, in the event of the current calamity befalling the species *Panthera leo*. The paper was stunned when not a single entry was submitted. The editor in charge of the contest came up with a phony winner—the Detroit Autoworkers, though it proved to be a shortsighted choice; when things deteriorated further there were definitely fewer autoworkers around than lions. The Yale Bulldogs, however, stuck with more traditions than they could handle, stuck also with their nickname. The original bulldog, stuffed in a trophy case in the school's gymnasium, took on a new and sadder significance.

As darkness began to fall, we headed the little skiff back to the island campsite. Dr. Johnson had caught no fish, but had not lost his abounding good humor. He was still trying to save the last bit of sourdough from his rusty hook, in a mistaken attempt at economy. The light was failing, and I watched his clumsy maneuvers with some dismay.

"Perhaps it's well that we're going back to Cleveland tomorrow afternoon," I said, making an unkind reference to his total failure as a woodsman.

"Why do you say that?" he asked innocently, looking up from his sticky labors.

"Because we're too isolated here. We have no idea of what's going on in the world. We may have some terrifying surprises waiting for us."

"You're an alarmist."

Yes, but not the way he meant. "It's situations like this," I said, "that so often breed subsidiary plagues and social unrest."

"You may have a point. It would be extremely unfortunate if, say, rats were among the next species to disappear."

That was an odd thing for him to say. For five minutes we glided across the turgid water, and I held myself in check. Finally I couldn't stand it and asked him. "Why would it be so bad if the rats died?"

He grinned. He knew he had scored a point; I was still well ahead, though, because he still hadn't cleaned his hook. "It's not rats that are so bad," he said. "As far as your plagues are concerned, I mean. It's the plague-carrying fleas *on* the rats. If the rats were gone, the fleas would have to find other hosts. And that has always meant humans in the past. The great black plagues of history have generally coincided with efforts to reduce the rat population."

"Oh."

"Rats!"

"Yes," I said wearily, "I know. Let's hope they thrive."

"No," said Dr. Johnson, his voice strangely muffled, "that was an interjection. I stuck myself with this hook."

Another metaphysical point for me. I could barely see his outline against the now-starry sky; one hand was raised to his mouth as he soothed the savaged thumb. He was a good friend, and I'll probably never meet his like again. Of all my coworkers, my costrivers after *scientia*, I guess that Dr. Johnson most closely filled my image of the truly wise man that I formed in my undisciplined schooldays. But it is always the *fittest* who survive, not, as popular thought has it, the strongest. Perhaps it was fate that kept me from bringing my own fishing equipment; perhaps I have earned some special favor of destiny, I know not. But I thank my lucky stars that it wasn't I fiddling with the sourdough in that boat.

When we pulled the little skiff up on the grass of our campsite, I noticed that Dr. Johnson was still sucking on his wounded thumb. "What's wrong?" I asked.

"It doesn't want to stop bleeding," he said.

"You must have stabbed it pretty deep."

"No, not so bad. It ought to have quit by now."

"Have you tried direct pressure?"

He sighed in the gloom. "I've been doing that for ten minutes."

I felt a tiny, cold glitter of something. Slowly the thought took shape. "You know what I think?" I said. "I think we've hit the big time. It's possible that a couple of days ago the special little bacteria that live in our intestines died off. You know, the ones that produce most of the vitamin K our bodies use. You need that vitamin K because it's vitally important to the clotting of blood. Hospitals give newborn babies doses of vitamin K because newborns don't have colonies of that bacteria in their bowels. Now, if that little bacteria is extinct, we're going to have a lot of people with blood that won't stop bleeding. And then there's going to be a rush on vitamin K. And then there won't be enough, and people won't be able to get their hands on it, and then—"

"I think you're getting carried away. That's not very scientific at all, is it? I mean, you deduce all this from the bad cut on my thumb."

"I'm not deducing," I said testily, "I'm hoping."

"It's grotesque."

"And then there'll be riots, but the officials will be helpless, and more and more people will start hemorrhaging. We'll have a world of hemophiliacs! And before anybody can do anything about it, it'll be too late. We won't have to wait until all the food vanishes." I was very excited, but worried, too, because my hypothesis was built on rather thin evidence.

"Your hypothesis is pretty shaky," said Dr. Johnson, echoing my thoughts in that winsome manner of his.

I decided to perform a serious experiment. I felt it prudent to know the truth before I returned to Cleveland, so that I might be ready for the worst. That night, after Dr. Johnson and I had retired to our sleeping bags, I pretended to fall asleep quickly. Dr. Johnson had no difficulty dropping off, after the long, exciting day on the water. I crept from my zippered bag and moved soundlessly to his side. I made a careful incision on the inside of his arm with my scaling knife, about one-half inch long and deep enough to start a copious flow of blood; I also could not avoid rousing him from his slumber.

"What are you doing?" he asked sleepily.

"Binding you with stout cords," I said, which is what I was doing at that point. I suppose I ought to have done that first; that's what experiments are for, to learn these things. I made a mental note.

He complained that the incision gave him some discomfort. I opened the first-aid kit and allowed him two aspirins, no water. Then I sat down to wait for results; the blood ran freely, never slowing down during a period of fifteen minutes. I tried to stanch the rivulet with a gauze pad, but that had no effect. By morning Dr. Johnson's heart had pumped enough of the viscid fluid to foul his sleeping bag beyond possible hope of cleansing. I said goodbye to my friend and went outside to wait for the boat to take me back to Cleveland.

* * *

It was very cold. The oil companies had stopped delivering fuel, and the day before, the Morans' apartment building had burned its last. Paul and Linda lay in the bed, bundled as warmly as they could manage, but still shivering and exhausted from a poor night's sleep.

"I ought to go out today," said Paul. "I could get us a stove that burned wood and stuff. And we'll need more food soon."

"Don't go, Paul. I'm sure the baby's due today. I just know it. You won't be able to find a doctor, and I don't want to be alone when it comes."

Paul threw back the pile of clothing and blankets angrily. "Oh, I don't know anymore," he said, getting up and pacing the floor. "I can't see that I'll be any use whether I'm here or gone."

"I need you, Paul," she said. "We need each other. We just don't have anybody else in the world anymore."

He looked at her, lying helpless beneath the ineffectual layers of material. Her face had become lined with worry; her hair, once her greatest pride in whatever shrill tint it wore, was matted and dull. The mythical glow of motherhood had somehow passed her by, but Paul didn't mind that. He saw her now in a way he had never imagined possible. The heavy weight of life in the newly hard times had crushed all the false, selfish values she had cherished. Without the neurotic need to create problems, she had become a saner, truer person. He hoped fervently that the same thing had happened to himself.

"You were right," he said flatly. "You were always right. We should have gotten out of the city when we had the chance. Now it's too late; we're stuck here."

"Only until the baby comes," she said. "Then we can leave. I know things will be better. There's no reason at all why we have to stay up North. If it's going to be this bad, we may as well go down where it's not so cold. We can even go to Mexico, maybe. And then we won't have trouble about food—we can just pick it off the trees." She smiled at him, and he felt very lonely.

"So what happens when the baby comes? That scares me out of my mind."

"You've been reading that book I gave you, haven't you? So don't worry. Mine isn't the first baby that's ever been born; just do what it says. Other husbands have delivered. Policemen do it all the time."

"What if something goes wrong?"

Linda forced another smile. "What's to go wrong?" she asked. Paul could think of several things without trying very hard, but he said nothing.

Paul stood by the window, praying that everything would turn out all right. Outside, the street seemed very hostile. The garbage had been accumulating for over a week, and as it spilled and blew across the sidewalks it gave the city a fearful, abandoned look. He thought that it was odd how closely the street's appearance matched his own inner landscape.

"How are your teeth today?" asked Linda.

Paul turned around and laughed. "You're about to have a kid right there by yourself, and you're worried about my teeth."

"If you're not in good shape, you won't be able to pull your weight," she said with a mock-serious expression.

"They're still bleeding a lot," said Paul. "They won't stop. I would have thought they'd stop bleeding a long time ago."

"You're not getting enough vitamins or something."

"I'm just tired of living off canned food. I'd love some good meat right now, but nobody around here's got any."

"I've been bleeding, too," said Linda in a small voice. "It started last night."

"I know. I guess it's natural."

"I never heard of anything like that. I just want it to stop. The mattress is soaked."

"Now *you're* the one who's worrying too much," said Paul.

"You know what I'd like?"

Paul sat by her on the edge of the bed. "No. What?"

Linda smiled. "I think it would be great if one morning we woke up and all the cockroaches in the world were dead. It could happen, couldn't it?"

"Sure," said Paul grimly. "But you know what everybody forgets in the middle of all his little problems? Maybe one morning the cockroaches will wake up and all the *people* will be dead. It could happen just as easy. I mean, if different animals and plants are going one after another, that probably means human beings will have a natural turn, too. From now on when we go to sleep at night, we'll never be sure if we'll wake up in the morning."

"I thought about that once, but I didn't want to mention it. Anyway, you *never* know if you'll wake up. You have to face that."

"There's a big difference," said Paul. "The idea of your own death is somewhere off in the hazy future. If you're our age, dying in your sleep won't be a serious probability for fifty years. But the extinction of everybody is different. I can't accept it calmly, but it's there and I can't fight against it. We'll never know. It could happen tomorrow."

"No, tomorrow is a day for new babies," said Linda. "I don't want to talk about death anymore. We're going to have a baby soon. It's going to have to grow up in this falling-down world, but it'll learn the new tricks fast. Our baby won't have any trouble. Then when we get old, he can take care of us; that's funny to think about. You have to look at it that way, too, Paul. It's not such an awful, hopeless situation. We've already made a lot of adjustments." She squeezed his hand, and he kissed her lightly. "We just have to make a few more, that's all," she whispered weakly, a first tear beginning to trail down her dry cheek.

"That's all," whispered Paul, watching the dark red stain around her grow slowly larger.

25 CRUNCH SPLIT RIGHT ON TWO

Eldon MacDay, No. 23, 6 foot 1, 225 pounds, a running back from Arizona State, realized where he was. It was a frightening discovery not merely because he was sitting at a round table in the dim private dining room in a restaurant in Euclid, Ohio. And not merely because he ought to be, really *should* be lying face down in the odd-smelling artificial turf in the new McGuire Coliseum in Cleveland, beneath a defensive end and an outside linebacker. That didn't upset him much, either; after all, the restaurant was a great deal more restful. The detail that really tore at MacDay's composure was his wife's presence at the table. His wife, Louvina. His wife, who had died over five years before. She was eating a steak, supposedly a Kansas City cut, and he could tell that it was excessively rare, just the way she always ate them. He could see the wine-red juice pooling up around the meat on her plate.

"That ain't no real Kansas City cut, Lou," he said.

"I know," she said, smiling. "I don't specially care."

"Just so's you like it," he said.

"I like it fine."

"All right." MacDay was getting more frightened. He wasn't supposed to be in their favorite old restaurant. He wasn't supposed to be in Euclid at all. But even worse, Louvina wasn't supposed to be *anywhere*.

"You sure you don't want some wine, honey?" he asked.

Louvina just smiled again. He hadn't seen that smile in five years, but it still made him feel the same way. MacDay shuddered. The waiter came to their table and asked if everything were all right; Mac-Day knew just what the man was going to say. He knew, without looking, that the waiter's shirt would be hanging out behind. MacDay stared at the tablecloth, but after a few seconds, though still afraid, he looked up. The waiter was walking slowly away. His shirt was just the way MacDay remembered.

"Are you feeling all right, Eldon?" asked Louvina. MacDay recalled that, too. The first time, though, five years ago, he hadn't known why she had asked it.

"I'm fine," he said softly. He knew that the next thing she'd say would be, "Why aren't you eating?"

"Why aren't you eating? Don't you like the steak?"

"It's all right, Lou," he said. "I just ain't hungry."

"But this is a celebration, baby," said Louvina. She paused, a fork-ful of baked potato, sour cream, and chives held in abeyance while she looked at him, almost shyly. "You know what we be doing tonight, Eldon?"

MacDay looked startled. He stared at his wife; her expression changed to bewilderment. MacDay *knew* what they were going to do that night. He *knew*.

And just as he opened his mouth to reply, he was hit by the Comets' middle linebacker, a rookie subbing for the regular who had been hurt early in the second quarter. MacDay had been kneeling in the artificial grass, one of the Comet defensive players hanging onto MacDay's ankles, another Comet player sprawled across his back. MacDay's mind cleared slowly; first, he felt the sharp point of the football jammed into his forearm near the elbow; then he felt the cold sting of the Cleveland winter air, a contrast from the controlled temperature of the restaurant; he opened his eyes, and the difference in light from the shadowy dining room made his head hurt. Then he felt the lingering shocks of the tackle, he heard the fading sound of the official's whistle, the voices of his teammates and the Comet players, then the background moan of the sixty thousand people in the stadium. He heard the voice of the Browns' quarterback, Tom Bailess, shouting, "Late hit! Late hit!" and the officials disagreeing. The Comet players got to their feet and walked toward their defensive huddle. MacDay opened his eyes wide and shook his head, then stood up and trotted to the Browns' huddle.

"All right," said Bailess, "second and seven. You all right, Mac?"

MacDay nodded. He felt a little bewildered, but you can't explain something like that to a head coach like Jennings.

"Okay," said the quarterback. "Thirty-eight Sweep split right. On three. Break!" The Browns' offensive team clapped once in unison and went into formation. MacDay was glad his running mate, Sonny Staley, the small halfback from Colgate, was getting the ball; Bailess could probably see that MacDay had been shaken up a little on the last play. MacDay was getting a rest, if he could accept blocking the Comets' 260-pound defensive end as a breather.

There was little time to think about the strange vision he had had only a matter of seconds ago. Already it was beginning to vanish, to fade in his memory. It had been only the collision, MacDay told himself; his head had hit one of the Comets, or the ground. He had been knocked out for a second or two. Now, though, while he watched Bailess set up behind the center, he had too much to think about. The quarterback, seeing the other team's defensive alignment, might decide to change the play at the last moment. MacDay listened closely to the signals; Bailess followed the Browns' digit system, calling out first the kind of formation the Comets were using on that play, then a single digit, then a two-digit number. If the digit were different than the "hut" number chosen by Bailess in the huddle, the Browns' players were alerted that a change was being made. The number that followed would indicate the new play. Any other digit would be a dummy, to keep the Comets guessing.

"Pro," shouted Bailess. "Three, thirty-seven. Three, thirty-seven." No change in the play. "Hut . . . hut. Hut!" On the third hut, the Browns exploded into concerted action. The Comets followed immediately. Bailess took the snap from center, spun around out of the way of the two guards pulling from their position, blocking in the direction of the sweep. Bailess faked a handoff to MacDay, who hit the line of scrimmage just after the guards ran by. Behind him, MacDay knew, the quarterback had given the ball to Staley, who was following the guards around right end. MacDay hit the Comets' big defensive end, who was trying to push him aside and get at the ball carrier. MacDay threw himself at the man low, hitting him just above the knees. The Comet player fell forward, pushing MacDay with him for a short distance. MacDay twisted, and he saw that the defensive man would hit him while MacDay was lying on his side. "Oh, hell," thought MacDay. "Here come a shoulder separation." The man fell on him heavily, knocking the breath out of MacDay.

"Are you all right?"

MacDay opened his eyes. His chest and back ached so badly that he couldn't catch his breath. His wife was looking at him with a worried expression. "You okay, Eldon?" she asked again.

"Sure, Lou," he said. He wasn't as upset as he had been before. In fact, he was grateful for the quiet moment, even if it were only a split-second dream on a cold football field.

"I said, you know what we be doing tonight, Eldon?"

"I know, baby," he said. He ate a piece of his steak. The game always worked up a terrific appetite in him.

"Well, I got a surprise for you." Louvina smiled shyly and reached down to the floor, where she had put her purse. "I got a present for you, honey."

It wasn't going to be a surprise; MacDay knew just what she was going to take out and give to him. Still, it was sweet of her. He wanted to act surprised, for her sake. "Aw, you don't have to get no presents for me, Lou," he said.

"Here," she said. "'Cause of what you got for me." She handed him a small black box. He opened it, and there was the gold ring with the garnet. He always wore that ring; the only time he took it off was before a game, when he had his hands and wrists taped. It was sitting on the shelf in his locker right now. Or, rather, the "now" he recognized; this episode in the restaurant was coded in MacDay's mind as "then." He took the ring from the box, making startled sounds and saying just the same words of thanks he had said . . . "then." He looked inside the band, and there were the words *Eldon + Louvina*. He put the ring on his finger.

"Don't say anything. Let me look at you."

Louvina hadn't said that. MacDay blinked, saw the bright blue, cloudless sky, heard the odd hush in the stadium, saw the faces of teammates, officials, and the Browns' team physician. "Oh, hell," murmured MacDay.

"I said, be quiet," said the doctor. The man pointed a pocket flashlight into MacDay's eyes. "There's only a minute and fifty-four seconds left," said the doctor. "You're out of the game." He turned to one of the assistant trainers. "Get the stretcher."

"Don't want no stretcher," said MacDay. "Let me walk off."

"You feel strong enough?" asked the doctor.

"If I ain't, there has to be two guys on the bench that I can lean on. I ain't going to be carted off like some goddamn stiff." Two of the Browns' players supported MacDay, and they walked slowly from the field, up the tunnel to the locker room. The spectators applauded furiously, in solemn but short-lived respect for his courage. MacDay paid little attention to their ovation.

The doctor ordered MacDay to rest on a training table for a few minutes. One of the clubhouse men came with a pair of long-nosed scissors and cut the tape from MacDay's hands. Beneath the tape, on MacDay's right hand, was the gold ring, the present from Louvina. "Oh, God," whispered MacDay.

"You really hurting?" asked the clubhouse man. "I been listening in here. I heard you really got your bell rung."

"Petie, you want to do me a favor?"

"Sure, Mac. What you want?"

"You go into my locker and get my rings. Both of them, the wedding band and the garnet ring."

"Sure, Mac," said Petie. "They be on the shelf?" MacDay nodded. The other man went to the locker, and MacDay watched as he opened it and looked around for the rings. In a few seconds he came back. "Here you are."

MacDay thanked him and took the rings. He put the wedding ring on his left hand. He held the garnet ring for a moment before he examined it. It was identical to the one he was wearing. "Petie," he said, taking off the other garnet ring and handing both of them to the equipment manager, "can you tell the difference between these two?"

"Huh? No, they look the same to me. This one's heavier, I think, isn't it? No, I guess not. No, Mac, you got me. Here, this is the one you was wearing." Petie handed the two rings back.

"Okay, Petie," said MacDay. "Thanks."

"Hope you feel better," said Petie. He left MacDay and went about his own duties.

"Just a headache," said MacDay, very quietly. "And something pretty damned freaky." He waited for the doctor to come back and finish his treatment.

The sounds of the crowd came into the locker room, though muted by distance and MacDay's own fatigue. He was still charged with nervous energy, worked up in the course of a week's preparation for this first game of the season. He wanted to go back out on the field, back into the game. He felt useless, lying on the training table, listening to the play-by-play of the end of the game on Petie's radio. His whole life was geared to taking the ball from Bailess and running at the other team; everything else was wasted time. He lived alone now, ever since Louvina's death. He didn't party with his teammates, rarely even spoke to anyone connected with football, except in the context of the game itself, at practice or on Sunday afternoons. After the season ended, no one knew what MacDay did or where he went. That was his private business, he felt. But no one knew how empty he was, how pointless and futile, when he wasn't running the ball.

MacDay had arrived at training camp in the same manner as in the previous several seasons: unannounced, unexpected, but nevertheless precisely on time. He said little to the other team members, to the coaching staff, even to the friendly, familiar employees of Hiram College, where the Browns trained. He was given his dormitory assignment and told that he would be rooming with a rookie running back, J. D. Lieger, MacDay's first white roommate. MacDay didn't even shrug; he just wanted to get into his gear and start working.

The training sessions were hard, much more strenuous than the regular season routines. Many of the veteran players had let themselves balloon up, fat and soft, during the off-season. The rookies had no idea of the kind of work that was expected of them in the professional world. Most of the players grumbled; MacDay said nothing, and his coaches had few complaints about his performance. He was ready to play the first regular game on the morning he arrived at camp.

The weeks at training camp passed slowly for MacDay, just as they had every year since Louvina's death. He was impatient for the real tests to begin. But he never let down, even when he was worn out with fatigue and the boredom of repetitious drills.

On the eighteenth of July, about two months before the first game of the season against the Comets, Coach Jennings announced at the breakfast assembly that the team had been the victim of some petty thefts. Jennings said that he was certain that the thief was a player, and that he expected that man to come into Jennings' office and apologize. The coach spoke some more about pride and integrity, then sighed and sat down. At three o'clock, just before the daily afternoon calisthenics, Jennings said that the thief had not had the guts to show up. In a low voice, the head coach said, "Well, then, gentlemen. Grass drills." Every member of the Browns' team knew what was coming; every one of them would have loved to have gotten at the man responsible—except, of course, the guilty man himself and Eldon MacDay.

Grass drills, or up-downs, were a conditioning exercise consisting of running in place, knees pulling as high as possible, for from fifteen seconds to half a minute. Then Jennings yelled "Down!" and the men threw themselves down to the grass, all together, so hard that an observer could hear but one sharp smack as their bellies hit the ground. Immediately, the coach yelled "Up!" and they all jumped to their feet, running in place again, doing this over and over, usually twenty-five times. By then, most of the Browns, veterans and the youngest rookies, were hardly able to stand. Jennings would give them a couple of minutes to rest, and then go on to a new exercise.

Today, however, was something special. The coach called "Down!" forty times, then fifty. While the players were running in place, exhausted, gasping, struggling just to keep their legs moving, Jennings said they'd stop when the thief made a public confession. No one said anything. Jennings shouted "Down!" After a few more repetitions, several of the players were left lying on the ground, too weary to lift themselves up again. The count reached sixty. Then sixty-five. MacDay began to see a haze forming in front of him. He felt as if he were working in a warm, sleepy fog. The bright, hot sun paled in the sky; the day darkened. MacDay was wrapped in a protective faintness, and the only outside influence that penetrated was Jennings' voice: "Down!" Seventy. Only a few players were still going. Some men were vomiting on the grass. Some didn't move at all, helpless and moaning. Seventy-five. MacDay was by himself, the last one on his feet. Jennings shouted his orders for MacDay alone. MacDay didn't know that. He was fascinated by what his oxygen-starved brain was showing him.

He saw a strange, wonderful scene around him. The grass field had disappeared. The college and the entire summer world had vanished with it. He was still running in place, jumping up and down at the head coach's command, but MacDay had forgotten that. The darkness had swallowed him up, then gradually lightened a little to show him the inside of a restaurant. He saw a table, and he saw Louvina. He saw his wife, just the way she had been on the afternoon before she had been . . . hurt. Nothing moved. Louvina seemed frozen, looking at him with an odd expression. She seemed so real that he could touch her. The table and chairs, the other people in the place—

MacDay could turn his head and observe everything to the smallest detail—all seemed caught in a suspension of time. He felt tears coming to his eyes. He wanted to hold Lou one last time. He wanted to say something to her. He opened his mouth to speak, but all that emerged was a hoarse groan. His legs would hold him no longer. The light failed again, and MacDay fell to the ground.

"Ninety," said Jennings respectfully. "And down." MacDay couldn't hear.

When MacDay came to his senses, he saw that the rest of the team had broken up into squads and were working on their specialties. Someone had put a wet towel across his forehead. He thought about Louvina, about the vivid, static tableau he had entered. His body was angry with pain, but he didn't pay attention to that. He wished that he could have just touched Louvina, just a little. But he hadn't been able to move nearer to her.

MacDay remembered that first flashback as he lay on the training table, staring at the gray, soundproofed ceiling. The game with the Comets had ended, and he could hear his teammates coming up the tunnel, yelling and congratulating each other. "That's one," he thought. "If they's all that easy, we gonna have a *good* time." He tried to take his mind off what had happened to him on the field, but his thoughts kept going back to Louvina.

During the previous summer at the training camp, he had never been able to speak to her. The flashbacks that he had experienced there were all exactly like the first—as though he had walked onto a stage set or an exhibit in a wax museum. Even during the preseason games, when he had three or four flashbacks during the course of each game, he was never able to break out of the paralysis that held him helpless in the restaurant. The flashbacks happened less and less frequently; it took MacDay a while before he understood what made them happen at all. At first, on the occasion of the grass drills, they were brought on by extreme physical exertion. After the first episodes, it had been four days before he had another, while he had been working at the tackling dummies.

The temperature went up over ninety-five degrees, but the coaches never noticed. They all stood around with clipboards, shouting. It seemed to MacDay that the coaches had their words written for them. Maybe they had scripts on their clipboards; one coach yelled,

"You ain't gonna get weather like this, come December!" about every twenty seconds; another coach kept repeating, "Keep your head up! Head up!"; the third coach, his voice gravelly hoarse, just chanted, "Drive! Drive! Drive! Drive!" MacDay was grateful when the dark haze began to form around him, shutting out the realities of the drill.

The flashbacks required pain, he learned. But during that stretch of weeks before the first regular game, the flashbacks were frustrating to him, for all that they gave him more incentive to work. The flashbacks cost more in exertion, as if his mind and body were building a tolerance to fatigue. If he repeated the amount of work that had given him a flashback the day before, he would only succeed in wearing himself out. He had to increase the pain. And, if he did that, all that he'd get in return was the same photographic vision. He wanted more, but he didn't know how to get it. He wanted to go to her, he wanted to touch her face one last time.

Then, that afternoon, on the field with the Comets, it had happened for the first time. He had seen Louvina move, he had sat down at the table across from her. They had talked, he had stared into those eyes that had been taken from him. He was too surprised to know what to do; still, the matter was out of his hands, it seemed, because he couldn't do anything that he hadn't done in that situation years ago. Nevertheless, he was awed and grateful. And he wanted more. He still hadn't touched her.

He had not told anyone yet about the flashback episodes. He was glad that he hadn't, now, because they seemed to be something different than he had first guessed. Working as the Browns did at training camp, MacDay could pass the episodes off as some kind of mental strain, some deficiency in diet. Now, though, the garnet ring moved the circumstance into an entirely different realm. He couldn't tell anyone, after that. The decision had been made for him. It also compelled him to try harder to visit Louvina again, as often as possible. It wasn't a dream or hallucination. MacDay knew that he was truly going back to her, back those five empty years. He much preferred sitting in that restaurant with her than doing whatever he had to in the present.

"You took a pretty good pop, huh, roomy?" said J. D. Lieger, Mac-Day's roommate, as Lieger came into the locker room.

"Yeah," said MacDay. "That happens to you, sometimes."

"So I'm told," said Lieger. "I hope I get to find out one of these days."

"You gonna have to beat out some gentlemen, if you gonna play," said one of the Browns' defensive backs.

Lieger grinned. "Ain't that why I'm here?" he asked.

"Naw," said Bailess, the quarterback. "You're here so our real runners don't have to get hurt taking back kickoffs and punts. You're what we in the trade call 'cannon fodder.'"

"What's that?" asked the rookie.

"Look it up," said Bailess. "Hey, Mac, how you doing? We missed you."

"Didn't sound like it on the radio," said MacDay. "I'm fine. Damn doctor done forgot about me. Either I'm all right, or I'm dying."

"Let me know which before practice on Tuesday," said Coach Jennings. "Here, this is yours." He tossed MacDay the game ball. MacDay only nodded. The other players congratulated him, but MacDay just thanked them quietly, swung his legs off the training table, and went to his locker to get undressed and showered.

On Monday, MacDay relaxed in his apartment, thankful for the day off following the victory over the Comets. He watched television for most of the afternoon, then went out to dinner by himself. He had an idea to drive out to Euclid to visit their old restaurant, but after he entertained the notion for a few seconds he grew unaccountably nervous. Instead, he drove to a large shopping center, ate dinner at a mediocre Chinese restaurant, then sat in a theater for a boring double feature. He left about a third of the way through the second movie.

The week's practice began again the next morning. He reported to the stadium, and the doctor gave him a quick examination. MacDay showed no sign of injury, for which he was grateful. He had more goals to work for than ever before, and his prime objective would have to be secret from Coach Jennings and his staff. Fortunately, the reaching of that goal was by the same route as the achievement of his more orthodox aims.

If getting hit hard was what it took for MacDay to return to Louvina, to see her move and smile and speak, then he was eager to pay that price.

"Okay," said Coach Jennings briskly, "let's go in and look at the films of the Comets' game. I know that was just the first game of the season, and the newspapers have given you the benefit of the doubt.

They say it's too early for the squads to have hit their best strides, or whatever those guys are saying these days. I know the game was just Phoenix, who haven't won a game since the dawning of Western civilization. And I know that we killed them. Nevertheless. *Nevertheless,* gentlemen, I'm sure that every one of you will find something instructive about these movies. Because every one of you did something crummy. The coaches will be circulating among you, to point up moments of special interest, to learn your views and opinions, and mainly to make sure that none of you gentlemen are falling asleep." MacDay sat alone, and he studied the films closely; he watched his own performance, which was creditable—139 yards gained in 27 carries, with one touchdown. Even Coach Jennings gave him a few compliments, a rare honor indeed. MacDay watched the actions of the linemen and the other blocking backs, trying to become even more familiar with them, even more efficient a part in the machine that was the Cleveland Browns.

But the movies were a torture for MacDay, as well. He was glad when they ended, when the team went out for calisthenics and drills. He worked through these, getting the pains and aches out of his muscles. After lunch Jennings had scheduled a couple of hours of scrimmages, beginning with a light workout, no tackling, and ending the day with hard-hitting exercises. MacDay was ready to hit.

"Look, Mac," said the head coach at lunch, "I don't want you to think that I'm handing out special favors. I don't do that kind of thing. You know that. But you put out 100 per cent Sunday, and I know that you'll give everything today, too. You're that kind of player. If I had forty players like you on the roster, the Browns wouldn't need me at all. So what I was starting to say was, I want you to use your own judgment. I don't want you to hurt yourself in practice on account of the rah-rah talk I use. That's just for the other clowns, to get them to perform. If you don't feel up to working out full this afternoon, lay off a little. Forget the scrimmages. Why don't you just run a couple laps? Tomorrow's good enough."

MacDay was a little startled. To his knowledge, the coach never spoke like that to anyone; the coach had waited until everyone else had left the cafeteria before he began, so that the players wouldn't think that he was playing favorites. It had been Jennings' experience that athletes rarely understood the real intentions of their coaches.

"I'm fine, Coach," said MacDay. "I ain't even hurting none."

"You're sure?" asked Jennings. "I mean, it don't do us no good to have you being brave today, and being out for Cincinnati on Sunday."

MacDay laughed. "Trust me, Coach," he said. Jennings only nodded, slapped his running back on the shoulder, and left the table. MacDay carried his tray to the service window and followed, out to the field.

The scrimmages started easy, about twenty minutes of touch-tackle plays run by the offense against the defense. Most of the players enjoyed this part of the workout every week; MacDay now thought it was the most irritating thing about his job. He longed to feel the hard jolt of a tackler cutting him down, or the deliberate shock as he himself blocked out a defensive player. After a while, Jennings began putting the Browns through plays under conditions more like the real game. MacDay smiled.

"All right," said one of Jennings' coaching assistants, "Mac, let's try a 20 Strong."

MacDay nodded. This was the play he had hoped for. He would take the ball from Bailess and run straight up the middle, right for the middle linebacker. Theoretically, the center would be controlling that man, and the rest of the line would be blocking straight ahead. MacDay would get no other blocking help, either from his halfback or the tight end. He would be by himself, and if any of the linemen missed their assignment, MacDay would be cut down, quickly. Bailess called the signals, took the snap, and jammed the ball between MacDay's arms. The latter lowered his head and bulled his way through the line. The linebacker spun around the center and was waiting for him. MacDay hit him at full speed. He was hoping . . .

It didn't work. After the play, the middle linebacker gave MacDay a hand up. "Wow," said the man, "you put a good hit on me." MacDay only grunted.

"No way, Warrick," said the assistant coach to the center. "That linebacker got around you like you was planted on Arbor Day. Can you try it again, Mac?" MacDay nodded. They ran the play again, and this time MacDay hit the linebacker as hard as he possibly could. This time, for a moment, a short while, he caught a glimpse of the darkened restaurant, the table, Louvina. Then, instantly, it disappeared. He was already getting to his feet.

"Let's try the 37 Weak," said the coach. In this play, Bailess gave the ball to Sonny Staley, and MacDay ran ahead of the ball carrier, blocking the outside linebacker. MacDay hit his man harder than usual for a scrimmage; the linebacker complained, but MacDay couldn't hear. He was seeing a clear tableau of the restaurant scene. Again, nothing in it moved.

So it went for the rest of the day, and the following days of that week before the Cincinnati game. MacDay took his hits aggressively, but all that he got for his pains was the same vivid but motionless tableau he had experienced during the training season. He had to have something special happening in order for him truly to go back there; it was only under real game conditions, when his emotional state or his physical energy provided an essential catalyst. So then, he realized, he wouldn't be able to visit Louvina until the Sunday game. He was disappointed, but at least he was beginning to understand the ground rules of the situation.

At last, after days of tension relieved by occasional, unsatisfactory flashbacks, MacDay went to the McGuire Coliseum for the game with Cincinnati. During the pregame preparations, he experienced an intense anxiety and anticipation, unlike anything he'd ever known before in his career. At one point, his hands shaking so much that he was barely able to dress, he considered asking the team physician for something to calm him. But the word would get back to Coach Jennings; the head coach would be displeased, MacDay knew. Jennings would wonder about any player who wanted to be quieted down before a game.

"This is for Lou," MacDay thought, as he and the other Browns charged out of the locker room, down the tunnel toward the field. "I got to break my neck to talk to her, I'll break my neck."

The Cincinnati defense was not as tough as the Phoenix team had been the week before. Coach Jennings was screaming excitedly on the sidelines, and the Browns' players not on the field were standing just out of bounds, shouting encouragement to their teammates. It looked as though Cleveland would be able to take a quick lead over their divisional rivals and that the game might be decided for good before halftime. This disappointed MacDay somewhat. If that were the case, it was possible that the Cincinnati defense might let down even worse; the Bengal players would feel that it was meaningless to risk injury in a losing cause. In that event, MacDay would have to take the game to them. He took the ball on one play and ran through a hole in the Cincinnati front. He saw the linebackers sliding down the line in pursuit. His instincts told him to cut back to the inside; his mind and his desires made him continue to the outside. A Bengal player hit him from the side, knocking MacDay's legs out from under him, and a second Cincinnati player knocked him out of bounds.

"Well, how do you like it?"

"I don't know what to say, Lou," said MacDay, before he was even able to focus his eyes. "How did you know what size?"

Louvina laughed. MacDay just stared at her; she was so happy that it hurt him, in a way. He remembered that she was dead, that she would die not so very long after they left the restaurant; for these last few years he had hated the world, the people in it, he had even hated God for letting someone with so much love be obliterated in such an offhand manner. He genuinely didn't know what to say to her, and he was glad to be bound by the situation. His self of five years past was in control, and he was just a spectator. But he was thankful for even that much. "It was easy, Eldon," she said. "You had that old ring you got for playing in the College All-Star game."

"Yeah, sure," he said. "But, damn it, honey, you didn't have to do it. I don't need a ring like this."

"Of course not," she said smiling. "If you needed the thing, I wouldn't have waited until now to give it to you. I love you, Eldon."

Even five years ago, even unaware of what was to happen, the older MacDay had been unable to reply for a moment. "I love you, too, Lou," he said at last, quietly. He reached across the table and took her hand. MacDay felt an overpowering emotion as their fingers touched. "Yes," he said to himself, "that's Lou. That's just the way I remember her."

"Listen," she said, "I'll be right back. I been crying all over my eye stuff here. I got to go fix it up."

"That's silly, Lou. You look fine. I don't want you to leave me here alone." MacDay's sentiment made every word of hers, every gesture painful, but infinitely wonderful.

"Oh, I'll be right back, I said," she said, rising from her chair. "I'm way ahead of you on the steak, anyway."

MacDay stood, too, and held her before she turned away to find the lavatory. He wanted to go after her, but his previous self wouldn't allow it. He took two steps back to his chair, and turned his ankle. It didn't hurt very much, but the memory of it happening the first time made the situation even more real to MacDay than the garnet ring had done. He sat in his chair, his mind a shifting mixture of feelings. He ate some of the steak, then rubbed his ankle, which was getting sore.

"Your ankle bothering you?" asked Bailess.

"It's fine," said MacDay. "I turned it a little making my cut."

"I didn't see much cut," said one of the Bengal players scornfully.

"That's why my ankle's giving me hell," said MacDay. Then he turned his back and went to the Browns' huddle. His ankle did bother him a bit, and he limped off the field when J. D. Lieger ran on to replace him.

"Thanks, roomy," said Lieger. "This is my big break."

MacDay nodded wearily. Jennings' backfield coach came over to see how badly MacDay was injured. "Just turned it a little," said Mac-Day.

"You want the doc to look at it?"

"Hell, no," said MacDay. "Let me catch my breath, and I'll be back in. I don't want no smart-ass kid like Lieger breaking one for no touchdown, not while I'm sitting on my ass." The assistant coach smiled and reported to Jennings. MacDay thought about his twisted ankle. It appeared that garnet rings weren't the only souvenirs he could bring back from the past. The thought entered his mind that . . . later . . . after they left the restaurant . . .

"All right, come on, let's go!" he shouted at the Browns on the field. It was third down and six yards to go for a first down. Bailess took the snap and ran back into the pocket, set up, then threw an incomplete pass to Lieger, who had circled out of the backfield. Mac-Day hadn't really been worried about losing his job to the kid, and he was sorry that Lieger hadn't been able to hang onto Bailess' pass. The Browns would have to punt.

"It worked," he thought. "I saw her again." His mind raced from one thought to another. He began to realize again what might happen when the scene developed further. He shook his head to stop those thoughts, and tried to concentrate on the game.

Just before halftime, MacDay went back into the game. On the second play from scrimmage he was given the ball on the 20 Strong, the run up the middle. He was intent on executing the play correctly, as always, but his main objective had changed. Rather than gaining yardage, his purpose now was to hit the middle linebacker as hard as possible. In this instance, it meant that MacDay had to do some quick shifting to get a good shot at the man and not draw the wrath of the coaching staff. He lowered his head and butted the linebacker. The man gave a little ground, then wrapped his arms around MacDay. The two struggled. MacDay cursed loudly, because he hadn't found the flashback he wanted so badly. "What the hell's the matter?" said the linebacker, as a second Bengal player came over to assist on the tackle, "you'll get your hundred-yard day, all right." The two Cincinnati players toppled MacDay, and the second man managed to knock the ball out of his hands. MacDay scrambled for the fumble, but a Cincinnati player recovered it. The Bengal players jumped up and shouted. The Browns walked slowly from the field. Bailess slapped MacDay's back.

"Okay, Mac," said the quarterback. "Even I blow one, once in a while."

"Not the way I did," said MacDay, upset that Louvina had been denied to him.

"Aw, it wasn't so bad," said Bailess. "Why, I seen fumbles kicked back and forth all the way from one end zone to the other. Yours was just a *little* fumble."

"Yeah," said MacDay as they reached the sidelines, "but it probably means we won't get back in the game until the second half."

"Yeah, is right," said Bailess, grinning. "Good boy."

Late in the game, with the Browns leading by a score of 31 to 13, with second down and five yards to go, Bailess called for a long pass. He looked around at the players bent over in the huddle and said, "63 Fly split right. On three."

"Oh, hell," said Nathaniel Coggins, the wide receiver. He spat on the artificial turf. "Hey, man, there's only three minutes left in this game. What you think they gonna do in three minutes? Why you want me to run my ass off? What for, man? You ain't careful, I just might accidentally pull a hamstring or something."

"Shut up," said Bailess. "Break!" They all clapped, and went to their positions.

"You don't never pull no hamstring when we're winning," said one of the linemen to Coggins.

"Yeah," he said, "you're right. I forgot." The play went off, but the pass was overthrown. The next play was 25 Crunch split right, MacDay carrying through the hole between left guard and tackle. He knew that time was running out; he had failed to get another flashback all afternoon. He was determined to do it now. He took the handoff from Bailess and charged into the Cincinnati defenders. A hole opened up for him, and in a few steps he was through. He raced down the length of the field; only a weak-side safety stood between him and a touchdown. MacDay gave a little fake with his head, then paused. The pause was just enough to let the Cincinnati player adjust. Jennings saw from the sidelines that MacDay seemed to have given up, and the head coach screamed; MacDay couldn't hear. The safety hit him high, and another defensive player recovered quickly enough to hit MacDay again, spinning him off his feet.

MacDay held his head. He felt terrible. He had quit, he had deliberately permitted that safety to crack him, when MacDay had had a certain touchdown. It was going to be difficult to explain. He wondered about the silence around him. Had his actions been that obvious? He lifted his head, and he was reassured.

Louvina was coming back to the table, accompanied by three other men. MacDay was worried; he always worried when she talked to strangers, whatever the situation. But he *knew* who these men were. He knew, but he realized that it didn't make any difference. He could only watch.

"Eldon," she said, "these here men are from Jackson. They say they saw you play ball at Hanson High."

"That's right, Mr. MacDay," said one of the men, taller than the other two. He didn't seem to be at all interested in meeting MacDay. His tone was grim, his expression blank.

"I used to live near you, as a matter of fact," said a second man, a black man. "On West Third Street, around the corner from Bar's Mike and Grill. You remember?"

"Sure," said MacDay. Five years ago he had suspected nothing. He had only wanted to eat his meal in peace.

"We were wondering if we could coax you and your wife into having a drink with us after you finish," said the first man.

"I'm sorry," said MacDay.

"Oh, it's all right, I think," said Louvina. "After all, this man tell me he used to bring your ma the paper. I mean, just this once, it'd be all right, wouldn't it, Eldon?"

"I understand that you're probably always besieged by fans," said the black man. "But my son is probably your biggest rooter. Next to your wife, of course." The black man laughed briefly. "I have this football in my hotel room. I bought it for Willie. I was really hoping you'd sign it for him."

"It be okay with me," said Louvina. "Maybe it would help the boy some. You're always saying how you want to do something for the community."

"All right, all right," said MacDay impatiently. He pleaded with his wife silently, his five years of helpless hindsight just as ineffectual now, trapped in his second chance. The five of them stood up; the third stranger, silent through all the conversation, took out a wallet and paid MacDay's check. Then they left the restaurant. Louvina walked with her arm through MacDay's; the two of them walked behind the three men.

"I'd like to ask you a question, Mrs. MacDay," said the tall man. "Why do you think your husband plays football? I mean, why does he go out there, week after week, and put himself in a position to get dangerously injured? One play after another, he runs right into a bunch of other men who are trained to cut him down. And winning a stupid football game can't be worth all that, can it?"

Louvina laughed. "They ask him that all the time. And Eldon always say the same thing. I don't say it as good as he do, but it has to do with wanting something bad enough. Eldon want to be *good*, is what he want. He want to be the best."

"That's not the reason I take all the pain," thought MacDay sadly. "It's for you, Lou. I hurt for you."

"No," said the tall man, "that's not why he goes out there and gets bruised. I hate to contradict you, Mrs. MacDay, but he goes out there because he gets paid a hell of a lot of money."

"Not all that much," said MacDay sourly.

The men ignored him. "And what do you think, Mrs. MacDay?" asked the black man. "If he gets paid so much for taking a risk, don't you think if we got paid ten times as much, we'd take a bigger risk?"

"What do you mean?" asked Louvina, frightened by the man's tone.

They had been crossing the parking lot of the restaurant. The silent third stranger had left their group to get his car. Now the tall man grabbed Louvina, and the black man caught MacDay in a tight hammerlock. The third man drove straight for them. "You see, MacDay," said the black man, "we gonna make sure you don't feel like playing.

The money didn't work, and the threats didn't work. Chuck here, why, he's gonna work."

The tall stranger waited until the car was only a few yards away, then he pushed Louvina in front of it. MacDay twisted free of the man holding him. He saw Louvina fall in front of the car. He heard her screaming, he saw her huge eyes, bright and staring, looking straight at him. "God damn it, not again," thought MacDay. He tried to run to her, but the black man tripped him. As MacDay fell, he never lost contact with Louvina's eyes. They seemed to grow even larger. He heard her, still screaming. "Please, God," cried MacDay, "not her!"

"What?"

MacDay could only groan. The heavy chest of drawers lay across his legs. He couldn't move. He just stared at the pieces of the broken mirror on the floor. He saw his face, contorted by pain.

"What did you say, roomy?" It was Lieger, calling from their other room. "What are you doing out of bed? The doc—" The rookie came into the bedroom, stopped, and ran to where MacDay lay twisted on the floor. He hauled the massive chest up off MacDay's legs. "Are you okay?"

MacDay just shook his head. He knew his legs were shattered, just as Louvina's had been. Crushed. He knew it would be nothing short of a miracle if he would ever stand on them again, let alone walk. "God," he muttered, "you got a great sense of humor."

"What?" said Lieger frantically. "Wait, I'll call the doc. You been out since you got popped. Jennings thought you'd rather come to here than the hospital."

"Sure," said MacDay faintly. "Hey, J. D., you better get the hang of picking your spots. You ain't gonna get all your spots picked for you. Not like this."

"You just wait, Mac," said Lieger, dialing the phone. "We'll get you to a hospital. You need it now."

MacDay knew that a chest of drawers couldn't have so thoroughly destroyed his legs. But how could he explain that he'd been run over by a car, five years in the past, in his own bedroom? Jennings would never understand. "That's it," thought MacDay. "No more games, no more seeing Lou. No more seeing Lou. Seen her die twice, now. That's enough, I guess."

"You'll be all right," said Lieger, who was near hysterics.

"It's all right," said MacDay to himself. He was curiously peaceful. The pain in his legs seemed to be a solid object, with a separate existence of its own. It didn't throb or stab; it was constant, rolling on with MacDay's own life. That made it easier to ignore. "It's all right. I been dead for five years already, anyhow. In a way. Ain't had no soul for five years. Been in Hell for five years. So for a few weeks, God has to lift the lid off Heaven for me, just to make me sweat. God, you sure a *bad* dude."

"You're crazy, Mac," said Lieger.

"Didn't know I was talking out loud."

"Sometimes, you're just plain crazy. No offense."

MacDay didn't answer. He was looking into the shards of mirror all around him on the floor. All he could see were eyes, huge eyes, the eyes of a dying person. He didn't know whose.

HARD TIMES

It was still early, not even eleven o'clock. The office of Justin Benarcek was quiet, calmer than it had been in many weeks. He heard no voices, just the rapid clicking of Miss Brant's typewriter beyond his richly stained door. Justin stood and stretched leisurely, taking a deep breath and letting an unfamiliar mood of well-being sweep over him. He went to the window and pulled back the heavy drapes.

Beyond the window it was a bright, clear August day. Sunlight streamed through the glass; the office was decorated in somber colors and dark woods, but the light overcame the oppressive atmosphere. The austere browns and heavy blues of his law books seemed more than just a shelter for the grim philosophy within. For no other reason than the beauty of the day, Justin felt happy. He was smiling, and he slapped the narrow windowsill in his good humor.

On an impulse he turned back to his desk. He buzzed his secretary on the intercom.

"Yes, Mr. Benarcek?" she said.

"Miss Brant," he said, assuming a formal tone, "I was wondering if you had an unbreakable date for lunch this afternoon."

Miss Brant hesitated, no doubt expecting a sudden burden of work from her boss. "No, sir," she said slowly.

"Then let's go down to the Shalibet," he said. "Maybe we could take the rest of the afternoon off and do something." Miss Brant said nothing for a moment, and then told him that she'd love to.

"All right, then. Call and make the reservations." Justin sat in his expensive leather chair, closing his eyes and enjoying the feeling while it lasted. The sun was warm on his neck. For a while he dozed, until the intercom woke him.

"Mr. Benarcek?"

"Yes, Miss Brant," he said, yawning. "Did you make those reservations?"

"Yes, sir. For one o'clock."

"What time is it now?"

"Twelve, sir. But there's a gentleman to see you."

"He doesn't have an appointment, does he? I thought I was pretty well free today." Justin was annoyed at the man already, for dispersing the warm, clinging, and rare sense of joy.

"No, sir. But he says that it's important. And he said to ask you if you remember 'The Trog.' He said you'd know."

The Trog! Bo Staefler, from his freshman year at Yale. It had been at least fifteen years since he'd even heard from Bo.

"It's all right, Miss Brant. I'll see him now. And don't worry; I'll be sure to get through before one. Give me a call in a half hour."

Justin ran a hand through his ruffled hair and straightened his tie. In a short while the door opened and Bo Staefler came into the office. He was balder, a lot heavier, but still the same huge, grinning man Justin had known so well in college. Justin stood and came around his desk to shake hands.

"Say, Justin, how are you?" asked Staefler.

"All right, Bo. Things are going okay. How are you?" Staefler just nodded. Justin suspected that his old friend was paying more than just a social call.

The two men sat down and talked about their shared foolishnesses of twenty years ago. Things Justin had gratefully buried in his memory were brought out and examined with a fierce, nostalgic pleasure.

"Remember those two old women we picked up?" asked Staefler, more comfortable now, his tie loosened and his jacket thrown over the back of his chair. "We got them drunk and took them back to the Taft."

"They weren't so old," said Justin, laughing softly.

"They were thirty if they were a day," shouted Staefler.

"And now we're crowding forty."

"Yes," said Staefler. Both fell silent, thinking.

"How about when Trofell and Hanson threw the chair out of the window in Wright?" said Justin, wiping a tear from the corner of his eye.

"Wait a minute, Justin," said Staefler.

"And they were so angry at being canned that they chained all the gates to the Old Campus shut."

"Justin," said Staefler, "I have to talk with you."

Justin sighed. "What is it, Bo?"

"I'm in trouble." Justin nodded; everyone who came to see him was in some sort of difficulty. It depressed him sometimes. That was why this morning's unexpected liberty had been so delicious.

Justin leaned back in his chair and played absently with a pen on his blotter. "Tell me about it. Start at the beginning, talk slowly, and don't leave anything out."

Staefler took a deep breath. "I killed a person, Justin. About a year ago. A woman. I was drunk and I honestly didn't know what I was doing. I don't even know who she was. I just left her there. No one saw me. The police have never been able to figure it out, but I can't stand it anymore."

"Why tell me, Bo? Why not just go away and forget it?"

"You don't know!" Staefler looked across the desk with a pitiable, pleading expression. When he spoke, his voice was strained and hoarse. "You can't imagine what I see, what I dream. The newspapers said it was *brutal*. It was. I . . . sometimes I . . ."

"It's all right, Bo." Every once in a while Justin fooled himself into believing that he could empathize with his clients, but he knew that their visions were, gratefully, denied to him.

"I just wanted to talk with someone, Justin. I haven't said a word before this. And you're a lawyer, a famous one. If ever something happens, I mean if the police ever . . . well, you know."

Justin didn't reply. He got up from the desk and looked out the window; forty-eight stories below, the city cowered away from him. Rooftops lay about him in random patches, covering the distance between him and the bay. Among the buildings the streets and the tiny vehicles ran like visceral messengers of a great concrete organism. The sun was still burning away, unchallenged by any cloud.

"You can do us both a favor, Bo," he said, his back still turned to his old friend. "Give me a phone number where I can reach you. Then go home for a few days. I don't know what to suggest. Maybe our Federal Services liaison can help you. But don't get yourself in an overwrought state. You won't be any good to anyone like that."

"Whatever you say, Justin." Justin could tell from Staefler's voice that he was weeping. "I don't have anyone now. I don't know what to do."

Justin went to Staefler's chair and grasped his friend's shoulder. "You're my friend, Bo. I have a responsibility to you." Staefler looked up gratefully. He stood and began to say something. Then he stopped, took his jacket, turned, and left.

Justin stood by the empty chair for a few moments, frowning. Yes, he had a responsibility to his friend. But he had a duty to the Federal Services, to the system that he served. The intercom's buzz brought him out of his reveries.

"Is that all, Mr. Benarcek?"

"Yes, Miss Brant. Let's go to lunch now. No, wait a second. Get me the office of the district attorney."

"Certainly, Mr. Benarcek. But I think you ought to lie down and take a nap."

"What? What are you talking about?"

"I mean it," said the secretary. "I think that you ought to take a nap."

Justin felt lightheaded. "Yes," he said, "you're right. I ought to take a nap."

The first thing that Justin saw when he awoke was a great, blinding light on the ceiling. Then he noticed the red, blue, and green wires at the corners of his vision. When he tried to move his head for a better view, he found that he couldn't.

Bit by strange bit, the scene grew more familiar. The unmistakable clean stink of a hospital. Hushed voices belonging to persons beyond his range of vision, speaking in an indecipherable jargon. Unpleasant sticky spots on his head and chest where, he now recalled, many wires had been placed.

He was in the Federal Services clinic.

He closed his eyes against the stabbing pain of the circular light. His mind was very dull, very drugged. He admitted his helplessness and surrendered. Soon the drugs would be flushed from his system, and the heavy, illegitimate security would expire. Justin relaxed into the lassitude and submitted to the busy hands of the medical attendants.

Hours later, dressed in a white, backless gown and sipping orange juice in bed, Justin was visited by a doctor. The man entered the ward briskly and walked to Justin's bed. He was harried and fatigued, but to Justin's still cloudy perceptions the doctor was at first only a white blur of lab coat and a short pendulum-swing of brown clipboard.

"Mr. J. Benarcek? I'm Dr. Ruggiero. How are you feeling?"

Justin wasn't quite certain yet. "Hmmm? What?" he said.

The doctor frowned. "Still feeling a little groggy?" he asked. Justin nodded, and the doctor riffled a few pages on the clipboard. "I'm sorry, Mr. Benarcek," he said. "You were scheduled for Recovery last night, about ten, but you had an extremely long test sequence. You'll be feeling sharper in another two or three hours. Shall I come back then?"

"No, it's all right," said Justin, setting the orange juice on the small bedside table and letting his head fall heavily to the pillows propped up behind him. "Did I have the test?"

"One of them. You're here for the Services complex, aren't you?" Justin didn't know. The question must have been rhetorical, because no one outside the Federal Services knew anything about the government's internal procedures. Justin had applied for a low-level office position; though he had no knowledge of selection techniques beyond the popular rumors, he hadn't expected anything as extreme as the hospital stay had been.

"You can prepare yourself for another couple of tests," said Dr. Ruggiero. "There is a standard battery of psychological instruments that we employ for applicants at your level. Well, I'll check back in a while. You can have all the liquids you want now, but I think it's best that we keep you off solid foods at least until morning." The doctor turned to leave.

"How did I do?" asked Justin.

Dr. Ruggiero turned again. "On yesterday's test? We can't tell yet. The tapes take about three days to evaluate. You won't be given the next one until yesterday's has been studied by your board. If at the end you are granted your job, the data will be put in your file, to which, under the law, you have access." The doctor sighed, and Justin smiled, knowing that even this man, enclosed so deeply within the Federal organization, could be unhappy with the government way. "If your application is rejected, you have the right to petition your board for an explanation. Of course, it may take the board a good deal of *time* to process your appeal."

"What happened? I mean, I don't even remember. I thought I'd just have to fill out some forms or take an exam."

The doctor laughed. "No, we don't bother with that. We never knew what they were measuring, if anything. In a few days we'll just feed you another controlled fantasy situation, lead you into it a bit, and turn you loose. You have no opportunity to cheat, and fluctuations due to changes in temperament or test conditions are kept to a minimum. I suppose that it's better this way." He stood by the side of the bed, lost in his own thoughts for a few seconds. He roused himself with a start. "Well, Mr. Benarcek, have a good afternoon. You know where the call button is? All right, I'll look in later."

The phone rang while Justin was taking a shower. He slapped the tap buttons angrily and hurried through the drier screen. He still made wet footprints on the thick white rugs as he crossed the living room to the phone. "Hello," he said.

"Hello, Justin?"

"Yes."

"Hi, this is Bo Staefler. You probably won't remember me, but we were in the same class at Yale. I'm in town and I thought I'd take a chance on calling you up."

"Bo! Of course I remember you! How are you? How have you been?" The damp chill of the living room was forgotten. Justin took the phone to a comfortable chair and sat down.

"Fine," said Staefler. "Look, my wife is with me and I want her to meet you. I've been telling her about you for fifteen years and she can't believe most of it. She's standing out here now, watching the car. Why don't you give me directions, or maybe we could meet you somewhere, whatever's convenient."

The two men talked for a few minutes more, making arrangements to meet in Justin's favorite downtown pub. After he hung up the phone, Justin finished his shower, shaved, dressed, and ordered a cab. The unit arrived in the street outside Justin's module in less than half an hour, much quicker than he expected. Indeed, the cab's warning buzz startled him from a short nap.

The pub was of the popular standard: dark, decorated in red plush and gloss black, with many polished steel fittings reflecting sun sparks of light from countless directions. Justin found Staefler and his wife waiting for him, their drinks half finished. Staefler rose from his seat when he saw Justin and, grinning, grabbed his friend's hand.

"Hey, Justin!" he said loudly. "Putting on weight and losing hair, but still the same clown from the radio station, eh?"

Justin smiled. "Married life's done more for your girth, I would say."

"Right," said Staefler. "My wife, Bunny. Bunny, this, of course, is the fabled Justin Benarcek." Staefler and Justin sat down, a signal for the waiter to appear at Justin's elbow. Soon the three were drinking and laughing, as the men spun out story after story of their college days together, only a bit expurgated for the sake of Mrs. Staefler's sensibilities.

It was well past midnight when Justin returned to his apartment module, a bit drunk and filled with a transient glow of fellowship that would fade with a good night's sleep. The evening had been more than pleasant; his law practice and an inner fear of social activity combined to keep Justin alone in his tiny room for weeks. And, he thought as he slid deeper into the warm trap of sleep, Staefler and his wife provided him with an image of the deeper relationship he denied himself.

Just before noon of the next day his secretary informed him that he had an unscheduled visitor. It was Staefler's wife Bunny, who had been shopping downtown while her husband was attending the textile show for which he had come to the city. Justin was happy to see her; the only woman that he dealt with in his carefully restricted life was his secretary, Miss Brant, and he never met her socially. In fact, he talked with Bunny Staefler for almost fifteen minutes before she suggested that they go to lunch. Justin would never have thought of it.

"Sure, Bunny. Do you want to go back to Johnny Jack's or try someplace else? We could have a leisurely lunch and meet Bo after his convention. I don't have anything else this afternoon to keep me around here."

"Whatever you like, Justin," she said softly.

Justin flicked a switch on his intercom. "Miss Brant," he said, "make reservations for two at the Shalibet. For about one o'clock. I won't be back this afternoon, and if you get those two briefs typed you can take the rest of the day off."

"Justin," said Mrs. Staefler, "do you think that we have time to run back to the hotel for a minute? I want to drop off these packages. I've been carrying them all over this great city of yours this morning and I'm tired of it. Anyway, if we're going to one of your elite restaurants I want to change out of these clothes."

"Sure, Bunny," said Justin, holding the door for her. Down on the street they got a cab; as the unit slowly traced a path through the heavy midday traffic, they chatted quietly. It was almost an hour later when they arrived at the Staeflers' hotel.

"Do you want me to wait here in the lobby for you?" asked Justin.

"Oh, come on up," said Mrs. Staefler. "It may take me a while to sort through the wardrobe. Anyway, you can help me decide." She smiled, and a quality about her smile startled Justin with a flush of illicit excitement.

Grabbing some clothes from the closet, Mrs. Staefler hurried into the bathroom. Justin went to the window and stared down at the thickly choked street. He felt mildly and pleasantly confused, as though unfamiliar emotions were competing just beneath his consciousness. Bunny Staefler was humming as she selected her costume. Justin heard the snap of the light switch, and the racket of the fan in the bathroom died. He turned to appraise her choice of clothing.

"Come here for a moment, won't you?" she said nervously, sitting on the edge of the bed, smoothing the low ripples of the bedspread.

Justin felt another rush of excitement, but said nothing. He sat next to her and waited.

"I want to talk with you, but I don't know if I can get this all out without embarrassing both of us." Justin looked at her, but she stared at her hands, still playing uneasily with the quilted cover. "I don't want you to think any of the usual things. I mean, that I don't love Bo or anything. Because I do. But I . . . I don't know, I need something."

Justin sighed and looked past her, distractedly staring at a cheap, lurid print on the wall of the hotel room. He knew what she needed, or what she thought she needed. But these situations were always so impossible.

Mrs. Staefler guessed what he was thinking. "It wouldn't be as if we were getting into anything huge, anything that we couldn't handle. We're going home day after tomorrow. We won't see each other again for years, probably. But I just want someone *close*."

All Justin could think about was how he felt when he had learned about Suzy's affairs. He frowned, unconsciously moving away from the lovely woman next to him. He stood, and she wouldn't look up at him. He heard her crying softly. He walked toward the door.

"Thank you," she said, sobbing. "But I think you ought to lie down and get some sleep."

"What?" asked Justin, astonished.

"I said that you ought to try to sleep."

"Yes," he said dreamily. "I'd like that now."

"Good afternoon, Mr. Benarcek." Dr. Ruggiero stood beside the hospital bed, his hand clasping Justin's wrist while he measured the pulse rate.

"Am I here?" Justin remembered nothing about the Recovery room this time. He had already been returned to his ward, but he was still very, very drugged.

The doctor laughed. "Yes. Pretty sleepy, eh? Well, I'll leave you in a minute. You had a difficult test this time. Your mind put up a tough defense. We had a lot of trouble imposing the fantasy on you. I have a feeling you're going to want to just rest for a while."

"I hope it's worth it," said Justin. His mouth felt strange, tingling as though it had been anesthetized, and he had trouble forming his words.

Dr. Ruggiero said nothing for a few seconds. "I don't know, Mr. Benarcek," he said. "Of course, I don't have any say in the matter, and the Federal knows what it's doing." He paused, and smiled ironically. "Anyway, it *tells* us that it knows what it's doing. And they decided this is the best way to eliminate the misfits. But I don't know. That test was pretty hard on you."

Even heavily sedated, Justin realized that the doctor was saying dangerous things. He hoped for both their sakes that no one was listening.

"It's all right," said Justin. "I signed the release form."

"No," said the doctor, "I don't mean just that. There ought to be a better way. This sort of thing used to be immoral." Dr. Ruggiero fell silent again, his expression indicating that he had finally gone too far, that he had said aloud the potentially fatal ideas that had been smoldering within him. He dropped Justin's hand suddenly. "I'll look in on you before I go off duty," he said, and turned and hurried from the ward.

A few days later they came for Justin again. They scooped him out of his bed and onto a cart. They fastened the straps around him and covered him with a stiff, clean sheet. An orderly injected him with a sedative, and before they had wheeled him to the testing laboratory he was already only semiconscious.

It seemed to Justin that he was once again a lawyer, and that Bo Staefler called him after a fifteen-year silence. They spent a pleasant afternoon together, enjoying an expensive meal and the company of two beautiful, costly women. He and Bo had gotten drunk, just like in their long-dead college days, and had somehow managed to find their way back to Bo's hotel, where they had collapsed in an inebriated coma.

Justin awoke feeling sick the next morning, and Bo consoled him by reminding him that it was Wednesday morning, and that Justin didn't have to go to work. Justin was horrified; he had never missed a morning worship since he had become a Professional man. The temple would know that he was not there, and the agents of Thomas and Charles, the Federal Services leaders, would want an explanation. For a citizen of his prominence there *was* no explanation. The Federal was a powerful force, an authority that could not be duped or offended. And it was a jealous body.

Bo laughed at Justin's fear. Bo tried to explain that missing one devotion in fifteen years was surely not so grave a sin. But Justin knew better. He had seen what had happened to certain of his associates who had thought that very thing. Bo was a small Mercantilist from a small town. The tireless eyes of Thomas and Charles were not so acutely trained on him. But Justin could not afford a lapse.

Bo became angry. He had not completely shaken off the liquor of the night before, and already had downed a good quantity of a synthetic whiskey provided by the hotel's management. He staggered a little as he walked to Justin. He grasped Justin's shoulder and tried unsuccessfully to look steadily into Justin's eyes. "Go on," said Staefler. "Run to your silly thing. Least I'll find out what kind of friend you are. Haven't seen you in fifteen years, and you'd rather spend the time kneeling in the dark. You moron."

Justin was angry, but his anxiety didn't allow him time to answer his friend. He realized that he may be insulting Staefler by leaving, and that he might irreparably damage their relationship, but he made his decision. He picked his coat up from the floor and went to the door.

"Wait a minute," said Staefler from behind him. "You have time to get some rest, don't you? I think that you ought to sack out for a while."

Justin felt amazingly well. He was getting used to the process, perhaps, and did not fight the doctors as much as they imposed their strange and painful ministrations. He still felt the effects of the anesthetic when he was returned to the ward, but to a lesser degree than in the previous rounds. Dr. Ruggiero was waiting for him when they wheeled Justin to his bed.

"You ought to be a little less foggy this time," said the doctor. "It was a very short episode. You reacted much more strongly, for some reason. I'm sure your religious training has been more strict than usual."

"Then I did all right?" asked Justin, for the first time in the long procedure feeling a hint of confidence.

"As I explained, I don't have the training or the authority to make any evaluations. But the psych techs brought you out of it in less than thirty minutes. That usually works to your advantage, unless, of course, you reacted quickly in the wrong direction." Justin looked startled, but his sudden fear was dissolved by Dr. Ruggiero's confident smile.

"I'm glad it's over," said Justin, rubbing his itching eyes.

"I suppose you are. It's an awfully hard thing to go through. Too hard, perhaps."

Justin was afraid of the man. Here he was, starting that same treasonous line of conversation. "I know I don't particularly want to do it again, but I'm sure it does what it's supposed to."

"There are other ways. Besides the pain and physical discomforts it causes you, don't you think it's unnecessary to force people to have encounters that their natural behavior would never allow? If you knew that there were other testing apparatus available, would you still do this?"

Justin looked around the ward. There were no other nurses or doctors around to overhear, and the other patients were either out at their own tests or asleep. But surely there was monitoring equipment. Justin agreed with what the doctor felt, but he was naturally hesitant to say anything.

"Here," said Dr. Ruggiero, dropping a slip of paper on the bed. "We've been around for a little while, now. When you get out, come by and see us. If you get your job we could have a little celebration." The doctor smiled wryly and left Justin alone.

The paper was folded in half, casually lying on the sheet for all to see. Justin picked it up before anyone might come into the ward. It said, "The League," with an address in the ghetto. Beneath that it said "Wed., 10 P.M." Justin understood immediately. Here was a secret organization, probably with revolutionary aims. He had never known; no one had ever heard of its existence. The doctor had said they had been around for some time. . . .

If the paper were found by the agents of Thomas and Charles it would be disastrous. Apparently Dr. Ruggiero knew more intimate things about Justin than he had admitted. The doctor had some reason to trust him. Justin carefully studied the address, tore the paper into quarters, and swallowed them.

Justin awoke on a narrow bed in a dim, cold room. His right arm was raised up on a shelf and he was being fed intravenously. A single light bulb on the ceiling flickered, making shadows jump crazily before Justin's dazed eyes. His body was aching and his head throbbed. He called out, but it was a long time before anyone responded.

A young orderly came into the cell, dressed in a soiled white coat. He stood at the side of the cot and looked down at Justin. Then he stopped the drip of the IV bottle and removed the needle from Justin's arm.

"What is this?" asked Justin groggily.

"You've just had your test. You remember. You wanted a Federal job. You've been under for a couple of days, so you ought to be a little out of it right now."

"I know. I remember that all right. I had three tests. Almost two weeks. Where's Dr. Ruggiero?"

"One test. There's only one test," said the orderly, rather bored. "Don't know any Dr. Ruggiero. Probably part of the fantasy."

"No," said Justin, his mouth suddenly dry, his blood rushing loudly in his ears, "he was there *between* the tests."

"Nope. You didn't have those tests. You just thought you did. We only give one test. Hell, they're expensive. You didn't do so well, you know."

Justin didn't understand, and he didn't realize the meaning of what the young man said. "It was *real*," he said.

The orderly just laughed and prepared a hypodermic injection. "Is this real?" asked Justin, just beginning to panic.

"Sometimes, once they've gone through this they can never be sure," said the orderly. He didn't bother to swab Justin's arm with alcohol before he gave him the injection. "But if you ever wake up from this, you'll know." In less than a minute Justin closed his eyes, despite all his fear and all his fighting, and he stopped thinking.

AT THE BRAN FOUNDRY

It was all so very strange. We were totally helpless, pushed about by people who did not even seem to be aware of our existence. We began to question the reality of it all, ourselves. Where were we? Could this actually be happening to us? At times we couldn't be certain of anything; at those times, we were desperately close to madness.

It all started as the annual Key Club outing. There was "Chico" Carresquel, Robin Roberts, Don Zimmer, "Dutch" Dotterer, Bobby Del Greco, Rip Repulski, and me, squeezed into Don's Tempest. Following us were Ryne Duren, Wayne Causey, Ike Delock, Sherm Lollar, Walt Dropo, Vic Wertz, Eddy Yost, "Whitey" Herzog, Gus Zernial, Reno Bertoia, and big "Bullet Bob" Turley, in Wayne, Walt, and Reno's cars. We also had two of the Kiwanis representatives with us. The adults were Mr. Zernial and Mr. Causey, Gus and Wayne's fathers.

We left Collinwood High right after school, at three-thirty. We drove out Lake Shore Boulevard, past Euclid Beach and Humphrey's field, past Euclid, past E. 222nd Street and further. We rode with our noses pressed to the windows because we had never been to Wickliffe before. We stopped when we got to the bran foundry.

The factory consisted of many large buildings, all connected by enclosed corridors many feet above the ground. There were catwalks that threaded the dizzy heights. The complex covered hundreds of acres; Mr. Zernial told us that part of the area used to be the old Shoregate Shopping Center. He told us how he used to go there as a child, to buy bags of plastic soldiers in the Woolworth's.

The enormous factory was ominous in appearance; it stood there, gray and dark brick-red, hissing black smoke into the late Greater Cleveland afternoon. The various buildings stood to left and right, and the chimneys and chemical-towers stuck up like fists for a great distance behind. Immediately before us, however, was a smaller yellow building, with many windows and a low roof to give it a less gruesome aspect. We walked along a narrow flagstone path; on both sides the lawn was trimmed to an even and compulsive shortness. On the lawn just before the door to the building was a white wooden sign-board with a glass door. The letters inside had been arranged to read: The Jennings Raisin Bran Corporation. Visitors welcome. Tours leave from the lobby 1 2 3 4:30. Personnel Office use Gate C.

Mr. Causey held the door open for us; all the rest of the guys went in, but I held back for just a moment. With the door to the lobby open, I could hear the piped music from inside. It was the sort of brisk, raucous trumpet and xylophone stuff that always meant "industry" in the Bugs Bunny cartoons that were made during the war. I looked back, across the vast parking lots jammed with the cars of the employees. I saw cut-off sections of grimy buildings, and tall derricks burning waste gases at the top like eternal flames of commerce. Mr. Causey was waiting, and I stepped past him into the lobby, immersing myself completely in the eager music.

We stood in the lobby for a few minutes. There were couches covered with dark-green leather, and coffee tables with copies of *National Geographic* and the house organ, *The Bran Bulletin*. Soon the bustling music built to nearly unbearable intensity, and just at the very peak, when we couldn't stand it any longer, a door marked *Private* opened. A personable man of middle age came out and joined us, shaking the hands of Mr. Zernial and Mr. Causey. As soon as he appeared the music quieted. Like magic, it became a divided string background to narration.

"Hi, fellows!" he said to the rest of us. He pronounced the "ow" in "fellows," smiling broadly.

Mr. Causey cleared his throat and spoke up. "I'd like to thank you," he said, "and I'm sure the Key Clubbers will join me in this; we'd like to thank you for taking time out of your busy schedule to show us around your marvelous installation here."

"Not at all, Mister, uh, Causey, is it? Yes, Mr. Causey. Well, let's get started. My name is Bob Jennings, and I am Chairman of the Board of the Jennings Raisin Bran Corporation. Come with me now, as we discover—The Wonderful World of Raisin Bran!"

The music built steadily so that during his last pause the cornets and French horns were calling through the lobby in ear-splitting fashion. Then it all hushed once more, like magic, waiting for him to make another pronouncement. It was eerie.

Mr. Jennings motioned us toward a pair of glass doors. He held one open for us, and we went through into a huge room filled with machinery making a deafening racket. Still, the background music followed us, audible over the crashing and pounding engines.

As we went through the door Walt Dropo stopped and said, "Are you *really* the head of the Corporation?"

Mr. Jennings smiled. "Yes, son, I am."

"Gosh," said Walt.

To the right of the double doors was a small, glass-enclosed office. Mr. Jennings said, "Please excuse me for a moment," and went into the office. He went up to a secretary at a desk, and spoke to her. We could hear everything that they said, as if it were being broadcast throughout the plant.

The secretary smiled; even from where we were standing I could see the perfect teeth. "Good afternoon, Mr. Jennings," she said.

"Good afternoon, Miss Brant," he said. "Is everything in order?"

"Yes, Mr. Jennings."

"Good."

Mr. Jennings came back to our group and stood by a huge, thundering machine. He put one foot up on a riveted plate, turning to us casually and smiling. From behind a massive stanchion he brought out a box of Jennings Raisin Bran. It apparently had been left there by mistake. He gazed at it meditatively for a few seconds, and then regarded our group once more.

"You know," he said, "I'm *glad* to be able to take time from my crowded working day to show you folks just how careful we are in making each and every box of Jennings Raisin Bran." The music was quieter now, playing something that I recognized as the Entry of the Gods into Valhalla from Wagner's *Das Rheingold*. It seemed to fit the ecstatic expression that Mr. Jennings made every time he said the words "raisin bran."

"Where's Walt?" asked Mr. Zernial. "What's happened to Walt?"

"Every day, we get dozens of letters from simple people just like you from all over the United States, asking me, 'Bob, how *do* you make Jennings Raisin Bran so good? Every box has that same home-made goodness that we have come to expect from the Jennings brand.'"

"Has anybody seen Walt?"

"I seen him," said Sherm Lollar, "last time I seen him was when we came in here. Maybe you could ask that guard over there, the one in the gray uniform."

"It's really very simple," said Mr. Jennings. "We here at Jennings Raisin Bran know how much you folks depend on the quality of every item that bears the Jennings name. And we're proud that you demand such high standards from us. It's our goal to make every box of Jennings Raisin Bran worthy of that expectation. We work hard to meet our own standards of excellence, and we're continually doing research in our up-to-date, expensively equipped laboratories to find even better ways of doing things."

"They really have armed guards right here in the plant," said Eddy Yost. "What do they need guards for?"

Mr. Causey glared at him. "Company secrets. Industrial sabotage. Now, quiet down and listen."

"For instance, let's begin with the raw materials. If you'll follow me right out these doors over here . . ." Mr. Jennings smiled, and indicated another pair of glass doors set into the side of the huge building. As we followed him I glanced around the plant, looking through the surging machines like gigantic trees in a restless steel forest. We went through a cloistered walk, and the music went with us, rising through brass or string passages, but making no progress with its exposition.

At the end of the corridor we went through some more glass doors. We were outside again; the sky was white, streaked with a heavy gray that promised rain. We were in a sort of open yard. Several railroad tracks crossed the area, disappearing quickly down avenues in the maze of buildings. Our guide went up to a group of men who were unloading box cars on one of the sidings.

"Eddy?" said Mr. Zernial. "Now what's happened to Eddy? And has anybody seen Walt yet? The rest of you stick together. I don't want anybody else wandering off. You could get lost around here, and I don't want anybody getting hurt. Frank," meaning Mr. Causey, "maybe I should go look for Walt and Eddy."

"Well," said Mr. Causey, "why don't we just wait a while? They'll probably find us out here. I mean, we don't want to lose *you*, too!"

I noticed that one of the gray-uniformed armed guards was standing to our right, leaning against one of the box cars, trying to appear casual. Reno saw what I was looking at.

"Mr. Zernial, do they have those guards following us? Do they think we're spies from Kellogg's or something?" he asked.

"They're probably guarding the bran shipment."

"We use, first off, only the finest Laurentian bran ore. Come up closer; make a circle around here so that you can see better. I think the boys are unloading a shipment right now. Hello, Tom. Hi, Bob, Larry. Ned. Mack."

We all noticed that Mr. Jennings knew the names of all the workmen. Just like Caesar. We gathered around him in a group, watching the men break open a large wooden crate. They pried open a few slats with crowbars.

"Oh, my God! Now where's Reno? He was standing right here a minute ago," said Mr. Causey.

"Look, if they don't want to learn anything, that's their business," said Mr. Zernial.

Mr. Jennings went up to the crate after his employees had broken open the top. He reached in and pulled out a handful of gritty red earth. He came back to us and indicated that we should hold out our hands; he passed the dirt among us.

"This is raw bran ore. It was recently dug out of the rich fields of ore located in the Laurentian highlands of Quebec, or from our own Mesabi range in Minnesota. It was shipped by ore boat through the Great Lakes right to our port on Cleveland's West Side, then loaded onto freight cars and rushed directly to our factory. To ensure freshness, the trip has taken less than two weeks from the time it left its natural rock bed to its arrival here."

"Mr. Jennings, I hate to interrupt," said Mr. Causey, "but some of our boys seem to have wandered off. I really don't want to cause any inconvenience, but perhaps I should try to find them before they interfere with some machine or something."

Mr. Jennings smiled. "No need to worry," he said. "They'll be no bother at all. I used to think these trips were stuffy, myself. Let them wander around and look at what seems interesting to them. They may learn more that way, anyhow. I'll have them paged from my office if they haven't come back by the time that you're ready to leave. Now, what say we follow this shipment of ore on its way through the many changes it must make before it reaches your pantry shelf?"

We followed him into another immense building. Inside were three furnaces, black with soot and standing several stories tall. We walked by the first two; men and women in dirty overalls turned and smiled shyly as we passed. Mr. Jennings nodded and smiled at them all. The music moved easily into a pleasant *andante*, signifying a transition. Where did the background theme come from? I began to wonder what was really happening.

At the last furnace Mr. Jennings introduced us to Gary Kibling. Mr. Kibling was in charge of Furnace Number Eight.

"Thank you, Bob. Hello, boys. I guess Mr. Jennings has shown you the raw ore outside, is that right? Fine. Now, the first step in making your raisin bran is the refinement of your ore. Of course, we can't make flakes out of the impure stuff that you saw. It would taste terrible. Well, our job is to melt it all down and get out all but the very best bran content. It's actually a complex operation, but I'll try to make it as easy to understand as I can."

Rip nudged me. "They have guards in here, too," he said. I caught Mr. Jennings' eye and smiled. He smiled back.

"This," said Mr. Kibling, "is a blast furnace, very much like those in use in the smelting of iron, manganese, and paper. The basic idea is that the pure bran, having the greater specific gravity, will sink to the bottom when liquefied. Your impurities, or slag, will float and be easily removed. This slag, by the way, is useful, too. It is employed as cheap cereal filler in most of your canned and frozen meat preparations that you buy in your supermarket.

"This furnace is almost one hundred feet tall. The lower part is your crucible. It is circular on the inside, and rises up to that cone-shaped part, which is the shaft of the furnace."

"Mr. Kibling?"

"Yes?"

"Are we safe?" asked Whitey Herzog. "I mean, why doesn't the melted stuff inside melt through the furnace, too?"

Mr. Kibling and Mr. Jennings laughed. "That's very naive of you, son, isn't it? We wouldn't be here if it were that simple. No, actually, the furnace is reinforced and water-cooled, so accidents, or 'breakouts,' as we call them, are very rare."

"But they do happen?" asked Don Zimmer.

"Yes."

"It must be terrible, then," whispered Mr. Causey.

"But, to continue," said Mr. Kibling. "Your raw bran is heated to temperatures exceeding twelve hundred degrees up in the shaft, in the presence of limestone and coke. The melted ore runs down into your crucible where the slag can be run off, and the pure ore tapped out as we desire. The pure bran that is formed is cast into ingots. At this stage the ingots are called 'pig bran.' They can be melted down again and again, each time being refined to higher and higher levels of purity, but we don't bother. Are there any questions?"

"Uh, it seems that Rip, Whitey, and Don have gone off somewhere with Mr. Causey," said Mr. Zernial nervously. "Did any of you notice where they went?"

"I think that they were a little shaky after that talk of 'accidents.' Perhaps they stepped outside," said Mr. Jennings, smiling. "We're going that way, too, so why don't we check?"

Again we went with him, though our number had now shrunk from twenty to twelve. Mr. Jennings stopped outside another of his buildings. The music became softer around us, and the wind grew colder.

"In here we have our own bran mills, where the pig bran ingots are rolled into usable sheets. We find it is cheaper to do our own milling, rather than send the ingots to be made into rolls of sheet bran at one of the local mills. This is because we use the finest-gauge sheets that can be made efficiently. Most of the job mills won't handle orders for double-O-gauge sheets.

"The ingots are passed between roller presses while they are still hot from the furnace. They are reduced in thickness time and again, until they are the legal limit for flakes. The sheets are rolled up and sent by that overhead conveyor to this building here, which is the stamping plant. I think we'll skip the mill room, because there isn't actually much to see, and because we're getting a little short on time. But if you have any questions at all, don't hesitate to ask. Let's move on, though, so you can get a good look at the flake stampers."

Everywhere we went we saw the silent gray guards. Sometimes they stood in groups of two or three, but even then they did not speak. They leaned uneasily against the door frames or the walls of the buildings, fingering the holsters of their guns. The syrupy music bathed them, too, but only succeeded in making them appear more ominous.

We went into another part of the factory. This building was the noisiest yet. Here the giant, greased machines took the sheets of bran and punched out the flakes that were packaged for our consumption. The room was filled with the constant, deafening slamming.

"These," shouted Mr. Jennings above the roar, "these are the flake stampers. There are twenty-seven different flake configurations, designed by our Art Department to be pleasing in texture and shape as well as in taste. As you know, each flake may be oriented in several different ways, by turning them right to left, front to back, top to bottom, or any position in between. Thus, there are thousands upon thousands of possible flake combinations, so that when you see them in your cereal bowl they appear to be random and unique in shape."

"I didn't know that," Chico whispered to me. From the corner of my eye I saw Mr. Jennings snap his fingers and nod toward Chico. I thought nothing of it, but a moment later Chico was gone. I saw one of the gray guards coming back through a glass door. He leaned casually against the wall, nodding his head slowly at Mr. Jennings. I didn't say anything.

"From here," Mr. Jennings said, over the stamping of the flake-punch machines and the louder but sweeter music, "the flakes travel down those chutes to the mixing room where they are combined with the other ingredients. I don't think we'll have time to visit the raisin-casting plant today, but you're all invited to come back again soon. In the mixing room the hand-lathed raisins and the powdered vitamins are added in carefully measured amounts. All these final operations are carried out under the supervision of a Federal Board of Food representative and our own efficiency expert. This is where that niacinamide and certified color are added. We also toss in about three percent non-nutritive crude fiber; on the Federal agent's lunch hour we get that up to twelve or fifteen percent. Then it's all shuffled together and packaged by the marvelous and expensive automated packaging machines. From there, it's only a short ride by truck to your local grocer's shelves. That's about it. Thank you for coming with me and discovering these new horizons in the continuing Adventure of Raisin Bran. Are there any questions?"

"Yes," said Mr. Zernial. "Where is everybody?"

"They're probably all waiting in my office by now," smiled Mr. Jennings.

"Mr. Jennings?"

"Yes? Speak up."

"Vic Wertz here. I was wondering about the way you glossed over the raisin part. Where do they come from?"

"They're mined in the abundantly rich Pennsylvania raisin fields, and shipped directly here by freight train."

"I think that I know what he's getting at," said Mr. Zernial. "Do you buy your raw raisin ore from the Pennsylvania strip miners?"

"Yes, sir. As much as we detest their practices, we feel that they are outweighed by the end product. We feel that we owe it to you, our customers, to use the finest basic ingredients that we can."

The rest of our group began to murmur among themselves. I looked up and caught Mr. Jennings' eye again. This time he didn't smile.

"Golly, Mr. Jennings," said Ike Delock, "we see your point, of course, but from an ecological point of view, I wonder if it *is* worth it. I'm going to bring this up at the next meeting of the World Affairs Club. I never realized—"

"Okay, that's it!" snapped Mr. Jennings. He looked over his shoulder; the gray guards had snapped to wary and expectant attention. "All right, get them! But save that one," he yelled, pointing his finger at me.

The guards grinned, running toward us. They drew their revolvers as they ran. They began firing at us. Mr. Zernial screamed; he fell to the floor first, and from beneath him a pool of blood began to flow, running in a stream under one of the stamping machines. We were paralyzed for the moment. My God, what was happening? Where could we go? The guards picked us off one by one, and I saw my classmates falling around me.

Mr. Jennings came up to me, in the middle of the slaughter. I was crying, I think; I remember noticing that none of the employees working the stamping machines even seemed aware of what was happening. I began to pound on Mr. Jennings' chest, screaming something incoherently.

"Don't worry," he said, smiling. The music was still around me, thundering climactically. "Don't worry, they have orders not to hurt you. You're going to be okay. Just take it easy." He began fumbling with my belt. He opened the snap of my trousers. I looked up into his flushed face with amazement. "No," I cried, "don't!" I hit his hand and then I punched him in the stomach.

He turned away from me for a few seconds. He was gasping; his shoulders were hunched over and his whole body shook. When he turned around again he had a box of Jennings Raisin Bran in his hand. "Here," he said, "take this. It will get you out of here alive. I shouldn't do this, you little queer, but I love you already. Go. Get out while you can."

I took the box of cereal from him and ran for the door. I turned to look over my shoulder, remembering what was happening to my friends. They all were lying on the floor now, still and twisted in their horrible deaths. The sound had died down around them. The music had stopped, everything was incredibly silent. People moved around me, deliberately, like a slow-motion movie. I saw Mr. Jennings reach into his coat. He brought out a blued-steel revolver. He was grinning crazily now; I knew that he wasn't going to let me get away. He pulled out the gun slowly. His hand moved across his body, he fired the gun. A gray mist shot from the barrel of the revolver; his hand continued across his body. The gray mist spread in front of me. I felt hot and prickly inside, and I knew that I couldn't move. The grayness turned to black around me, shot with red and yellow flashes, turned back to gray, then to white. I woke up.

I was lying on the concrete driveway outside. The first thing that I could feel was the pain of the cinders cutting into the side of my face. It was beginning to get dark, and rain was falling in a cold drizzle. The noise from the factory had lessened, but I was still aware of a pounding ache in my head. As I came more to my senses I found that I had been wounded in my arm, and from my right shoulder to the elbow my jacket was soaked dark with blood. I couldn't move the arm, and it hurt terribly. I had difficulty getting up, but I managed. I found the box of Jennings Raisin Bran on the ground near me and, remembering what Mr. Jennings had said, I picked it up and carried it with me.

I was lost among the tortuous alleys of the factory, but after some time I stumbled on the right road. As I was leaving I passed a sign indicating that one of the dark brick buildings was the Puffed Wheat division. I knew then that I had to come back soon.

I must go back to see the cannons. I must see if they shoot the wheat from cannons, shoot it just like they say they do on TV.

CURTAINS

It seemed to Sergeant Weinraub that they only had two kinds of weather on the battlefield. Sometimes it was unbelievably cold, so that the ragged little troupe huddled beneath torn blankets and tried to thaw its bandaged fingers with warm cups of thin coffee. Just as often it was blisteringly hot, and the weight of the rifle alone was enough to drive a soldier crazy. On the endless marches beneath the fiery sun the soldiers dropped pieces of equipment to lighten their burden; their trail could easily be followed, as one essential item after another was discarded in the dust. Then later, when the weather grew suddenly icy, the men cursed themselves for losing the very things that might keep them alive. There was never any moderate climate; it was either cold or very, very hot.

Today it was sweltering beneath the blazing sun. The seventy-five men were resting in the scant shade of a few stumpy trees. Weinraub looked at them for a moment. They leaned against the gnarled trunks wearily, eyes shut, faces shiny with sweat, beards black, mouths open. No one talked. No one smoked or laughed. They all sat there, panting in the heat, waiting for Weinraub to order them to fall in. He was in no hurry, himself. But they had a mission to accomplish.

Sergeant First Class Steve Weinraub was trying to put up a good front for the men. The command had fallen to him suddenly, and he hadn't adjusted to the responsibility yet. But that made no practical difference at all. He was expected to perform as though he had been trained for the job. He walked over to one of the men. "I want to talk with you, Corporal Staefler," he said.

The man looked up. He said nothing. Weinraub sighed and sat down in the dirt next to Staefler. "I'm going to hand you some of my old duties," said the sergeant. "Now that I have to look after all seventy-five of you, I don't have the time anymore."

"Sure," said Staefler flatly. "Like what?"

Weinraub slipped out of his pack's harness and rummaged among his personal effects. He brought out a small black book. "This is the company record book. I want you to carry it from now on. You can see how I've been working it. Just keep track of the reviews, paste them in, make the appropriate notes. It doesn't take that much time, but I just don't want to be bothered." Staefler took the book, looking past Weinraub, still too exhausted to waste energy talking. "I got the new *Stars and Stripes* here," said Weinraub. "Why don't you cut out the review on our next rest stop?"

"What did they say?"

Sergeant Weinraub turned the pages until he found the right place. "'On The Home Front,'" read the sergeant. "'By Brigadier General Robert W. Hanson.'"

"Hanson!" said Staefler. "How did we rate him? I didn't think he bothered to notice us poor slobs."

"He was right out there, last time," said Weinraub. "I saw him. I figure Lieutenant Marquand must have heard ahead of time."

Staefler spit into the dust. "Yeah," he said softly. "I wish I'd known."

"'And then there's Delta Company,'" said Weinraub, continuing to read from the magazine, "'a rather shabby troupe seemingly dedicated to defending our borders in the tritest ways imaginable. This week, in preparation for the first great offensive of the war, rumored to be a massive invasion of the European enemy's homeland, Delta Company attempted to consolidate its gains of the previous months. There was no secret about the importance of this performance. But, for some reason, the company dragged out the oldest, silliest ploy known to modern warfare. Dressed in civilian clothes, the company divided itself into two equal "gangs" and staged a sort of teen-age street fight. I don't know about my colleagues, but I myself have grown excessively weary of such tired examples of low-level creativity.'"

"Uh oh," said Staefler. "Sounds like he didn't like us."

"Yeah," said Weinraub. "'The farce continued in predictable fashion until the company's senior officer, Lieutenant Rod Marquand, cried out against the injustice of the soldiers' fate and threw himself on an opponent's switchblade knife. Although the stunned look on the face of the poor soldier holding the blade was worth a few minutes of the tedious exhibition, Marquand's cheap tactic destroyed whatever tiny shred of interest the performance may have generated. When will we have enough of sordid emotionalism and such sensational novelties as Marquand's? I suspect not until the officers responsible have learned to their dismay the results they may earn; we can hope these officers will take heed from Marquand's poor example, but I fear that's asking too much. We shall see.' "

"I want to know something," said Staefler. "You're telling me that Lieutenant Marquand got himself killed to save us, and this idiot Hanson is saying it was all for nothing?"

Weinraub closed the magazine and handed it to the other man. "Seems like it."

"And now you're in charge?"

Weinraub nodded. That was the same question he kept asking himself.

"I know what you better not do," said Staefler bitterly. "You better not throw yourself on any bayonets."

"Right," said Sergeant Weinraub. "Okay, men," he called. "Fall in."

Over a year before, when the war first began, Weinraub and others like him had been very excited. He could remember the declaration itself with strange clarity. The Representative of North America had appeared on television one evening after dinner. There had been no advance notice. The situation-comedy rerun had ended, the station had played a couple of commercials, and then the handsome face of the Representative filled the screen. Weinraub had glanced across the room at his wife, who was sewing. "Hey," he said. "It's the Representative." She had looked up and smiled, but otherwise had shown no interest in what the Representative had to say.

"Good evening, my fellow citizens of North America," he said. "I come before you tonight to make an announcement that will affect you all, and to explain the situation so that you may understand the reasons behind my decision. As of midnight tonight, New York time, the North American people will be officially at war with the people of Europe. It has been many years since our two great continents have engaged in such a conflict, but nevertheless I feel that you will all support me now, and come to the defense of our noble land."

The next morning the newspapers reported plans for the first draft call for the North American Havoc Forces since the end of the African war six years before. Seized by the powerful patriotic spirit, Weinraub had not waited to be called. He was proud to be the first citizen of his tiny Pennsylvania hometown to enlist. In the months since then he had distinguished himself in a modest way, enough to warrant promotion to sergeant first class. And now, with the fruitless death of Lieutenant Marquand, Weinraub found himself in command of an increasingly discontented force. He understood that the North American invasion of Europe could be adversely affected, even ruined, by the performance of his Delta Company. But he didn't like to think about that.

The Delta Company was only one small theater of operations, of course. But one couldn't hide from the critical gaze of the Representatives. Even though the little band of soldiers thought themselves isolated and ineffectual, so mythic a figure as General Hanson had been assigned to observe one of their actions. Weinraub had no idea if Hanson would be there again in four days, when Delta Company was scheduled for another. Weinraub thought about the review, and prayed that someone out of the NAHF would be sent.

The column marched slowly, shuffling through the dry dust of the road. The sun was going down at last, but the heat did not abate. When it got too dark, Weinraub called a halt, and the men moved off the trail to make camp for the night. He threw his own things down next to Staefler.

"You got any ideas yet?" asked the corporal.

"Yeah, I'm working on something. Nothing definite. Nothing I want to talk about yet."

"You'd think the NAHF guys would give us a break," said Staefler, still burning over the bad notice Lieutenant Marquand's sacrifice had received. "I mean, we're on the same side."

"I don't think so," said Weinraub. In the light of the campfire, he could see that Staefler was giving him a quizzical look. The sergeant hurried to explain. "Well, look," he said. "Sometimes we get an African attaché assigned to review us, sometimes an Asian, sometimes even a European. And they're the enemy. But they're all answerable to their particular Representative, and those guys are a lot rougher on their juniors than you think. The military liaison fellows have an awful short lifespan unless they play clean. As a matter of fact, we can usually count on worse treatment from one of our own than from some neutral power. That way the Representatives won't think the NAHF man is favoring us."

"And the whole system works fine," said Staefler. "But only as long as the Representatives are honest. What do they get out of it? I could never understand that. They must have some kind of deal worked out. And if the Representatives aren't on the level, what we're doing is really kind of pointless."

"Shut up, corporal," said Weinraub sharply.

"Sorry, sir." Staefler spit into the dust again and moved away from the fire. A couple of the privates waited until Staefler had gone, then moved into the circle of firelight.

"We heard about Lieutenant Marquand's review," said one of the men. "We were wondering if it was true."

"Yeah, Nicholl," said Sergeant Weinraub. "*Stars and Stripes* didn't seem too thrilled."

Another man tossed a few branches into the fire. "Was it really General Hanson that wrote the review?"

"Yeah. He's one of the *new* critics. I don't really know what they want."

"We better find out some way," said the second man. "Any idea what's going to happen with the Evaluation?"

"Not yet," said Weinraub. "Lieutenant Marquand had a fine record going until that idiot Hanson spoiled it. The Evaluations have been pretty good to us. We haven't lost that many men, and the NAHF has gained a lot of ground on our account. This one flop shouldn't hurt us too bad."

"Maybe if we look at what's happening on the other fronts, we can get a better notion of what they want," said Nicholl.

"I don't know," said Sergeant Weinraub. "Some South American company did the Battle of Maldon thing. You know, a losing cause but loyal warriors, fighting to the last man to avenge the death of their stupid leader. I would have figured that would really tickle the audience, the whole company of them going out in a huge blaze of glory. But the review just said something about 'pyrotechnic nonsense.' They want simple, basic stuff these days. The tear-jerkers aren't getting points anymore."

"I heard where South America is really losing," said a third soldier. "Asia managed to wipe out most of the Brazilian coast a couple of months ago, and the SAHF is going all out. They wasted that whole company for a major retaliation, but I guess it didn't work out."

"Asia killed off the Brazilian coast?" asked Nicholl. "I didn't know about that. I was just down there about four years ago."

"From what I hear, you won't be able to go back there for a while," said Weinraub. "It's going to be a long time before it cools down."

"What about Africa?" asked the second man.

"Nothing for sure," said Weinraub. "Rumors are that Africa's going to declare against Asia. That would be good news for South America."

"I don't know that they'd be much good," said Nicholl. "We took care of most of Africa's bigger production companies seven years ago."

Sergeant Weinraub stood up, his cramped legs aching. "You got to remember that the Representatives try to keep their own domains in the running," he said. "The Representative of Africa is as shrewd as any of them."

"Yeah," said the second soldier, "and I bet they all got some kind of helping-hand fund to dip into."

"That's pretty rotten talk," said Weinraub. "I'm tired of hearing you idiots going on like that. It shows a lack of discipline. Lieutenant Marquand was a good officer. He didn't allow that kind of thinking, and I won't, either."

There were a few mumbled "Yes, sirs," but Weinraub paid little attention. He was looking for Staefler. The new action had to be planned, and the necessary matériel requisitioned. Weinraub found Staefler sitting among a group of men, all of them arguing loudly about the death of Lieutenant Marquand.

"Corporal," said Weinraub, "would you come here for a minute? We have less than four days now, and I want you to help me go over the outline."

"All right," said Staefler. He stood and followed the sergeant to where a couple of privates were setting up the senior officer's tent.

"Sit down," said Weinraub. "I wish these guys would finish putting up the HQ already. Never mind, we can talk here. Frankly, I want your advice. I've never planned an entire action by myself; it's also no secret that you're the most talented man in the company, now that Lieutenant Marquand's dead."

"Thank you, sir," said Staefler. "I'm pleased you feel that way."

"Not at all. But it does load certain responsibilities on you. The rest of these soldiers don't really have much to worry about. A couple of them win parts in each action, but every time there's less to choose from. Do you follow me? Every one of us *wants* to be used. I mean, that's why we're here. We all want to give the best performance we're capable of; otherwise the EHF will crush North America, and then there'll be no stopping them. But the commanding officer has it a whole lot harder. He has to compromise between spending all his talent on one big action, and reserving material for the next one. And most of all, he has to exercise judgment in choosing his own role."

"You making a dig at Lieutenant Marquand?" asked Staefler angrily.

"No, no. I was just trying to say that I have to play an active and important part, but still keep myself able to continue in command. It's a very critical job of planning."

"I think the best thing now is to play it conservative," said Staefler. "It's pretty clear that the brass isn't looking for the kind of stuff we were giving them at the beginning of the war."

"Yeah, right," said Weinraub. "Straight out of Clausewitz. He always hated the kind of complicated stratagems our newer officers are so crazy about. Clausewitz said the best thing was just to hit the enemy in the face, hard."

"Hanson's bunch of critics is going back to old-fashioned themes," said Staefler thoughtfully. "We have to come up with something traditional. Make it short and simple. When I was in school, my coaches never stopped telling me that the professional athlete needs concentration, total commitment, and good form. The guys that don't make it are looking for easy ways around the hard work."

"All right," said Weinraub. "Instead of trying to burn out the observers' mind with a flash of brilliant footwork, let's come up with something nice and substantial." The two men chatted while the privates completed putting up the company headquarters. Then Weinraub and Staefler went into the tent and began drawing up the first outline of the action.

The next morning, as Weinraub was eating his spare field rations, a soldier called into the tent that a command jeep was approaching along the road.

"Thanks, private," said Sergeant Weinraub, hurriedly putting on his trousers and buttoning his tunic. "That has to be the brass with the Evaluation of our last action. Have the men police the area. I don't want a prejudiced audience for the next one." He felt a tightening in his stomach, a fearful anticipation of what the Evaluation would say. He knew that at the same moment a copy of the Evaluation was being presented to the staff of the Representative of North America. All of the NAHF, in effect, was waiting anxiously with him.

He stepped out of the tent, into the torrid sun. The men were frantically trying to give the place an organized appearance, but the jeep was already rattling to a halt on the dusty track beside the camp. Weinraub took a deep breath and walked toward the waiting officers.

Before he had gone halfway, the sergeant realized that General Hanson himself was waiting in the jeep. Weinraub suddenly felt lightheaded; he wasn't sure that he could put on a cool show now, knowing what kind of an Evaluation he could expect. He took another breath, saluted, and presented himself to the officers.

"Sergeant First Class Weinraub, acting commanding officer of Delta Company," he said, his mouth dry and his head still buzzing.

General Hanson returned his salute. "I've admired your work, Sergeant Weinraub," he said. "I've had the pleasure of following Delta Company for several months now, though I've only actually reviewed one of your actions."

"Will you be reviewing us again, sir?"

Hanson gave him a quick smile. "It's against our policy to advise the troupes along those lines, but, yes, I'll be writing the notices for your next action. That's three days from now, isn't it?"

"Yes, sir. We hope you like it, sir."

"I do, too," said the general, giving Weinraub a piercing look. Even though Hanson was compelled to be impartial, it was clear that he was still a superior officer in the NAHF, and his private desires were in no way affected by his public duties. He reached into his tunic and took out a sealed red envelope. "Here is the Evaluation of Lieutenant Marquand's last action. I want you to study it. I want you to realize the importance of what you're doing, and take the appropriate precautions. Use your judgment, and use your good taste. I'm confident we won't have any more mistakes from this company. All of North America is counting on you." The general's driver started the jeep's engine at a signal from Hanson, and Weinraub took the envelope and saluted. Weinraub stood in place while the jeep's wheels spat gravel and dust, then clattered away down the road. He tore a strip from the side of the red envelope and slipped out the Evaluation sheet, meanwhile walking slowly back to the tent. When he got there he lay on the folding bunk and read the paper.

"Sergeant Weinraub?" It was Corporal Staefler.

"Come in, corporal. Hear the bad news."

Staefler entered the tent and sat in the single camp chair by the bunk. "How bad is it?"

"You remember how Fox Company made some terrific coup and won a staging area in the South of England?"

"That was two or three months ago, right?"

"Yeah," said Weinraub. "We really needed it; without it we wouldn't be able to launch any kind of attack. We had to get on the offensive. Well, not only did the Europeans recapture that staging outpost, but three flights of long-range bombers got through the aerial defenses and wiped out Baltimore, Washington, and Charleston, South Carolina."

Staefler stared for several seconds, stunned by the harshness of the Evaluation. "They got *Washington?*" he said at last.

"That's not so bad," said Weinraub wearily. "The NAHF had twenty-four-hour notice, and everything important was evacuated. What really hurts is the loss of the English base. We're right back where we were a year ago. The Europeans are taking their time, knocking out our cities one by one, and we haven't had the first shot at hitting them on their own ground."

"It's really up to us to get that base back, then," said Staefler.

"Yeah, we got to make it good. An advisory note in the Evaluation reported that some European troupe did an awful fine job in an action a few days ago, and when they get evaluated we may be in for a real tough time."

"There's at least three guys in the company from Baltimore and Washington. It'll be hard telling them the news. Especially since they still haven't gotten over the rotten review Lieutenant Marquand got. They all respected him. He was the damn best officer I ever knew."

"Look, do me a favor. Find out which of our men had families in those cities, and send them in to me. With the lieutenant gone, that's another ugly thing I have to do." Staefler gave him a sympathetic grin, turned, and left the tent. Weinraub was lost in thought until another corporal called in to ask if the men should be formed up for the day's march.

"No, thank you, corporal," said Weinraub. "We'll be staying here for a while longer. Let the men relax. I think I want to begin shaping up the new action." He was interrupted again a short time later by the men affected by the European raid. He handled the diffcult task and dismissed the shocked soldiers with a few words of condolence. Then he went back to the job of devising a simple and effective action.

About noon, Weinraub left the tent to find Corporal Staefler. The men were engaged in various improvised recreations: baseball, boxing, or just plain loafing. Staefler was standing in a circle around two huge soldiers, both of them naked to the waist and trading punches to the cheers of their fellows. Weinraub touched the corporal on the shoulder. Staefler immediately began to break up the fight, thinking that Weinraub disapproved. "No, don't interrupt them," said the sergeant. "Come on, I want you to hear what I've planned."

"Is it done?"

"Just about," said Weinraub. "If you help me put the finishing touches on it, we'll have almost three days to prepare. That's about thirty-six hours more than usual. There won't be any excuse for a foul-up."

"Great, but what can I do?"

Weinraub pulled a dead branch from one of the twisted trees as he passed. He was silent for several seconds, dragging the stick in the dirt and trying to frame what he wanted to say. "You know as well as I do that you're the best of the lot, Bo," he said finally. "There isn't time for modesty. If we don't do a first-class job this time out, the invasion may never get going, and who knows what the Representatives will award to the Europeans. This is going to be your show. I have to lead from strength, and you're it."

Staefler was stunned. "Look, sergeant, don't get me wrong. I've been nearly bursting for months now, waiting for Lieutenant Marquand to let me carry the ball. I knew I could do one hell of a good job. But now I'm not so sure. It's not that I'm afraid of what it means personally. I don't suppose any of us are, really. But this is such a *big* thing. . . ." His words faded away; the two men stopped along the side of the road, and Weinraub studied the corporal intently.

"It's not just for me," Weinraub said. "It's not even for all the other guys in the company. And it goes further than just this one crummy theater of operations. We got to do it for Lieutenant Marquand. So he didn't die for nothing."

"When you start the locker-room pep talk, I know you're desperate," said Staefler, grinning. "I can't say how much I'm glad for the chance. It's just that I'm not sure I can stand this kind of pressure."

Weinraub clapped the other man on the shoulder. "I've thought it all out, Bo," he said. "There isn't another soldier in the troupe that I can trust on this one."

Staefler shook his head. "Yeah, well, we'll see," he said. "What's it going to be?"

"I figure World War II. It's clean, direct, and there's a lot going for it as far as audience identification. It will be a simple demolitions job, an ambush, and a single act of heroism. You'll have a sort of long solo at the climax. I stole the idea from a movie."

"Great. I didn't want to say anything to you before, but I thought World War II was the best choice. Have you made up a list of supplies?"

"Yeah," said Weinraub. "Come on back to the HQ tent and I'll give it to you. Get on the phone and have the stuff sent out as soon as possible. We need a good river with at least one bank wide enough for the action and the audience. NAHF Dispatch has two full days to find us one around here, so we may even get a rehearsal in."

"That would be nice for a change," said Staefler, more confidently.

Later that day the list of equipment, uniforms, and weapons was radioed to the NAHF depot. Weinraub was informed that the nearest suitable river was some three hundred miles away; the trucks would arrive about noon of the following day, and the company would arrive at the site in the late afternoon or evening. They would have only a couple hours of daylight to sketch out the positions for the action, and a little time the next morning before the audience began to arrive. It was unfortunate that the river was so far away, but Sergeant Weinraub had wisely written a simple scenario that had no complicated movements. Only Staefler had to understand his part perfectly. If he performed well, the whole action would be an impressive success. And Staefler was the best soldier in the company.

When the trucks and the matériel arrived the following day, Weinraub called his men together to explain the action. "I'm going to split you up now," he said. "Fall in in a straight line and count off by threes." After the soldiers had done so, he detailed the men numbered 1 or 3 to be Americans, and all the No. 2s to be German soldiers. This put the American forces about twice that of the mock Nazis, fifty to twenty-five. The troupe changed into the appropriate uniforms supplied by the NAHF quartermaster corps, loaded the American equipment into the American trucks, the German equipment into the German trucks, and climbed into the remaining space for the long drive to the river.

Weinraub and Staefler were both German soldiers, dressed in the field-green trousers and jacket, high black boots, and peaked cap of officers in the Nazi *Waffen-SS*. They rode in a light open Volkswagen personnel carrier, with one of the other members of the company as driver.

It was after eight o'clock when the company got to the chosen site. Weinraub got out of the Volkswagen jeep and walked slowly down to the bank of the river with Staefler. "This is fine, Bo," said the sergeant. "We'll camp on this side tonight. The American troops will go on ahead; there's supposed to be a bridge a little over ninety miles farther downstream. I'll run through the plan with them now and synchronize our watches. Then they'll leave to take their positions. After that, it'll all be up to you and me."

The American forces consisted of three regular transport vehicles and two jeep command cars. They were well on their way before darkness fell, and Weinraub gathered the remainder of his men, all dressed in the field uniforms of the *Waffen-SS* or regular Army, some wearing the insignia of the Combat and Construction Engineers. "All right, listen up," he said. "The first thing, the important thing we have to do is throw a light bridge across the river here. The water is just under eighty-two feet wide. We've got plenty of authentic bridging equipment, so the only problem is going to be time. We may have to work right through the night, and give the performance tomorrow on little or no sleep. I'm sorry. If NAHF Dispatch could have found us a suitable site a little closer, we could have had more time to plot out the action. Never mind.

"In the back of one of the trucks are a couple of dozen eight-foot sections of the *Leichte Z Brücke*. These are portable steel sections that are joined in two parallel rows across the river, and then connected by a wooden platform roadbed that is also cut into sections in one of the trucks. We're going to need to improvise supporting stanchions where the *Brücke* units meet. That's twenty-two junctions. Siekewicz, I want you to pick ten men and take care of that. Meanwhile, I want to meet with Corporal Staefler, Private Wilson, Private Segura, and Corporal Leskey. The rest of you start working. Corporal Naegle's had experience with this type of operation, so while I'm busy in my meeting he'll be in charge."

The troupe worked strenuously, far into the night. By the time Weinraub had finished his conference, the bridge extended almost halfway across the river. Men waded chest-deep in the black, moon-sparkled water, securing the Z sections to short pillars constructed of rock and sturdy tree limbs. After the sections had been laid across the water, there would remain only the simple task of putting down the roadway and fastening it with light girders. The whole job ought to be completed before 4 A.M.; Weinraub was satisfied.

"Is there going to be any problem?" asked Staefler nervously. "I mean, you said you got the idea from a movie."

"That's never been any trouble at all," said Sergeant Weinraub. "The critical staff doesn't care where we get our source material, as long as the action is carried out with skill and integrity."

"I'll bet your mother would kill you, if she could see you now."

Weinraub looked startled. "What the hell do you mean?" he asked.

"Nothing," said Staefler quickly. "I mean, just that you're all dressed up like some Nazi butcher. And with a name like Weinraub, too."

"I see what you're getting at. No, my parents were Lutherans."

"I didn't mean anything by it," said Staefler. "I don't know. I guess I'm just trying to work off some of this stage fright."

"Sure. Come on, let's see if anybody's got the coffee going."

The bridge inched its way across the river and, at last, it reached the other side and was secured to the opposite bank. While the men, stripped to the waist, exhausted now by their labors, fastened down the sections of roadbed, Weinraub ordered the company's three demolitions experts to place explosive charges along the length of the bridge.

"Are we going to blow the thing up tomorrow?" asked Private Wilson.

"If everything goes well, we will," said Weinraub. "I want all the charges wired in series, so that one push on the plunger will set off the entire length of bridge. After you men finish that, we can turn in."

"Thank God," said Corporal Leskey. The soldiers set to work, and the tasks of laying the roadway and secreting the explosives were finished within the hour. Sergeant Weinraub congratulated his men and let them get some sleep, knowing that the inspection group would arrive right on time the next morning.

It was only nine o'clock when Weinraub was awakened by the

sound of the jeeps. They pulled to a stop fifty yards from Delta Company's camp; the reviewing committee walked slowly toward the men, chatting and laughing easily among themselves. Once more Weinraub felt an irrational anger, wondering how those critics would feel if they had to go out and be judged, week after week. Belonging to a combat troupe was hard work. The hours were long and the rewards were few, beyond the knowledge that one was helping the war effort against the Europeans. But the worst thing was the emotional strain of performing. Weinraub could never completely conquer it.

The reviewing committee was setting up folding chairs. Corporal Staefler, as usual, had assumed the responsibility of directing the committee to the best vantage point and assisting in whatever trivial favors the critics required. Weinraub guessed that it was keeping Staefler's mind off his solo.

Soon it was time for Weinraub to order his men to their places. He gathered the fragment of his company and ran through the general instructions once more. "Above all else," he said, "don't get in the way. I don't want any of you spear carriers ruining the action. If something seems to go wrong, *ignore it*. You may be wrong yourself. Let Corporal Staefler or myself handle any emergency." He gave Staefler and Segura their special directions, and then waved the soldiers to their places. Staefler and Weinraub took a position in a sandbag bunker near the committee's seats. The two *Waffen-SS* officers were armed with MP 40 submachine guns and Walther Pistole 38s. With them in the bunker were five sharpshooters, one soldier manning an MG 42 machine gun. The other men were scattered about the clearing, some protected by bunkers or foxholes, others sheltered behind stumps and boulders.

Weinraub nodded to one of the privates, who gave the signal by radio to the American forces waiting across the river. In the stillness the sergeant could hear the roar of the transport trucks as they were started up. Looking through his field glasses, he soon saw the first of the convoy approaching the river and the bridge. Weinraub took a quick glance behind him; there had been a rumor that the Representative of North America himself might observe this crucial action. A seat had been prepared for him, but it was empty. General Hanson caught Weinraub's eye and nodded grimly. The sergeant returned his gaze to the far side of the river, where the first of the American trucks was rolling onto the bridge.

In a sudden instant of panic, Weinraub swung the glasses to the ignition device, sitting isolated in the middle of the clearing for dramatic effect. The box was small and green, standing up in the mud, its familiar T-shaped firing mechanism making the situation obvious to the observers. He scanned the device through his glasses, but everything seemed to be in order; the wires from the explosive charges were connected properly, he thought. In the matters of armaments and equipment, he had to trust the skill of his engineers. He hoped for his own and Lieutenant Marquand's sake that they hadn't fouled up.

The plan was simple. The Germans would wait until the entire American convoy was on the bridge, then blast it all to pieces. There was a murmur of approval from the reviewing committee. Weinraub had planned well. The simple, classic idea had gained him a positive edge already. The sergeant smiled to Staefler, who grinned back nervously.

Suddenly, a shot cracked from one of the German bunkers. A groan went up from the audience, but Weinraub only smiled again. That was Private Segura, firing on schedule. It seemed as though he had revealed the plan prematurely; the American trucks came to a sudden halt in the middle of the bridge. Infantrymen poured from the backs of the vehicles, running out along the bridge and lying flat, searching for the hidden ambushers. Weinraub gave the signal, and the three German machine guns opened fire. Four Americans died immediately, trying to rush the German position. Seeing that, the rest of the Americans sought shelter. The Germans were all safely hidden, and it was the Americans who were caught in a predicament. Sergeant Weinraub shouted to Corporal Leskey to run out and blow up the bridge. Of course, Leskey knew that he'd never make it. He was proud that Weinraub had chosen him. Before he had gone ten yards, an American marksman had cut him down. The reviewing committee applauded, suddenly realizing the interesting situation Weinraub had developed. It seemed to be a stalemate. If the Germans could somehow destroy the bridge and its occupants, or if the Americans could somehow manage to overrun the Nazi position, the action would be a great debut for Sergeant Weinraub.

Muffled shouts were heard from the bridge. Most of the American soldiers ran back toward the trucks; it seemed that they were going to try and drive across, ignoring the dense storm of shells coming from the German emplacements. Before they achieved their goal, half of the Americans were slain, sprawling horribly on the white wood planking of the bridge. The others tried hastily to pull the bodies of their mates out of the path of the trucks. More Americans were slaughtered. At last they gave up and sprinted for the safety of the trucks. Four American sharpshooters remained at their posts near the end of the bridge to cover their fellows' attack.

Weinraub signaled again. Private Wilson ran out to the ignition box, making perhaps twenty yards before an American bullet ripped through his neck. The trucks had almost reached the end of the bridge. "Now," cried Weinraub, slapping Staefler's back loudly. In the midst of the action, the corporal would have no time to feel anxious. He had a job to do. The idea was for Staefler to race to the box, nearly succeed, and then be shot by the American snipers. Dying, he would fall over the T-plunger and blast the bridge and the enemy in a last dramatic, heroic gesture.

It worked perfectly. Just before he reached the igniter, several rounds of fire caught Staefler, jerking him about like a kite on a string. He clutched his abdomen and looked straight at Weinraub. "The plunger," muttered Weinraub, clenching his fists. Behind him the committee was perfectly still. The trucks were moving, the first one just inching off the bridge onto the bank. "The plunger!" screamed Weinraub. "Fall on the plunger!" Staefler was obviously in great pain. His knees buckled; he knelt in the mud of the clearing, his jaw slack, and stared at the ignition box. At last, just when Weinraub was about to go mad with frustration, Staefler fell over the plunger.

Nothing happened.

Weinraub felt tears on his cheek. Not caring about the bullets whacking into the sandbags, he ran out to Staefler. "You idiot!" he shouted, grabbing the suffering man. "The plunger! Why didn't you push the plunger?"

Staefler stared at him, his eyes half closed. He still held his lower abdomen, where the tunic was fouled with a rapidly spreading bloody stain. "*Zünden*," he whispered hoarsely.

"What the hell do you mean, '*Zünden*'?"

A bubble of red froth burst on Staefler's lips and trickled down his chin. Weinraub looked up helplessly. Confused, the American soldiers had stopped their unscheduled progress. The committee was on its feet. The sergeant could see General Hanson already stalking back toward his jeep. "We closed after one performance," said

Weinraub bitterly. He dropped Staefler to the ground and knelt by the igniter. One of the soldiers called out to him.

"It's not a plunger," said the soldier. "I don't know, maybe the NAHF made a mistake, or Staefler gave them the wrong order number. It's got a key where it says 'Zünden.' You got to turn the key."

"They'll probably wipe us out in an aerial bombardment for this," said Weinraub, sobbing. He picked up the ignition box and turned the key in the Zünden socket. The bridge exploded in a boiling orange-and-black cloud, harmlessly as all the American vehicles and personnel were by now safely on the German bank. Weinraub stood and looked around him. His men, dressed in Nazi uniforms and American, their expressions showing only despair, all holding their weapons slackly, turned toward him to hear his orders. "We got to keep going, though," said the helpless sergeant. "That's the way it's done. The show's got to go on." Then he savagely kicked the twisted body of Corporal Staefler.

HOW IT FELT

A studied carelessness. It was a phrase that held a peculiar fascination for her; its paradox of attitudes struck her as sophisticated in a way that she, herself, was not. Adopting a studied carelessness of manner could make her appear more sophisticated to her friends.

It was late at night when Vivi came to this conclusion. She was standing beneath an immense tree in the congregation area of her home. The tree was one of her favorites; its bark was tough, black, scored with a vertical network of furrows. Its limbs were dressed with dangling shawls of Spanish moss, which Vivi had created in imitation of Alhu's trees. Vivi's friends, for the most part, had never seen Alhu's, and they frequently remarked on Vivi's imagination. She always smiled, but said nothing when they complimented her.

The stars frightened her, and as she stood beneath her tree she kept her eyes down, refusing to look through the tangle of leaves into the threatening face of the night. She tried instead to imagine how her friends would react when she assumed a new personality. Moa would be the first to notice. Moa was always the first; Moa would raise her eyebrows and whisper something in Vivi's ear: how bored Moa was growing, how tired Moa was of wandering through a lifetime without events, how much Moa welcomed Vivi's eccentricities. Moa would kiss Vivi as a reward. They would spend the day in repetitious sexual gratifications.

But then it would become dark. Vivi would be terrified by starlight, seized by a hatred of the moon. As always, Moa would not understand, and she would return to her own home. Vivi would be alone, as she was every night.

Vivi sighed. Even her fantasies were empty.

The branches above her head rustled. Vivi laughed bitterly. "It won't work," she thought. "You can't trick me that way." Vivi didn't look up into the muttering boughs, where stars waited like determined voyeurs among the leaves. She felt the rough side of the tree a final time, rubbing her fingers painfully over the stone-hard ridges. Still staring into the grass at her feet, she moved slowly away.

A thin wall ran across the congregation area, roughly parallel to the narrow brook. The wall was seven feet tall and four times that distance in length. It contained various devices that dispensed food and drink, as well as whatever other luxuries her companions required. Another wall, beyond the grove of the congregation area, held the transportation unit. Still other service units, scattered about the several square miles of her open-air house, provided everything Vivi or her friends could ever desire.

The carefully trimmed lawn changed to clumps of grass, then to isolated brownish stalks of weed growing in a narrow track of sand and pebbles. Vivi sat down at the edge of the brook. She dipped her hand in the water; it was a pleasantly warm temperature, the same temperature as the air in her home. The temperature of both was constant. Trees grew along the opposite side of the brook, and their leafy branches prevented the stars' reflections from frightening Vivi. She was bored. She was young, but she was bored. Nevertheless, she couldn't yet retire to her sleeping area. It was still too early in the night to lie on her back and stare at the evil constellations, letting the infinite horror of space invade her mind. If she did that too soon, then nothing would be left to pass the remainder of the night. She couldn't face that possibility.

"Vivi!"

She turned around; the thin wall blocked her view of her visitor, but she recognized the voice. It was Moa. "I'm here by the brook," said Vivi.

Moa walked around the wall and joined Vivi at the edge of the water. "I thought you'd be here," said Moa. "I want to show you something."

Vivi felt a sudden excitement. "Have you found something new?" she asked.

"I'm not certain," said Moa. "You'll have to help me."

"Of course," murmured Vivi, a little disappointed.

"I've brought Tagea. I hope you don't mind. He's waiting in your passagerie. He gave me the idea."

"No," said Vivi. "I don't mind."

"Good," said Moa, standing and pulling Vivi up beside her. "Let's use your transportation unit. It'll be quicker." The two women splashed across the brook and through the small stand of trees. They came out on a wide meadow, which was part of Vivi's sleeping area. It was here that, during the daylight hours, she and Moa shared the often tedious pleasures of their bodies. Vivi did not have to keep her gaze fixed on the ground; alone no longer, she found no terror in the stars. She wondered what new thing Moa had discovered.

"She comes to me more often than to any of the others," thought Vivi. "It is because I have emotion. It is because I can entertain varying states of mind. Moa cannot. None of the others can. Only I. And the price of this lonely talent is panic." Vivi walked beside Moa, trying to hold her pace down to Moa's languid speed. On the far side of the meadow was a ravine. They climbed down into it; Vivi enjoyed the humidity, the feel of the mud beneath her bare feet, even the biting of her insects. She glanced at Moa. Her companion's expression was no different than it ever was. Moa was without emotion.

They scrambled up the other side of the ravine. Vivi saw the man Tagea waiting by the wall. He said nothing when the two women appeared. Moa led the way, and Vivi followed. They stepped through the portal of the transportation unit; the unit, tied into the TECT system buried deep beneath the surface of the earth, transported them to Moa's chosen destination. Vivi blinked rapidly as she walked across the threshold. Wherever they were, it was now bright daylight.

"This is a new world," said Moa.

"I found it a few years ago," said Tagea. "It amused me, but now I've given it to Moa."

Vivi yawned; it was the first outward sign of her new campaign of studied carelessness. She would be unimpressed, not at all curious. She said nothing. She could see that Moa was disappointed.

"That sun in the sky is the center star of the Wheel of the Sleeper," said Moa. "I recall your hatred of stars. I remember that this star seems specially malignant to you. We have come here for several reasons, one of which is to prove to you that you have nothing to fear."

"Ah, Moa," said Vivi quietly, "you won't understand. It is not a product of objective thought, this terror I feel. It is something else, something that you cannot share. It is my burden alone."

"It is your *illness* alone," said Tagea. He stared at Vivi, shielding his eyes with both hands against the glare of the odd sun. Vivi did not answer, though her anger almost caused her to scream. But that would not have been in keeping with her new self.

"Are you unwell?" asked Moa. "You do not appear to be as unsteady in your responses. You are repressing the irrational personality that is your chief asset."

Vivi shrugged. Moa took her hand and led her across a field of waving blue grasses. Tagea followed them; Vivi could hear him muttering to himself. It was a habit of his, whenever it was obvious that he was being excluded from the immediate sexual situation. The three people walked for several miles. Vivi was becoming increasingly fatigued; at first, the magenta tint to the sky intrigued her, but that lasted only a hundred paces. The irritating tickle of the grass occupied her for another hundred. Then there was nothing. The horizon was empty. There was only Moa, still holding her hand, and Tagea's smug monologue behind them.

"Why are we here?" thought Vivi. Surely in her search for diversion, Moa had found something of interest. It must lie beyond the endless blue sea of grass. Vivi couldn't allow herself to ask the question aloud, however. She was establishing her character. Moa, who had no emotions, needed time to notice and analyze the difference.

It was a difficult thing, being the only person left with true feelings. Vivi often cursed her emotions; they interfered with her relations to Moa and the others. Vivi was more of a creature, a temporary entertainment than an equal to them. She wished that she could throw her feelings away, strip them off as all the other people had done generations before. But then, again, she was glad of her affliction. Her emotions helped her pass the awful hours. She never had to search the world—and other worlds—for amusement.

"You are oddly silent," said Moa.

"It is a mood," said Tagea. "Several of her moods include silence. I would have thought you'd have catalogued them all by now. Perhaps this is 'spite' again. Or 'petulance.' We've had them all before. I have long since grown weary of them. They are so limited."

"Is he right, Vivi?" asked Moa. "Is it another emotion?"

"Oh, I don't know," said Vivi. "I'm just being quiet. Is there something I should be saying?"

"No, of course not," said Moa. "But you're usually more responsive." Vivi only shrugged once more.

They emerged finally from the broad prairie, coming out on the bank of a small, muddy river. On the opposite bank was a collection of artificial buildings. Vivi forgot her new personality for a moment and gasped in surprise.

"Those are homes," said Moa. Her voice sounded pleased that Vivi had at last reacted. "They're like our homes, in a way, except that these low-level creatures trap themselves within physical limits. They must be surrounded by the products of their labor. It is a peculiar and annoying form of pride."

"I ought to defend them," said Tagea. "After all, I discovered them. They think I'm some kind of universal authority. It was amusing for a short time, but it didn't last."

Moa frowned. "You can't protect them now," she said. "You gave them to me."

"Yes," said Tagea. "I had no intention of interceding. I was only considering alternatives."

"Are you going to kill them?" asked Vivi. She said it with her air of studied carelessness, so that it didn't seem to matter to her whether Moa answered or not.

Moa walked down to the river's edge. She scooped up a handful of stones. "TECT will help me, even here," she said. "Watch." Moa extended her arms. The water began to churn violently. Rocks from the bed of the river and from the solid ground tore themselves loose and piled up to make a bridge. "I won't kill those creatures directly," said Moa. "Maybe indirectly. We'll see."

Vivi crossed the rock span behind Moa and Tagea. She wondered at how simple it had been to graft a new point of view onto her personality. It was no effort at all to maintain her unconcerned attitude; it was now the most natural thing to wander about with her companions, unimpressed, unaffected, somewhat weary. Moa was already puzzled by Vivi's behavior, but Tagea, the possessor of decidedly inferior mental powers, hadn't yet noticed. Vivi felt less than she had anticipated; she had hoped for a different wealth of worldliness, but had acquired little that was remarkable. She understood that this was how Moa had lived her entire life, without measurable degrees of emotion. It was an attractive quality in Moa. Vivi hoped it would be the same in herself.

"Look," said Tagea. He pointed toward the nearest of the buildings. A small gathering of creatures had formed.

"What do you think of them?" said Moa.

"Nothing, as yet," said Vivi lazily. "I notice that they have covered their bodies with furry containers, even though the sun is uncomfortably warm."

"Do you wish to converse with them?" asked Tagea.

"Don't you want to love them, or be afraid?" asked Moa.

Vivi stretched and yawned. "Are we in a hurry to return?" she said. Moa shook her head. Vivi waited. Moa raised her eyebrows and shook her head once more.

The creatures shouted at them as the three walked through their town. Moa and Tagea took no notice. Vivi was startled by the creatures' appearance at first, but after a short time she found their ugliness monotonous. Moa led the way beyond the stinking settlement; Vivi noticed that her feelings were fewer and weaker than ever before. She was pleased. She walked across a broad, stony plain and climbed several low hills on the far side. At the top of the tallest of these hills, Moa turned and pointed back in the direction they had traveled. "There," she said. "That's the community of the native creatures. You can see the smoke."

"It is much more pleasant here," said Vivi.

"The path is unbearably steep," said Tagea. "The rocks in the soil are uncomfortable to walk upon. We will only have to repeat the journey, to get home."

"Where we are, TECT is," said Vivi. "TECT will take us home from here."

"I had planned to walk all the way back to the point where we arrived on this world," said Moa. "It will be an adventure."

"Yes," said Vivi. "An adventure."

"Boring," said Tagea.

"Be seated," said Moa. Vivi and Tagea glanced at each other, then made themselves as comfortable as possible in the dry dust of the hilltop. Moa licked her lips and walked a few steps away from them. She faced away from the creatures' village, toward a vast, gray body of water in the distance. "That is an inland sea," she said. "It is larger than any sea on our world except the sunset ocean." Moa raised her hands toward the water. Perspiration appeared on her brow and on her upper lip. She held her position for many minutes. Vivi said nothing. Tagea was not even watching. Moa's body glistened with sweat. Her concentration was complete; her connection with TECT deepened until Moa quivered with a dangerous power.

"I've seen this before," said Tagea. "I think I've seen *everything* before."

"So have I," whispered Vivi. "But there's no one that can match the taste and delicacy of Moa's technique. I had hoped that we'd see something new, though."

"There's still time," said Tagea. "We'll be here for quite a while, if I know her."

The outline of the giant sea was blurred by distance. Still, Vivi could see that it was changing shape. Moa pointed one hand at the water, but swung the other slowly toward the neighboring hills. Carefully co-ordinating her devastating strokes, Moa splintered the ground at the edge of the ocean, and crushed the small mountains that stood between her and the water.

The hills turned from a rich blue color to an ashen gray. Moa pulled moisture from them, desiccated them, crumbled the ancient bones of rock into a fragile powder. The hills collapsed in great clouds that obscured Vivi's vision for a long while. Moa waited until the storm she had created subsided; the day ended with Moa standing, posing. Tagea slept. Vivi practiced her lack of passion. At dusk the air cleared. The dust settled into low mounds on the plain, white and sterile. Moa let loose the waters of the sea, through channels and fissures she built among the dead hills. The water rolled quickly, noisily at first, until Moa gestured. The ocean became sluggish and thick. The water contracted.

The night passed quietly. Vivi watched the ocean shrink in its new course, until the entire inland sea had shriveled to the size of a small pond. By then it was nearly dawn.

"Have I missed anything interesting?" asked Tagea.

"A pyrotechnic display," said Vivi. "Much more energetic than her usual, I suppose. Watch."

The pond that was all that remained of the ocean sat between two mounds of white powder. The water was a dark green. Moa pressed her fingers together, and the water bubbled. It shrank even further, rolling into a sphere of black substance. The sphere wasted away into a mere ball the size of a fruit, the color of the powdery hills. Moa extended her hands, and the ball began to spin. The ball bounced across the distance separating the hills from their creator. It became lighter, finally rolling as softly as a hairball to its finish at Moa's feet. She nodded, and bent to pick up the round clump of stuff. She held it for a moment, and dropped it back again. She forgot it. Moa said nothing.

Tagea yawned, and Vivi merely stared. Moa was not yet finished; she had only begun to block out her work. Vivi could not visualize the totality of Moa's project, and thus could not understand the reasons behind each of her specific, sure touches. Still, Vivi did not wonder. She would not give Moa that ever again.

After a time Moa stopped. Her arms fell to her sides at last, her bunched back muscles relaxed. To Vivi, Moa seemed to shrink, to withdraw within herself. She became human again. Moa turned to her friends and sighed. "I will study your reactions now," she said.

"A trifle overdone, don't you think?" asked Tagea.

"You always say that," said Moa. "I don't care to hear your opinion. I want to relish our Vivi's. This has all been for her benefit."

"I have seen it before," said Vivi. "Not all together, of course. But you're only stringing one trick after another. I want something different."

Moa stared. "Where is your dismay now?" she asked. "Where is your awe? I need it, Vivi. I'm hungry."

"I'm tired," said Vivi.

"Give me your fear," said Moa. Vivi said nothing. Moa turned toward the village of the creatures. She merely pointed. There was a distant, hollow noise, and the settlement disappeared in a muffled explosion.

"You killed them all," said Vivi.

Moa nodded. She made the ground open up beneath the wreckage of the town. Just as suddenly, as the debris tumbled into the crack, she made the earth close up. There was no sign that any living thing had ever passed by that place.

"We must delight our friends with this," said Vivi. "This is no doubt an entertaining moment. But it has gone on too long. You've always lacked discipline, Moa."

"Yes," said Tagea. "Let's go back now."

Moa's eyebrows twitched. "I've never known anger," she said. "I've never known hatred or admiration. But frustration is common enough among us. It is an itch. It must be scratched, one way or another." She put out her hand again. Tagea jumped to his feet, as though he were a marionette. His face contorted in pain. His arms and legs wobbled in the cool evening breeze; they looked like there were no longer any bones inside to give them a normal human shape. Still Tagea jerked about. Finally, Moa let him fall to the ground. He collapsed into a heap, like a doll filled with sawdust. His corpse turned bright, glossy pink. Vivi moved quietly to his side and touched him. His skin was hard and cold, like polished stone. As Vivi watched, Moa turned Tagea's body into a small, perfect cube of pink crystal.

"Tagea?" asked Vivi.

"He's right there," said Moa. "How do you react?"

Vivi looked up with an expression of studied carelessness. "He was more tiresome than he knew," she said.

Moa raised her hand again. Vivi raised her own. The two women stared at each other. At last, Moa dropped her arm. "I'm dead," she said. "You were my only pleasure."

"It's a pity you can't enjoy all this for its own sake," said Vivi, indicating the ruined world.

"I used to," said Moa. "Many years ago."

"I'm going home." Vivi contacted TECT, and gave the mental order to be transported back to her house. When she arrived, it was once again night. She was very tired; she went to her sleeping area. Vivi was strangely glad that she was alone.

The meadow was cool, her sleeping temperature. The air was filled with pleasant flower scents. Vivi's birds twittered in the distant trees. She lay in the tall grass, preparing herself for her day's greatest, final pleasure. She opened her eyes to the stars, waiting for the wave of utter horror to sweep through her.

It never happened.

BITING DOWN HARD ON TRUTH

for Julie and Butch Roe

It was the second week in December; the weather was actually fairly mild, bright, clear, temperature in the high fifties. The yard was brown and grassless. Where rain had made mud a few days before, there were hard, dry ridges of a lighter buff color. The high gray walls around the yard were close and cold.

BOOK ONE: Healthful Sport in the Cool, Clear Air

Mac was playing middle linebacker, as usual. He was of medium height but very thin, with an ascetic face, narrow shoulders, and small hands. On his right was Willie, as complete an opposite for Mac as one could hope to find: tall, heavy, well-muscled. On Mac's other side was Sam, Willie's wife. She was the shortest of the three, though she was built as solidly as her husband. They stared ahead at the other team. The opponents were coming up to the line of scrimmage; their quarterback flicked his eyes across Mac's team, examining the defensive alignments. Mac looked past him at the fullback, who was Mac's responsibility. Willie watched the halfback; Sam watched the tight end.

"I will observe their fingertips," thought Mac. He had been taught that the fingertips of the other team's linemen could give the impending play away. "If the play was a pass, an inexperienced lineman might have his weight on the balls of his feet, as he prepares to pull out of position and drop back to protect the quarterback. On the other hand, if the play was a run, and the lineman would be blocking forward, his weight might be supported by that hand, and his fingernails would show white." Mac glanced at the appropriate fingertips, but he picked up no clues.

It was fourth down and four yards to go for the opponents' first down. There was less than a minute to play, and the other team was behind by six points. They were going for the first down.

The center snapped the ball. The other team's quarterback faked a handoff to the halfback, who ran toward the sideline; Willie followed. The quarterback faded back with the football and faked a pass; meanwhile, the tight end ran a square-out to the other sideline, and Sam followed. Mac was going for the quarterback. Mac saw the man hand the ball to the fullback. "Watch the draw!" shouted Mac. "Draw! Draw!" The running back took the ball and ran through the vacated middle of the line. Sam recovered and came back to help on the tackle. Mac hit the runner low, knocking the man's feet out from under him. At the same time, Sam hit the runner again, higher, and the other team was stopped short of its first down. Willie jogged over and helped Sam up, then gave a hand to Mac. The three defensive players left the field, happy and tired. For all practical purposes, the game was over.

On the sidelines, Mac saw Jennings staring at the defensive team. Jennings said nothing, gave them not even a smile by way of congratulations. In his eyes, the defense had merely done its job. Mac looked away. One of the assistant coaches said something and laughed. Mac nodded wearily. The assistant coach slapped Mac on the back of his helmet.

"I have always thought that invigoration was one of the worst of impositions," thought Mac. "I have always thought that invigoration was one of the worst of impositions." He repeated the line to himself again and again, hoping that he would remember it the next day. He took a deep breath, and his chest ached and was sore. He took another deep breath.

BOOK TWO: Interesting Facts About Implements of War

The room was wide and long; the low ceiling made the room seem like a slot in a desk or an empty drawer. The walls were gray, the same color as the ceiling, a little lighter than the floor, which showed the marks of years of traffic. The lights were dim, and the large windows let in little additional illumination. Willie looked around the hall, waiting for the lecture to begin. Through the windows all he could see were the immense walls. The chairs in the room were filled; Sam sat in her place sixteen ranks ahead of Willie, twenty-two files to his left. Mac was nine ranks behind Willie, and forty-one files to his right. Willie opened his notebook. The page on which he had made his notes at the previous lecture was gone. There was no writing at all in the notebook. Willie clicked his ballpoint pen and wrote at the top of the first page *Lecture*. Then he sat back uneasily and waited for Jennings.

After a few minutes, Jennings came in and went to his podium on the short platform at the front of the room. "Good morning, ladies and gentlemen," said Jennings. "Today we have some bombs to look at. I hope you take adequate notes. I do not want any failures on the examination. I'm sure that you do not want to fail, either. Take adequate notes."

Willie noticed for the first time that there were, indeed, three large objects on one side of Jennings' platform. They must be bombs, Willie decided.

"What we have here, ladies and gentlemen," said Jennings, "is what you call your regular AN/M65A1 general-purpose bomb." Jennings walked over to the tallest of the bombs, which was almost exactly as tall as he was, which was almost exactly six feet tall. "That is, again, your what you call your Alpha November slash Mike Six Five Alpha One. I called this beauty a general-purpose bomb. Can anyone recall from our previous discussions how this beauty is delivered? Come, come, ladies and gentlemen." Jennings waited a moment, smiling coldly. "From aircraft, ladies and gentlemen. From your so-called aircraft. It is a thousand-pound bomb, ladies and gentlemen. Much too heavy for a man to carry on his back, I'm sure you will agree. Perhaps a few of you could imagine it buried in the ground like a mine, with only its detonator sticking up in the air. But, consider. What a job, ladies and gentlemen, to dig the hole, to lift it down into the hole. Ah, ladies and gentlemen, perhaps a jeep runs over this beauty! Like killing a mosquito with a howitzer. Make a note, my lovely intelligences. We drop these beauties from aircraft."

Willie wrote in his notebook,
AN/M65A1 . . . *general-purpose* . . . *1,000 lbs*. . . . *dropped from the skies.*

Jennings continued his lecture. Along with the first bomb was a medium-sized bomb, which Jennings identified as an Alpha November slash Mike Seven Eight five-hundred-pound nonpersistent gas bomb. The third bomb was a small Alpha November slash Mike Eight Eight two-hundred-twenty-pound fragmentation bomb. Willie noted all three, then thought about making a sketch of each. They looked pretty much the same to him, except for their different sizes. In that case, he decided, the sketches would be relatively pointless. Thinking the lecture must be over, Willie closed his notebook. Jennings hadn't finished, however.

"Ah, yes, ladies and gentlemen," said Jennings sternly, a sneer as evident in his tone of voice as in his expression, "will any of you tell me what is meant by a 'general-purpose bomb'?"

Not one member of the audience ventured a reply. Jennings slapped his thigh impatiently. Willie looked over toward Sam's seat; he thought about the other men who sat between them. When the lectures ended, and they all marched back to their cells, Willie noticed that some of the men whispered to Sam in the halls. He had never seen one of the men touch her. That would be too much. He had once hurried through the crowd to catch up to one of the creeps; Willie had seen the man bend forward during a lecture and make some comment to Sam. She had not reacted, not even made a gesture of annoyance. Still, afterward, Willie had followed the man and pushed him against the gray concrete brick wall. Willie had made it seem like an accident, in case anyone were watching. In a few seconds he had doubled the man over with three quick blows, then vanished into the streaming crowd. Willie hated the kind of creeps who leered at his wife.

"If no one can devise an adequate response," said Jennings in a slow, quiet voice, "we may have to cancel all reinforcement rations. We may even have to schedule additional punishment." One man, thirty-eight ranks in front of Willie and twenty-seven to his right, stood and nervously indicated that he had an answer. "Go on, Larry," said Jennings. "Let's hear it."

"An all-purpose bomb is one that, well, like you said, you drop it from a plane," said Larry. "You're trying to destroy or at least hurt some kind of target. You're trying to blow the thing up. The target, I mean. As opposed to photoflash bombs or gas bombs or like that."

"No," said Jennings. "Not 'all-purpose bomb.' The term is 'general-purpose bomb.' I'm sorry, Larry. Your answer was good enough to get the rest of these clowns off the hook. I'm sure you're happy to hear that, ladies and gentlemen. But, Larry, I'm afraid it wasn't precise enough to get *you* off the hook. Now, now, ladies and gentlemen, no rustles of annoyance. Let's have no little murmurs of pique, out there." Jennings laughed briefly. He nodded to a man uniformed in gray, who was standing near one of the exits at the front of the room. The man walked to Larry's seat and escorted him from the room. There were no further whispers or sounds from the audience.

Willie watched his wife's head, now bent over her notebook in study. The man sitting behind Sam, the same man Willie had beaten on the previous occasion, slouched in his seat. Willie still didn't like the way that guy looked.

"All right," said Jennings, "get the hell out of here."

The audience stood up and began walking toward the exits. Willie flipped his notebook open again; the notes that he had taken on Jennings' lecture were already gone. He shrugged, closed the notebook, and tried to catch up to Sam.

BOOK THREE: The Intelligent Use of the Mystic Impulse

The alarm bell rang, and Sam woke up. She yawned and stretched, then remembered that it was Sevenday morning. She hated Sevendays; she always wondered why Jennings couldn't let them sleep a little later. They didn't have any work to do, after all. She put her head back on the pillow and waited for Grigarskas to come by. Sam's cell was still dark. It was about half an hour before sunrise; the lights on the top of the gray walls around the yard were already turned off. She felt warm and sleepy.

"All right, Sam," shouted a woman on the other side of the cell's door. "Let's get going. You may be a Lion, all right, but the rituals won't wait for no Lion. Get your ass moving."

"I'm up, Miss Grigarskas," said Sam, unhappily throwing back the thin gray blanket and swinging her legs over the edge of the bed. It was Sevenday. Time for rituals. Then reinforcement—and punishment.

Sam dressed quickly. She brushed her hair and splashed a little water in her face from the pitcher on her bureau. Then she went to the window that occupied the entire wall opposite the door. The window was made of plastic, a single thick sheet of the stuff, mounted slablike in the gray concrete blocks of the building. It wouldn't break; it was about eight inches thick, and when Sam put her palms against it, it was very cold. All she could see was the high wall across the yard. She couldn't see anything beyond the wall. The yard itself was patched with blackness and lighter areas of gray, some fifty stories below her.

Sam left her cell and joined the crowd of women in the hall. They were all walking quickly toward the elevators. The Sevenday rituals were held in the vast assembly hall in the lower part of the same building in which she attended Oneday, Threeday, and Fiveday lectures. The hall was large enough to accommodate everyone from every dorm building. The hall was so immense that a person standing in its center could see none of its walls. From that vantage point, it was like standing on a dim, featureless plain. Only the checkerboard pattern of tiles on the floor reminded one that the room was, after all, inside a still larger building.

Sam was proud that she was a Lion. Willie, her husband, was only a Raven, and their friend Mac was a Soldier, one level below Sam. Few of the other women in Sam's dorm had risen above Occult, the second level in the ritual.

During the walk from her dorm to the assembly hall, Sam wondered if she would see Willie during the ritual. They would likely get together later; it seemed probable to her that they would receive reinforcement, because of their performance on the football field in the Fourday game. Sam hoped that Willie wouldn't do anything to disrupt the ritual; his angry jealousy had caused him to start fighting, right in the middle of the Sevenday services. It had happened several times, and each occasion cost him whatever progress he had made through the levels. He always had to begin over again, as a Raven. It never seemed to bother him, but it caused Sam private embarrassment.

Sam entered the assembly hall. On the seven large doorways were repeated murals showing Mithra slaying the bull. Inside, the gigantic hall filled her with awe, as it did every Sevenday. She took her place with her fellows, the other men and women who held the rank of Lion. While she waited for everyone to arrive, she looked toward the vast congregation of Ravens, hoping to see Willie. She couldn't find him in the crowd.

Jennings entered after a short while, dressed in the white and gold robes of the Pater patratus. "Nama, Nama Sebesio," he called.

"Nama, Nama Sebesio," answered the congregation. Jennings then ritually greeted each group, beginning with the other Patri. He gave each degree its particular and secret sign, and he was acknowledged by the chief of that degree. After the Patri, Jennings saluted the Runners of the Sun, the Persians, the Lions, the Soldiers, the Occults, and finally the Ravens.

The ritual itself held little interest for Sam. She had never had any enthusiasm for it, and even less faith in the meaning of it all. She thought of other things, and made her responses out of habit. After quite a long time, Jennings gave the crowd his Sevenday benediction and walked slowly from the hall, attended by seven groups of seven Patri. A bell was rung when he had left the assembly hall, the signal that the remainder of the congregation was free to depart. Sam sighed, and hurried toward the group of Ravens. Willie met her; Sam put her arms around his neck and kissed him. He frowned. "Not here, Sam," he said.

She laughed. "I love you, Willie," she said.

"I know, I know," he said impatiently. "But can't you wait? You know I don't like you hanging on me all the time."

"Sure," she said. "Sure, Willie."

BOOK FOUR: A Pleasant Interlude in the Rigors of the Week

On Sevenday evenings, reinforcement or punishment was given to everyone, according to the judgment of Jennings. Punishment was a terrifying thing; it, all by itself, was enough to motivate Mac, Sam, and Willie. They played as hard as they could during physical training, even Sam, whose appreciation of sports could be excited in no other way than in the hope of avoiding punishment. The three friends studied diligently during the lectures, even Willie, whose academic interests were virtually nonexistent. And they made a great show of enthusiasm for the Sevenday ritual, even Mac, whose intellectual pride prevented his involvement on any level other than avoiding punishment.

Reinforcement was not, in itself, a pleasurable thing. Reinforcement was only the lack of punishment.

Every Sevenday evening, half of the people were punished. Precisely half. And the rest waited fearfully in their cells, praying that they would be passed over for another week. The punishment was delivered in different forms: in the food, in the water, in the air, on tactile surfaces so that it might be absorbed through the skin. Jennings had more ways of administering the punishment than his charges had of avoiding it. It was no use to refuse a meal, abstain from drinking, or shun one's cell. The white-uniformed trustees would observe whether a person listed for punishment was serving his sentence. If not, the punishment would be rescheduled for the next day, increased, and the person penalized for time missed on Oneday. That would mean automatic punishment the next Sevenday.

Punishment was terror. Punishment was being trapped within one's own mind, helplessly frightened beyond endurance, until one became a shrieking animal. The memory of past punishments was often enough to induce a spontaneous recurrence. This, too, was cause for punishment. As the time for distribution of punishments approached each week, Mac, Sam, and Willie grew increasingly nervous. Even this Sevenday, when they had no reason to expect punishment, each sat in his own cell, anxious and cold. Perhaps there hadn't been enough people listed for punishment to make up the needed 50 per cent. Perhaps Jennings had picked people at random to fill the quota.

The warning bell rang. In every dorm, on every floor, the agonized screams of the unlucky people filled the corridors. Those who had earned reinforcement were relieved; every one of them felt the same intense gratitude. Every one of them wore the same rather silly smile. They stood up, shuddered once in nervous reaction, and went out to meet their friends.

On this particular Sevenday, Sam and Mac joined Willie at the latter's dorm to watch an old movie and then play some pinball. Jennings had announced at the Fiveday lecture that the movie would be Philip Gatelin and Roberta Quentini in *Slaves of Blood*. It was one of Willie's favorites. Mac always enjoyed Gatelin's old adventure pictures, and Sam had never seen the movie before. They took seats as close to the front of the dorm's rec room as possible. They sat in silence through the entire movie. Mac wanted to point out special sequences to the other two, but he restrained himself. Willie laughed and applauded during the love scenes and the battle scenes. Sam was entertained but said little.

"Well, then, Prince Collante," said Gatelin, in the role of Gerhardt Friedlos, based on the character made famous by Ernst Weinraub's trilogy of novels, "we seem to be alone."

The evil prince smiled. He removed his huge plumed hat and his black, gem-studded gauntlets. He dropped these articles to the richly patterned carpet of his apartment. "Yes," he said languidly, "we are quite alone. I have planned this moment well. You may expect no aid from your, ah, comrades."

Friedlos laughed. He leaned easily against a gigantic mirror. "You may discover that in my difficult journey here, I have taken the liberty of disposing of your guards. You, also, may expect little succor from that quarter."

"I am not dismayed. Observe," murmured Prince Collante. He undid the sword belt that girdled his hips. "I ask that you do the same, in the interest of delicacy. I have assembled a wide variety of blades, there, upon that divan. You may take your choice, and then I shall make my own. There is no reason to hurry."

"As you wish, Collante," said Friedlos, likewise unbuckling his scabbard and casually allowing it to fall to the floor. He turned and went to the divan. Sam cried out.

"Watch," said Willie. "Just be quiet and watch."

While Friedlos was carefully examining the swords, Collante unsheathed his rapier, which he had not let fall from his hands, and attacked Friedlos' unprotected back. With one quick slash, Collante opened a long, bloody wound in Friedlos' right arm.

The audience booed. Mac and Willie laughed at their reaction. Friedlos was equally without anger as he turned to face his antagonist. "I see that you have leaped to a somewhat unfortunate conclusion," he said. "If you had not always been so eager to flee our appointed confrontations, to leave the actual swordplay to your underlings, you might have learned that I fence with my left arm. That lesson will cost you dearly." Friedlos snatched a rapier and came quickly to his fighting posture, his torn right arm hanging lifelessly at his side, the sleeve of his satin shirt soaked red with his blood. The audience cheered him through the scene, as Friedlos and Collante fought back and forth across the prince's magnificent room.

"He did it all himself, too," said Willie. "I always wanted to be Philip Gatelin when I was a kid."

"Me, too," said Mac. "Until I found out about him."

"I didn't never believe any of that stuff," said Willie.

"Quiet," whispered Sam. "Watch the movie."

Friedlos' sword caught the prince's, and his blade slipped down the other's, until their basket hilts clanged together. Smiling grimly, Friedlos made a quick circular motion with his wrist, and Collante's sword flew across the room. "Now, you fools!" cried the evil prince. Five secret doors opened, and five guards dressed in the uniforms of the Suprina's guard rushed to Collante's aid. Friedlos made no move other than to engage the nearest guardsman.

"Oh, hell," said Sam. "The prince is a creep."

"You're getting the hang of it," said Mac. He immediately regretted saying anything.

"What?" asked Sam.

"Nothing," said Mac.

"Quiet," said Willie. "Watch the movie."

BOOK FIVE: A Slight Fracture in the Façade of Life

When Sam awoke the next morning, her cell was brightly lit by sunlight shining through the clear plastic wall opposite the door. The day was beautiful, though evidently windy, judging by the sheets of paper blowing in unrhythmic gusts across the yard, so far below her room.

There ought not to have been any light in the cell when she got up. The sun should not yet have risen. Everything should still be black. Sam was frightened.

Even if the alarm bell had rung and she had slept through it, Grigarskas would have made sure that Sam got up in time for the Oneday lecture. Sam couldn't understand what had happened, but she knew what she had to do. She had to get dressed as quickly as possible and run to the lecture hall. And she had to be prepared to be punished the following Sevenday. Sam got herself ready with tears in her eyes.

She opened the door to her cell. It was dim beyond, much darker than her cell. It was also not the corridor that ought to have been there; Sam stepped out curiously into a marvelously decorated room, filled with grotesque, expensive objects and a perplexing jumble of colors and textures. For a moment, she did not know where she was. A man she had not seen spoke to her. "You are never late, are you, Friedlos?" said the man.

Sam smiled. She recognized the tall, dark man who lounged so impudently on the far side of the chamber. "Well, then, Prince Collante," she said, "we seem to be alone."

The man smiled in reply. He took off his bizarre feathered hat and his heavy black gloves. "Yes," he said, "we are quite alone."

Sam listened to Collante, knowing what he would say, what he would do. She felt a thrill of excitement; if this strange affair developed in the same way, exactly as in *Slaves of Blood*, it would be fun. She had a momentary flash of panic: Collante was at least eighteen inches taller than she, and with a comparable reach and strength, not to mention the fact that Sam had never touched a sword in her life. She was momentarily terrified that she would depart the script and her life at the same moment, with Collante's rapier spitted right through her. The feeling passed; she spoke her lines with no conscious prompting, and she trusted that her movements would be similarly directed. "You, also, may expect little succor from that quarter," she said confidently.

Anxiously, Mac dressed and left his cell. No one else was about. The corridors were oddly, oppressively silent. He ran to the elevator. He hated the sound his heels made on the black-and-white checkerboard tiles. The noise echoed.

Outside, the day was very cold, though bright. There was no one in the yard. The walls stood out against the deep blue of the sky; the walls were as blank as dreamless sleep, taller than anything built by men should be. The only sounds were the clumsy noises of Mac's feet as he ran across the distance to the lecture hall. The wind was cold, and Mac's cheeks and ears stung after a little while.

"Jennings isn't going to be crazy about this," thought Mac. "I don't think anybody's missed a lecture in years. And it has to be me, huh? Terrific." He felt a cold, heavy feeling in his bowels. He was a little lightheaded with fear, and his ears buzzed. "Jennings isn't going to be none too fond of this trick."

"I am not dismayed." Mac looked up in surprise. He had just pushed open the door of the lobby in the lecture hall. He turned around, but there was only a satin-padded door with a silver knob in the shape of a dryad and a goat copulating. Mac turned around again. The stranger was removing a belt with a scabbard from his waist. "Observe," said the man, whom Mac had no difficulty identifying, but more trouble accepting. "I ask that you do the same, in the interest of delicacy."

"Delicacy," thought Mac scornfully. "I know exactly why, you creep. I seen this before." He wondered for a moment what he was going to do, realizing that he was not Philip Gatelin, and, even more, he definitely was not Gerhardt Friedlos.

"As you wish, Collante," said Mac, wondering where the words had come from. He removed his own sword belt, amazed that he even had one. He relaxed then, understanding that the situation was some sort of fantasy and that matters were likely out of his control. He turned to the divan to make a choice of swords, knowing what was certain to happen. He tried to turn, to watch, to prevent Collante's stroke, but he couldn't. The swords on the divan caught his interest with their variety and excellence.

Willie woke slowly; he snorted when he saw how late it was. He got dressed, neither more quickly nor fearfully than usual. Willie had seen many horrible things in his life, and he had flinched at none of them; his outlook had been proved right, time after time. Every horrible thing had gone away, eventually. He yawned as he walked to the elevator in his dorm. He crossed the yard, perhaps a little more hurriedly than usual, but not so much as to make him out of breath. The cold air finished the job of waking him up, and he liked the almost savage wind that cut so forcefully through the layers of his clothing. Willie could appreciate anything, human or otherwise, that earned his respect. Jennings had long ago earned Willie's respect. The wind was a lesser thing. The walls were nothing at all.

Willie pushed through the lobby doors of the lecture hall. He heard no voices, saw no one, was surprised by the chillness of the building. It seemed like the heat had been turned off during the weekend and not raised again on Oneday morning. He shrugged, and waited for the elevator to take him to the lecture hall.

The elevator arrived, its warning light blinked on, then off, and the doors opened. Willie entered. It was the only time that he had been in the elevator—any elevator, in any building—alone. He pushed the button for the seventy-third floor.

Suddenly, he felt a great tearing pain in his right arm. The pain spread up through his shoulder and began to throb. Willie stifled a cry. He raised his arm slightly to look, and the movement sent a blaze of agony through his body. The arm had a long, jagged wound and was bleeding swiftly, soaking his sleeve. Even though the pain was growing, becoming unbearable, Willie refused to cry out. The wound looked familiar. He only casually wondered how it came to be there; he was mildly startled when he began speaking, almost without his conscious knowledge. "I see that you have leaped to a somewhat unfortunate conclusion," he said.

The man standing behind Willie was the devious Prince Collante of Gaedre, cruel pretender to the throne of Breulandy and reputed intimate of the Suprina Without a Name. Willie only smiled coldly. Collante had attempted to take advantage of Willie's confidence and trust, by weakening what the prince thought was Willie's sword arm. The prince had made a fatal error.

The two men fought then, across the gaudily appointed apartment of the prince. They overturned furniture and decorations whose price could have purchased any throne in Europe. Willie said little as they struggled, listening to the prince's desperate pleadings, enjoying the man's panting and wheezing, as Collante tired. Soon, Willie knew, soon Collante would spring his final trap. Willie was ready, whatever that gambit might prove to be. Willie was always ready.

"Look," cried Prince Collante exultantly, "behind you!"

"No," said Sam, "it won't work." She knew only that the dark man stood before her, unarmed.

"I think he's right, this time," said Mac. "I think he means it."

"Of course I do," said Prince Collante.

"Of course he does," said Willie. "Look."

The three friends turned, and five men dressed in the uniforms of the Suprina's guard were running toward them, swords raised threateningly. Collante laughed scornfully, and walked slowly from the apartment.

"Another time, my prince," called Sam, Mac, and Willie in unison. The prince stopped on the threshold and saluted them gallantly, laughed again, then went through the door and closed it behind him. The three friends could hear the click of the lock.

There was little time for words. Sam faced to the right, Mac to the left, and Willie faced forward. Protecting each other's sides, they waited for the charge of the guardsmen.

"Simple," said Mac. "It's very obvious, I think. It was all part of the reinforcement. Something new."

"Wonderful," said Willie sullenly. His arm had actually been badly wounded, and it was now carefully dressed and bandaged.

"I wonder how much was real," said Sam. "I wonder if we could have gotten away."

"Away?" asked Willie. He really didn't seem to have much interest in the discussion.

"Sure," said Mac. "If we knew what to do, we could have gone out right through the front gate. I'll bet there was nobody around. Maybe Jennings was testing us. Maybe he was giving us a chance."

"I think it was all a mistake," said Willie.

"It couldn't have been real," said Sam. "But maybe."

"Maybe," said Mac, with a thoughtful expression.

"Oh, hell," said Willie. It was still Sevenday evening. He wondered how he was supposed to take notes the next morning, at the Oneday lecture.

It was the fifth week of Quintember; the weather was hotter each day, more humid, so that the air conditioning made the plastic slab windows steam up. The world outside was invisible through the wet haze, or else, when someone rubbed the stuff away, the yard below looked blurred and unreal. The high gray walls around the yard were close. They looked like death.

BOOK SIX: The Elegance of Useless Activity

The old year ended, the pageantry of Jennings Day passed, the mild weather of December changed into the windy coldness of Unuary, Diuary, Tertuary. Quatober brought spring. Like a hungry cat, greedy for prey, the hot weather attacked and took possession of the year. By the beginning of Quintember the temperature had climbed into the midnineties and remained there, day after day, sultry night after night. The humidity matched the thermometer's readings, and the air seemed heavy and almost unbreathable. Sam hated it, Willie abided it, Mac loved it. Jennings didn't seem to notice, and the white-uniformed trustees simply couldn't.

It was the fifth week of Quintember. Nearly half the year had gone by already, a year that had begun with the usual promise and illusion:

a year of potential reinforcement, of minimal punishment. Willie had planned to record the number of Sevendays that were given to each, but dropped the scheme shortly after the first of Diuary. Sam had shown interest in his project, but when he quit she said nothing. In Quintember he couldn't even remember why he had begun. He learned nothing.

It was baseball season, of course. Because of their success on the football field, Willie, Sam, and Mac had been allowed to play on the same baseball team. Willie was the catcher and batted fourth. Sam was the first baseman and batted eighth. Mac was the shortstop, even though he was left-handed, and batted second. Willie didn't enjoy being a catcher, any more than he enjoyed being a linebacker. He liked batting clean-up, though.

The pitcher, a woman named Sheila, looked toward Willie for his signal. He decided on the slider. Her fast ball didn't have much zip on it, but her breaking stuff was working. She nodded, went into her windup, and threw. The batter swung and topped a roller to Mac at shortstop. Because he was left-handed, and because Jennings had decided that Mac had to play that position, Mac had developed a unique method of fielding ground balls. If they were hit to his right, he would be out of position and off balance to throw the runner out at first. Consequently he had to stop the ball, take one more step with his left foot, plant it, and pivot so that he faced toward the outfield, and snap the ball underhand to first. It cost him almost a full second more than a right-handed shortstop, and his throws were often low and in the dirt, but a lot of practice with Sam had made their infield as good as any. Jennings never said anything or showed that he was at all pleased whenever Mac made one of his odd fielding plays; still, Willie was aware that their team had the best record of reinforcement in the entire league.

Willie stood up behind the plate, waiting for the next batter to take her place. He looked out at Sam, who stood behind and to the left of first base. It seemed to Willie that the right fielder had been murmuring to her at the end of each inning, as the fielders ran off the field and into the dugout. He would make sure this time. He would keep his eye on the right fielder, on his lips; Willie didn't care how foolish he looked, standing still after the last out, staring out apparently in a daze. If that man were making whispered suggestions to Sam, the team would soon need a new outfielder. Willie didn't care what Jennings would do—and Willie knew exactly what he would do.

Sometimes Willie wondered if Sam understood how much she meant to him. Willie suffered a lot of punishment because of her. She always said that it was pointless, that Willie did things for silly reasons, that he imagined things. But Willie could see what those creeps were doing. Sam couldn't, for some reason. She always saw only the good in people.

The opposing batter struck out on four pitches. Willie fired the ball down to the third baseman; the ball traveled around the infield, until finally Sam tossed it back to him. She looked very tired. She hated the heat and the tropical air. The game still had a few more innings; Willie wished that Jennings would put in a replacement for her. He knew that Jennings wouldn't.

The third batter swung on the first pitch and hit a high pop foul. The female pitcher yelled, "Sam! Sam!" Willie stayed out of the way, and Sam ran over and caught the ball, which had blown back in front of the pitcher's mound. That was the third out. Sam smiled at Willie; he looked at his wife, then turned and watched the right fielder. His experiment would have to wait another inning. Willie walked with Sam back to the dugout. "Is that guy bothering you?" he asked.

"What guy?" she said.

"The right fielder. Dicky."

"No," said Sam, frowning. "Are you trying to get him in trouble, too?"

Willie watched one of his teammates walk to the plate as he removed his catcher's gear. "I just want to know if he's giving you a hard time. I'll bust him up, is all."

"He's not," said Sam. "Dicky just says, 'Way to go' or something like that. Like anybody else would say to anybody else on the team."

"Anybody else ain't my wife."

"You're up next," said Sam. "Stop worrying."

"I can't help worrying, when I see what those creeps try to do. You tell that Dicky that if he don't shut up, I'm going to bust him up."

Sam said nothing. She just went and sat by herself in the corner of the dugout. She looked like she was going to cry. Willie was angry, and he couldn't understand what she was feeling bad about; she ought to be glad he was looking out for her. He let out a loud sigh, shrugged his shoulders, and went to the bat rack.

BOOK SEVEN: Even in This Day and Age We May Learn from
Experience

At the end of the Threeday lecture, Jennings had smiled and
promised the audience a surprise on Fiveday. "I have a real treat in
store for you," he said, clasping his hands behind his back and rocking
on his heels. "I have something so unusual, you won't want to miss
the lecture on Fiveday. I think you'll really enjoy it. I think it's something you'll remember for a long time, something you'll want to tell
all your friends about. Don't be late on Fiveday. I don't want to say
anything more about it now, but I'll give you just one hint. It's something that's really worth getting up to see. Even you, Paola," he said
warmly, looking at a plain, somewhat simple-minded girl who sat
about twenty ranks from the front and who had a reputation for
being consistently tardy, "even you might want to make a special
effort to get here early. It's a once-in-a-lifetime opportunity, and it's
something you won't likely ever see again. I guarantee you all a fas-
cinating lecture on Fiveday. Are there any questions?" The room was
silent, as it was supposed to be. Jennings' smile had disappeared, and
he looked slowly across the files, from his left to right, searching
hopefully for someone whispering, someone fidgeting to leave. He was
disappointed. "All right," he said at last. "Get the hell out of here."

That had been on Threeday. After the lecture, and for the next two
days, everyone had wondered what Jennings' surprise could be. Naturally, there were many guesses, but no one had any more information.

On Fiveday morning, Sam woke up at the bell. The sun was up,
filling the cell with weak but already warm sunlight. The day was
clear, as usual for that time of day in Quintember; later, after three
o'clock, the sky would cloud over quickly and there would be a brief
but intense storm. Then the clouds would dissipate, and the sky
would be clear through sunset, and the stars would shine down like
bright specks of glass on a velvet cushion. The early-morning haze
made the walls seem vaguely unreal, not as formidable as usual, somehow like the false sets used in movies or plays. The colors of the walls
and the yard below were diluted, all mixed with grays and water. It
was a pleasant feeling. Sam stretched and smiled. She remembered
that Jennings had promised them a surprise at the lecture. She dressed
quickly and dashed a few drops of water in her face—as a Lion, her

use of water was severely limited—and walked to the elevators. The other women in the dorm greeted her, and they all spoke together in hushed, excited voices. Jennings' surprise had them all helpless with anticipation.

Sam walked across the yard to the lecture hall with some of her friends. She looked toward Willie's building, but she couldn't see her husband. She was hot and sweating by the time she arrived at the lecture building; the air conditioning inside felt good. Inside the lecture hall, Sam stood for a moment before going back to her seat. The podium that Jennings used had been removed. So had all the screens and maps and other equipment at the front of the hall. People came and went to their seats. Sam looked at Willie's place; he was there, but he was not looking toward her. She tried to attract his attention, but finally she gave up and went to her own seat. Mac came in a few minutes later and waved. She waved back, then opened her notebook. She wrote *Lecture, Fiveday, Quintember 35, 0042* at the top of the page. Under that she wrote *Jennings' surprise*. Still, Jennings had not arrived. Sam sighed. She twisted around to look back at Willie. She couldn't catch his eye. She thought about sending him a note; it would have to go sixteen ranks back and twenty-two files across. By the time it got to him it would only be a limp mass of pulp. Sam closed her notebook and waited. After a little while she opened the notebook again and underlined what she had written. Then she began to draw little designs in the left-hand margin, on the outside of the vertical red line.

"Good morning, good morning, my little wonders," cried Jennings. Sam looked up, startled. Jennings rarely spoke like that. "Ladies and gentlemen, today is the day you've all been waiting for. Today is the day I promised that I'd show you something spectacular. Well, I hope you've rubbed the sleep from your eyes, ladies and gentlemen. I hope you're ready to take adequate notes. Ladies and gentlemen, I want to remind you that, as unique as today's presentation may be, it will still be material for your examination. I'm sure that you do not want to fail your examination, ladies and gentlemen. Though your eyes may be amazed, I hope your note-taking faculties will remain unimpaired. Let us begin." The audience waited in utter silence, thousands of ball-point pens poised expectantly.

"Fine," said Jennings. "All right, Sigurd. Tell the boys to roll in the first one." A helper went through the black drapes behind Jennings. A short time later he returned, pulling a rope. On the end of the rope was the tail wheel of a Messerschmitt Bf 109E single-engine fighter plane. Three other men helped push the aircraft into the open space at the front of the lecture hall. It filled most of the area, and with the low ceiling and dim lights, the plane looked grotesquely out of place, like a beached whale in the cloisters of an Austrian monastery.

The helpers disappeared through the drapes, and Jennings walked slowly in front of the airplane. "Fine, fine," he said. "Ladies and gentlemen, what we have here is your what you call regular Messerschmitt Bravo Foxtrot One Zero Niner Echo. Good old plane. German. Used in World War II. Good old plane." Jennings patted the low, swept-up wing of the aircraft. His voice had become strangely emotional. He stared at the propeller, gave it a little push with one hand, dragged the hand back along the plane's fuselage, and ducked under the wing. He turned again and spoke to the audience. "You have to love this baby. For a while, there wasn't anything that could knock it out of the clouds. It was a good old plane. Now look. Here it is. A relic, if you please, ladies and gentlemen. A relic from the past. We're studying. We're not hiding from it. You can sit there, ladies and gentlemen, take your notes calmly, coldly, without the least trace of passion. I don't give a damn." He was near hysteria. Sam was frightened. No one made a sound.

Jennings raised his head, shook it. "Ah, hell," he said. "Jorge, open the drapes. I'm not going to drag these babies out one at a time. That's stupid. Open the drapes." The helpers opened the drapes, and there were three other airplanes in a row. Sam stared; the planes were beautiful, in an odd way. Their smooth lines, their look of efficient design impressed her, even though she didn't understand what she was seeing. The bombs and the rifles that Jennings introduced on regular lecture days held little fascination. Sam noted their names and numbers, tried to learn their individual characteristics, only because not to was an invitation to punishment. But the planes were beautiful.

"What we have here, first, behind and to the left of the Messerschmitt, is another German World War II bird. You have your regular Junkers Juliet Uniform Eight Seven dive bomber, the Stuka. An early model, a little ungainly perhaps, but unstoppable until somebody tried. I had a lot of trouble getting one of these. I just hope you appreciate it." Sam was curious; this wasn't like Jennings' usual lectures at

all. Surely there was more to learn about the history and characteristics of these planes than their names. Perhaps Jennings was waiting for someone to show initiative. Maybe he was waiting for someone to ask a sincere and interested question. Sam wondered if anyone
would.

"And this," said Jennings, pointing to the plane directly behind the
Bf 109E, "is your regular North American Papa Five One Mustang
fighter-bomber. A good old plane. Looks great, doesn't it? They don't
make them like that anymore. The last one is the justly famous Royal
Air Force Hawker Hurricane, what you call your fighter-interceptor.
They used these babies with Spitfires. The Hurricanes tackled the
German bombers while the Spitfires took out the German fighters,
often those very same Bravo Foxtrot One and so on. You don't care,
do you? I mean, none of this means anything to you, does it? These
could all be made out of flour and water, and you'd react the same
way. As long as you don't get punishment on Sevenday, right? Well,
look. Nobody will be punished Sevenday. Nobody. No matter what
you do between now and then. I don't care. Get the hell out of here."

Sam felt an unpleasant chill run through her. Everyone sat still for
a few moments. There was no talking. Jennings hurried from the lecture hall; the helpers struggled to get the airplanes back behind the
drapes and through the freight elevator's doors. At last Sam stood up.
She waited for Willie to meet her. "What's going on?" asked her husband.

"I don't know," said Sam. For some reason, she was crying.

"Well, don't cry," said Willie. "I don't like it when you cry. I don't
know what to do."

"I'm sorry," said Sam. "I'm not doing it on purpose."

"Then why are you crying?"

"I don't know."

"Look," said Willie. He held out his notebook. "I took notes, like I
always do. And they're gone already. Just like always."

"Of course," said Sam. "Mine too."

"I wonder why he bothers," said Willie, looking at the door
through which Jennings had left. Hundreds of others were leaving
now, hurrying back to their dorms.

Sam was very unhappy. She wondered why Jennings had behaved
the way he did; she felt that in some way, the audience had let Jen-

nings down. She didn't know what to do. "I feel sorry for him," she said.

"Sorry?" said Willie, snorting contemptuously. "For Jennings? Well, I don't. Just so long as we don't get punishment this week. I'm glad about that."

"Want to look at the planes?"

"No," said Willie, looking around, noticing the other men who were taking furtive looks at Sam. "Let's go to lunch."

BOOK EIGHT: Even the Gifts of God Come Wrapped

Mac stood with the rest of the Soldiers in the immense ritual chamber. Jennings had promised them all that there would be no punishment that week; even so, Mac had risen before the alarm bell and hurried to the assembly hall. Delgado, the trustee in the white uniform, had shouted into Mac's cell, but Mac had already showered and shaved, and was walking back from the lavatory. "I'm not in there, Mr. Delgado," said Mac cheerfully.

"I see that, Mac," said Delgado sullenly. "And if I could think of a good reason for you to be awake so early, I might not put you on report."

"It's Sevenday, that's all. I just don't want to be late."

"I can see that you're very devout," said Delgado. "Just watch it, that's all."

"Sure, Mr. Delgado." Mac finished dressing and walked slowly to the assembly hall; he was one of the first to arrive, and he chatted in a low voice with some of the other Soldiers. They all wondered whether Jennings would act as oddly during the ritual as he had in the Fiveday lecture.

"I was sorely tempted not to come this morning," said one of the Soldiers.

"Me too," said another. "If we're not going to be punished, well, to tell you the truth, these rituals get to be a little thick after a while."

"I watch them like movies," said Mac. "It's kind of an interesting thing, if you approach it the right way."

"You're nuts," said the first Soldier. Mac only smiled.

Jennings arrived early. Not all the worshipers had assembled, but Jennings nevertheless ordered the great doors to be closed. "It's a good thing he said no punishment," thought Mac. Jennings greeted the various orders, and was saluted in return. The ritual continued in its prescribed formula. Mac looked toward the Lions, but couldn't make out Sam; he looked toward the Ravens, and thought he saw Willie, but he wasn't sure.

"I want to say something," said Jennings, at the beginning of his sermon. His tone was conversational, a sudden contrast to the deep, stilted words he used during the rest of the ritual. "Be honest. How many of you would attend these rituals if they weren't mandatory? Just clap your hands." There was a loud roar of applause. "Now how many would stay in their cells, or visit with friends?" The applause was somewhat softer. "Now," said Jennings, sitting on one of the steps leading to the altar, "we'll try again. How many of you would come here on Sevenday mornings voluntarily?" This time the applause was much quieter. "All right. That's good enough. We'll stop there. Nama, Nama Sebesio."

The congregation called back, "Nama, Nama Sebesio."

Jennings stood up, shaking one fist. "You damn fools! You just told me you damn well wouldn't come here if I didn't make you do it, yet you keep on muttering your responses. Don't you feel a little crazy, doing that?"

"No," thought Mac, "I don't feel dumb at all. You're making us come here. You're still making us give the responses."

Some of the people in the vast hall began to whisper. Near Mac, some people, men and women, began to weep. There was a sudden rustle of noise. Jennings looked around himself angrily. "Get out. Get the hell out of here," he said loudly. The assembly hall was so huge that Jennings could not possibly see the people lined against the walls; they could not hear him, but a wave of motion began from the center of the hall and moved toward the exits. Mac smiled sadly. He walked along, his head bowed in the dim light.

"It's a very interesting psychological experiment," thought Mac. "He's given us such a rigid life, and now he's removing the laws we've always used as props. It's pathetic, when you realize how simple he is. And these poor people! They're helpless. Their granite idol is wobbling on its legs. But you can't tell them anything. You can't prove that there's no danger, that Jennings won't fall and crush them. The only thing left is to sit back and enjoy it."

Mac looked back over his shoulder. Hordes of people followed him toward the doors. Thin beams of spotlights still outlined the crooked

form of Jennings, who waited alone in the center of the assembly hall.
Mac sighed. He seemed to be alone in understanding the power of
Jennings, and the man's arbitrary cruelty. "Goodbye, Pater patratus,"
thought Mac. "Maybe really goodbye."

BOOK NINE: The Tiny Imperfections Make It Valuable

Willie went to Mac's dorm and rode up the elevator to Mac's
eighty-fifth-floor cell. Mac stood by the transparent wall. Willie sat on
the cot. "I don't like it," he said. "It made me feel nervous. I don't
like it at all."

"You're not supposed to like it," said Mac, not turning around.
"Jennings is doing it on purpose. He's trying to shake us up, for some
reason. Don't pay any attention to his act. It's as phony as everything
else he does. It's just that now he's being more obvious about it."

"Well, then, that's what I don't like," said Willie. "I'll go along
with it all, as long as I know what's happening. But, God, if Jennings
is going to change all of a sudden . . ."

Mac faced his friend. Mac's expression was amused. Willie
frowned; he didn't see anything to laugh about. "Jennings isn't changing, all of a sudden," said Mac. "That's what I just said. He's consistent with his plan, whatever that is. You're playing right into his
hands."

Willie sighed. "We have to play right into his hands," he said.

"Then don't worry about it."

Sevenday afternoon was quieter and tenser than usual. People stood
in small groups, talking in low, frightened voices. Jennings' behavior
at the lecture and at the ritual chamber had disoriented them. Willie
complained of an upset stomach and a persistent jittery feeling. Mac
told him to relax, or Jennings would lead Willie and the rest of the
crowd into a mass breakdown.

"So why would Jennings do that?" asked Willie. Mac could only
smile and shrug.

The two men strolled over to Sam's dorm, about an hour before the
usual time for punishment and reinforcement. Generally, everyone
spent that particular time of the week alone in his cell, in the event
that he had been marked for punishment. This week, with Jennings'
promise of no punishment for anyone, people were out and visiting

earlier. The movie for that week was .38 *Caliber*, with Dan Calvin as Sheeky Bordinaro. Willie didn't want to miss any of it.

Sam, Mac, and Willie sat in the rec room and waited. Mac went to the snack bar and got them soft drinks and potato chips. The time passed slowly, and the rec room began to fill up with people. Sam held their seats, and the two men went over to the pinball machines. Their favorite machine, a garishly colored model called Hi-Lo Express, was idle. Mac took his turn first. "Sam's good on this machine," he said, after the ball registered a meager five hundred points for him and then dropped out of play.

"I don't understand it," said Willie, laughing. "We play this thing every chance we get. We work at it. We take our pinball playing serious. Then Sam'll come over, hardly paying attention to which machine she's playing, and beat the pants off both of us."

"Natural talent," said Mac solemnly. He watched Willie score sixteen thousand points on his first ball. It was Mac's turn, his second ball. He pulled out the spring plunger. The warning bell on the rec room's wall rang. Mac let go of the plunger. The silver ball shot into play, hit a few bumpers, dropped down toward the flippers, then fell out of play.

"You really blew that one," said Willie. "You didn't even touch the flippers. What's the matter? Too fast for you?" Mac had a total score of twelve hundred and forty points after two balls. Mac said nothing. "Are you okay?" asked Willie. Mac's hands gripped the sides of the pinball machine. His knuckles were white. His lips were drawn back from his teeth in a kind of animal snarl. Slowly, as Willie watched, Mac's legs seemed to collapse. Mac began to sink toward the floor. Willie caught his friend and supported him. Mac screamed. It was a crazy sound. It was punishment.

"Hey, Sam," cried Willie. "Sam, give me a hand. Come here and help me." Willie tried to hold Mac up while his wife hurried to them.

"What is it?" she asked, her face pale.

"Goddamned Jennings, is what it is," said Willie. "He said no punishment, remember? What does this look like to you?"

"What should we do?" Sam remembered her own punishments well enough to know exactly what Mac was going through. She knew he ought to be in his cell. She knew that, in his agony and his insane terror, they would never be able to get him to his dorm.

"I don't know," said Willie. "Put him down here, I guess. We can watch him here. Poor sucker." There were other shrieks all around the rec room, as others were consumed by their punishments. Those who had not been marked looked around helplessly. Shortly afterward, the movie started. Willie looked at Sam. She had been crying. She was staring at Mac, who lay contorted on the cold tiled floor of the rec room. "Come on," said Willie. "We can't do a thing for him until Jennings finishes."

"Can we just leave Mac here?"

"Nothing will happen to him. It's almost as good as being in his cell. He'll be out of it by the time the movie's over."

On Oneday morning, Willie woke up. The dorm was strangely quiet. After the movie the previous evening, everyone had gone straight to his dorm; Jennings' apparent act of treachery had angered and bewildered them all. Willie was still too confused to know just how to react. What could they all do? Nothing. It was very simple. They could do nothing.

There was a knock on Willie's door. "All right, Mr. Zepkin," shouted Willie. "I'm up. I'm getting up." The knock sounded again. Willie swore softly, swung his legs over the edge of the bed, and went to the door. It wasn't the uniformed trustee who had knocked. It was a woman.

"Good God," said Willie, realizing that he was still naked. "What are you doing in this building now?"

"I had to see you, Mr. Bordinaro," said the woman breathlessly. "I got your name from the DA's office. You don't know who I am. Nobody does, not in this town. I have to trust you, Mr. Bordinaro. I'm in trouble."

Willie stood quietly for a moment, shifting from one foot to the other. He looked out into the corridor; no one else was in sight. There were no other sounds. He stared at the young woman. It was, of course, Diane Hogarth in the role of Gussie Demoyne, from *.38 Caliber*. Willie recalled how he, Sam, and Mac had been drawn into *Slaves of Blood* some months before. A slow grin lit his face, just as it had Dan Calvin's in the movie. "Step into my office," he said. "Don't mind the bed. In a little while it will seem perfectly natural to you." He leered at her; she swept by, ignoring his remarks. She went to the window and looked out in silence. Then she turned suddenly, surprising him, and began to cry. Willie immediately regretted his words. He felt helpless. "Sit down," he said. "Stop the tears. I can't start helping you until you stop crying." He tried to get dressed unobtrusively. She looked past him, into a camera that wasn't there, and smiled weakly.

Sam paced back and forth, the length of her small cell. Gussie Demoyne sat on her cot and watched her. "Wait a minute," murmured Sam. "Let me think. Wait a minute."

"I don't have much time," said the strange woman.

"None of us ever do," said Sam, reading the lines of Sheeky Bordinaro. "We all manage to forget that. Sometimes somebody remembers. He gets panicked. That's what pays my rent." Still, all the time she said those words, she thought other things. "What did we decide, the last time?" she wondered. "What should I do? Is Jennings really leaving it all open? Could I really walk out the gate?"

"I don't have the time to play wise old man with you," said Gussie Demoyne. "If you won't help me, I'll get another name from the DA." She rose and started toward the door.

"Hold on," said Sam. "Yeah," she thought, "hold on. I can't think. I don't have time to plan. It isn't Oneday morning. It's still Sevenday night. Willie's going through this same scene, right now. Mac's still being punished. Oh, my God."

The other woman stopped and turned. She looked pleadingly at Sam. "Okay, sweetheart," said Sam. "You've convinced me. At least for the next hour. After that, the convincing gets harder and more expensive. I'll have to see the color of your dough. Even those baby blues of yours won't get you around that. Otherwise, I'll be happy to give you another name. No sense in bothering the DA's office. They're screwed up enough over there."

Gussie Demoyne smiled, sniffed, then ran over and threw her arms around Sam's neck. "Thanks, oh, thanks, Mr. Bordinaro!" she cried.

"Call me Sheeky," said Sam. "What am I supposed to do?" she thought. "Should I just try to leave? Should I wait for Willie to come here?"

"All right," said the other woman. "All right, Sheeky."

"It's simple," said Willie the next day. "It's really simple. Jennings is just messing up. That's all. And we got to figure out, right now, is how to take advantage of it next time."

"Sure," said Sam.

"No," said Mac. "It can't be that easy. Do you think it was a coincidence that I was punished? I had him pegged the last time. I'm sure of it. If I hadn't been punished, I would have led the three of us out of here. Right out under his nose. He's giving us the chance. I think he's doing it on purpose, to make us think we can beat him."

"We can beat him," said Willie. "Next time."

"We'll just need some plans," said Sam. "In case one of us is punished, the other two will know what to do. Or if two of us are punished."

"We can't beat him," said Mac insistently. "He only wants us to think we can. To make us docile. I don't know. I don't really know his reasons. But it can't be that easy."

"Why not?" asked Willie. "Why couldn't it be that easy?"

"I don't know," said Mac. "It just never is, that's all."

It was the fourth week in Sextuary; the weather was dry and pleasant, with the sky so blue and bright that beneath it peoples' faces looked washed-out gray. The ground in the yard was moist and rich; the air had an exciting edge to it, not cold, like the winter, but just—exciting. Still, the high gray walls around the yard were solemn and perfect.

BOOK TEN: Taking Them as They Come

About an hour before the first game of the football season, Sam sat in front of her locker, having her wrists and hands taped. Willie's locker was next to hers, but they rarely spoke before a game. She was generally too nervous and tense, and Willie hated having to coddle her feelings. Instead, they just pretended to concentrate on their game plans; once they got out onto the field and started their warm-up exercises, everything was all right. Sam's anxiety disappeared as soon as she ran through the tunnel and saw the coffee-colored field and the vivid, frosty-white yardlines. She kept up a chatty stream of conversation from then until the end of the game, with Willie, with Mac, with the assistant coaches on the sidelines, with the other players. She liked to taunt the people on the other team.

A woman named Kath stopped by Sam's locker. She was a new member of the team, a large woman, a defensive end replacing a man named Sherman, who had not been seen since the middle of the baseball season. "What you think?" asked Kath.

"That depends," said Sam, her voice hoarse and croaking. Sam would feel the jitteriness and sour stomach until they left the locker room. "What are you talking about?"

"I mean Jennings," said Kath.

"Jennings is all right," said Sam warily. The assistant coaches were Jennings' men, the uniformed trustees were Jennings' men, probably most of the other people were, too. Sometimes Willie hinted that he thought Sam was spying for Jennings. Sam never bothered to reply to that. She knew that Willie was serious.

"Sure," said Kath, staring at her cleated shoes. "You know what I mean. I mean, well, he's been acting so damn crazy lately. And I don't know what he expects. In the game. If it was only like it used to be, I could understand. Mac was telling me—"

Sam held up one hand, unwrapped yet by the clubhouse man. "You don't have to pay strict attention to Mac. You'll learn that, if you stay with the team. Mac will repeat everything for you anyway, sooner or later. And he gets these theories of his. You'll see."

"Still, he said that Jennings was just using us," said Kath. "The crazy act is just another way of getting what he wants out of us, and that we shouldn't fall for it."

"Can you suggest something else we can do in the meantime?" asked Willie, in a sullen voice.

"I want to finish getting taped," said Sam. "And you better be damn sure you got your assignments straight," she said to Kath, "because I'm in no mood to save your skin all afternoon if you get trapped to the outside."

"Don't worry about me," said Kath, with a forced laugh. There was silence, an uncomfortable amount of it; finally Kath shook her head and went back to her own locker. Willie had never looked at her, and he said nothing more. Sam had never looked up at Kath, either. Sam watched the man winding tape around her wrist and palm.

One of the men on the punting team stood up and spoke. "Before we get on with the usual pregame prayer and stuff," he said, "I want to welcome the new members of the team and wish them luck. I don't mean I wish them luck in the game. We don't need luck. We need teamwork. I mean I wish them luck *after* the game if they mess up." There were a few meager laughs. "Now I'm going to ask Danielle to lead us in our—" The man was interrupted by the rodentlike squeak of the door to the coach's office. Everyone fell silent, looking in that direction. Jennings entered the room.

He wore gray trousers and a maroon sport coat, a dark blue shirt, and a black tie. He had a gray snap-brim hat on his head, and he carried a clipboard. He handed this to one of his assistants who followed him from the office. "I want to say something," said Jennings. He needed nothing to gather the attention of the team members. Jennings paused for a tiny instant. "None of you ever met a young man who used to be on this team. His name was Bo. That's what we all called him. Bo. But you've heard of him, you know what a reputation he had and what he meant to this team. Some of the other people, on other teams, called him 'The Trog.' He was big, and he was fierce. But he was a gentle person, and that was why I and his teammates called him Bo, instead of the nickname he had earned. Still, he was proud of 'The Trog.' One day he said to me, 'Coach,' he said, 'if ever the team is in a close one, and the breaks are beating our boys, tell them to give it all they've got, and go out and win just one for "The Trog."' I don't know where I'll be then, Coach, but I'll know, and I'll be happy.' Those were about the last words he ever spoke to me. That's something I've never told anyone before. Well, this is the beginning of a new season. We had a damn good season last year. But this is a new season. Last year's scores are in the record books, not on the scoreboard outside. But if you can find just a particle of the devotion, just a minute scrap of the love and determination of that kid Bo, well, all I can say is, I know he'd be happy. Well. That's all I have to say." Jennings' voice had begun clear and forceful, but as he recounted his story, it changed. It grew slower and thicker, choked with emotions that he had never shown until recently. Under other circumstances, his audience might have been moved. Instead, they were seized with fear. Jennings' words and tortured expressions left them feeling helpless, leaderless. Their great source of constancy and security faltered before their eyes. He turned, one hand raised to his eyes. His shoulders shook as though he were sobbing.

"Goddamn it," said Sam softly. "What the hell are we going to do?"

"We're going to make them eat the ball, that's what," said Willie. "And not because of some damn good old boy named Bo, neither.

Because if we don't, we'll spend Sevenday evening twisting on our bunks trying to keep from swallowing our tongues."

"But what about Jennings?"

"Are you all right, Coach?" asked one of the other players. Jennings didn't answer.

One of the assistant coaches leaned close to Jennings' ear. Sam watched carefully, hearing some of the man's words, lipreading the rest. "Where we going now, sir?" he asked.

Jennings' reply was low but audible, his voice steady. "Gotta give the speech to the other team," he said. Sam was sure that she was the only one of the players who heard. The others were too involved in shouting promises of dedication and valor.

"The trouble with real life," said Sam to herself, "is you never really have the option to punt."

BOOK ELEVEN: Strategy Is the Shell, Tactics Is the Rifle

Mac sat in his seat in the lecture hall, waiting for Jennings to arrive, wondering how the man was going to act. Jennings' performances seemed too theatrical to Mac, too transparent. Now that Mac believed that he had a secret insight into Jennings' manipulative practices, other details that Mac had previously taken for granted acquired new significance. The lecture hall itself was no longer unsettling; it had evidently been designed to make the audience feel vulnerable, the low, oppressive ceiling having that psychological effect. Mac leaned back in his chair and smiled. He no longer felt vulnerable. He was only amused by Jennings and his rather juvenile tricks.

The muttering voices in the audience quieted when Jennings walked into the lecture hall. Mac studied the man as well as he could, from the distance of nearly fifty ranks. Jennings did not seem particularly distracted, as he had been on several recent occasions. He walked quickly to his podium, shuffled a few papers, then stared briefly across the vast, ordered collection of faces. His voice, when he spoke, was steady, deep, and as full of authority as ever. Mac smiled again; he was delighted that Jennings was in such control, that the intellectual puzzle that Jennings seemed determined to develop was of the most complex variety. "Good day, ladies and gentlemen," said Jennings. "Good day to you all. I hope you have taken appropriate notes during the course of the past several lectures. The more observant among you will have noticed the trend I have been taking. That is, for the sake of the least observant among you, away from the cruder and more unsophisticated of weapons, through the armaments of intrinsic poetry and beauty, and finally to those implements of war that succeed through their apparent lack of menace. I have chosen this method of discourse for definite reasons. If you cannot understand these reasons, you will have some difficulty with the examination. If you find yourself unable to fathom my purpose, I highly suggest that you seek out the advice of someone among you who does understand. I do not want you to do badly on the examination, and I am sure, very, *very* sure, that you agree." Mac laughed quietly and opened his notebook. On the first page, as blank as all the others in the notebook, he wrote *Fiveday Lecture, First Week in September*. He clicked his ball-point pen shut, closed the cover of the notebook and clipped the pen to it, and put the notebook in his lap. Then he yawned and slouched down farther in his seat.

"Let us begin," said Jennings. "I would first like to say that what we have today is obstacles. Obstacles, my ladies and gentlemen. We encounter various kinds of obstacles in life, do we not? Who will say that we do not? Of course we do. We find obstacles in our paths, no matter where those paths may lead. Even if the goal is something as trivial as emptying one's bladder, sometimes there are obstacles." Jennings paused, in the event that the audience might want to laugh. There was no laughter. Mac frowned; it was one of Jennings' rare lapses in taste. Perhaps, though, Mac thought, perhaps the lapse in taste had been intentional, not a lapse at all. Perhaps—

"—imparting knowledge," Jennings was saying. "A bomb is as good a weapon as any. But it takes no delicacy, no refinement at all to turn a city into scraps and shards. Or an army, for that matter. An airplane is gorgeous, sometimes. Who will deny, who among you, my ladies and my own gentlemen, will deny the utter loveliness of your regular Lockheed Foxtrot slash Niner Four Starfire tactical fighter? You will recall the movies we saw several months ago. You will recall the beauty. If you pause to reflect, it will all come back to you. Still, there are greater attainments within the panoplic field. There is yet the music of genuine cultivated skill."

Jennings had that, all right, thought Mac. Genuine skill. It was becoming more and more obvious. Jennings' own behavior had been carefully planned to parallel the development of his lectures on weaponry. When Jennings had discussed bombs, grenades, rifles, and armored vehicles, his manner had been heavy, contemptuous, and authoritarian. When he had lectured on aircraft, submarines, guided missiles, and small arms, he had been almost sensitive and emotional, like the connoisseur of food or art might act toward the absolute idealization of his dreams. Lately, while the topics had changed gradually to gas warfare, guerrilla tactics, and methods of obfuscation and misdirection, Jennings had seemed crafty, sure of himself once more, but more mysterious than he had ever been. Mac understood at last. He wondered if anyone else did. He wondered if the knowledge would be practical.

The discussion of obstacles had begun. Jennings was pointing to a screen on which a slide of old German antitank obstacles was projected. "These are dragon's teeth, ladies and gentlemen," said Jennings. "Note them well." Mac unclipped his pen, opened the cover of his notebook, and wrote *Obstacles*. "These are, as you see, truncated pyramids of, oh, I would guess reinforced concrete. Does that sound reasonable? Concrete pyramids? What do you think they might be used for? You, there. Chico." Jennings pointed to a young man in the seventeenth rank.

"They are antitank obstacles, sir," said Chico.

"Very good," said Jennings. "Excellent. No punishment this Sevenday for Chico." Mac shook his head, smiling. He knew that Jennings was only pretending that he had forgotten that he had just finished instructing the audience on the purpose of the obstacles. Jennings' actions were easier to predict, and that helped ease the constant boredom.

"They put these in rows," said Jennings. "The teeth in the front are lower than the teeth in the back. That way, a tank running over them is made to tip up. Clever, eh? And subtle, eh? And beautiful in its own way, eh? What do you think, Maureen?"

A woman only a few seats away from Mac stood up. "I quite agree," she said, and sat down again.

Jennings laughed. "No punishment this Sevenday for Maureen," he said. Mac knew that, despite those words, Maureen had just as good a chance of being punished as anyone else. Another slide was shown, of double-apron barbed wire. Mac wrote *Obstacles* again, beneath the previous entry. He stopped listening to Jennings, believing that he had learned all that he could from the man. He spent the rest of the lecture period writing the word *Obstacles* in single columns down the pages of his notebook.

BOOK TWELVE: Finding Time in a Busy Schedule

The warning bell rang. Willie sat up in bed, startled, bleary with sleep. He yawned and stretched; he smiled when he remembered how Jamison Hawke, in the role of Gror the Wild Man, explained his survival in the African jungles: "When I wake up," said Gror, "I wake up all at once. I don't lounge comfortably, I don't rub my eyes. I don't raise my arms above my head and wonder about how cold the bathroom floor may be. I am awake, and I am deadly, for the jungle is always deadly. If I indulged in the luxury of a slow awakening, it would be my last." Willie loved the old Gror movies, as foolish as they seemed in the years since their initial popularity. Willie tried to be as much like Gror as he could; the difficulty was that he only remembered about waking up "all at once" after he was already awake. For the thousandth time, Willie realized that were he in Gror's place, Willie would have been jungle food a long time ago. He licked the odd, unpleasant taste from his lips and swung his feet over the edge of the bed.

A loud bang sounded on the cell's door. "All right, Willie," came the trustee's voice. "No time for no little Raven to be all tucked in tight. Get your ass out of that bed."

"Ass is out," called Willie, frowning. "Mr. Zepkin, sir."

"You ain't kidding." The man's high-pitched laugh faded as he went along the hall, checking on the others. Willie stared at the cell door and held his hand out at arm's length, the fingers spread. Then, slowly, he closed the hand in a fist. It was a very obscene gesture, which he had learned from one of Gatelin's first pictures, *The Silver Sergeant*.

It was Sevenday morning, clear, dark, the stars cut off abruptly by the top of the gigantic walls, the lights on the rim of those walls already turned off. It would be light soon.

"Here's the famous Raven, getting dressed for Sevenday rituals, one of his favorite times of the entire week," murmured Willie. "Here's the Raven, almost unable to control his excitement, as he skips washing, brushing his teeth, and combing his hair in the nervousness and sincere religious passion that grips him every week at this time."

He spat on his floor, pulled on the special, drab vestment of his rank, and left his cell. The halls were crowded with others on their way to the assembly hall; Willie nodded to some, spoke to few, ignored most. He was already thinking about reinforcement. And about punishment.

The assembly hall itself never failed to annoy him. It was so obviously one of Jennings' great schemes to impress his audience. Willie was irritated by that; he refused to be intimidated into respecting Jennings. If the man couldn't do it with his own personality or his own actions, owning a big room sure wasn't going to do it for him. The great doors with the murals of the tauroctonous Mithra had been flung open, and slowly moving streams of people were passing through. Willie tried to push his way through. "No need to hurry," he thought. "This is dumb. Just slow down. Everybody'll get in. Slow down." But he still pushed, unable to stand the stupid way people ahead of him were walking, staring blankly, wasting his time.

Willie took his place in the ranks of the Ravens. The lower levels of initiates took their places against the walls of the tremendous assembly hall. The Ravens, the very lowest rank, were so far from Jennings' speaking platform that none of them could hear the man's words, and some of the weaker-eyed among the Ravens couldn't even see him. Only the other Patri, the Runners of the Sun, and the Persians could hear Jennings easily. The Lions and the Soldiers could hear him often. The Occults and the Ravens were kept informed of Jennings' pronouncements by means of messengers who made whispered reports at frequent intervals. Willie never listened very closely to the messengers, either.

After quite a while, the rest of the initiates arrived and took their places. Willie stood, nervously fidgeting, wishing the entire ritual were over, wishing the business of the week's punishment and reinforcement were over. He thought of Sam and tried to look toward the group of Lions. Most of the Lions stood against the same wall as Willie's particular cult of Ravens, about half the distance to Jennings' platform. It was much too far to make out Sam's form among the others. Willie recalled that their friend Mac, had been elevated from the rank of Soldier to that of Lion. Mac would be in the same temple as Sam, although probably not in the same cult. Just as well, thought Willie. Sometimes Willie was suspicious even of Mac's attention to Sam.

Jennings arrived and took his place. He greeted each group of worshipers. A messenger hurried to the group of Ravens and reported that Jennings had mounted the platform. Willie made an impatient face. Another messenger came and said that Jennings had ritually greeted each rank. Willie stopped listening. The morning passed slowly. The only motion came from the shuffling of the messengers, who reported each step in the ritual as though it had never happened before.

Some minutes after the sermon, Willie was aroused from a shallow doze by an irregular noise in the ritual hall. A low buzzing was originating from the ranks between the Ravens and Jennings' platform. It sounded like clamor. There was never any clamor during the ritual. Risking punishment, Willie whispered to the Raven next to him. "What's happening?" he asked.

"I don't know," said the woman. "I can't see. People are standing up. I thought I saw Jennings bend over up there. Maybe he had to get sick."

Willie laughed, but his humor faded. If anything, it meant that the ritual would take longer than usual. If anything, it meant punishment.

"It was really scary," said the messenger, his voice hoarse and shaken. He had no ritual words to rely on. He was speaking as one person to a group of curious listeners, without the benefit or protection of his position. "I never saw anything like that. It was a Runner of the Sun, I think. I only saw the guy for a second or two. It had to be, or else another Patri. They're the only ones close enough, right? He jumped up on the platform, and then he said something. I couldn't make it out. One of my friends said it sounded like 'Get the hell out of here.' That's crazy. I don't know. Then he just put a knife in Jennings' throat. Jennings went down. That's all. I got to go." People were screaming, frightened, trying to be heard. Others, more thoughtful, were trying to question the messenger; it was no use. He pulled away from the crowd and moved on.

BOOK THIRTEEN: The Election of a Fitting Climax

Mac sat at the head of his cot, his back against the gray wall, his knees drawn up. Sam sat at the foot of the cot, her hands folded in her lap. Her face had a sad expression. Willie stood by the cold plastic slab of a window, staring out at the walls across the yard. After a few seconds of silence, he turned around and looked at Mac. "You know what your trouble is?" he said.

Mac sighed. "No. Tell me. What is my trouble?"

"You think you know everything about everything, that's what," said Willie. "You thought you had Jennings figured out. You kept telling us how you had Jennings figured out. You were very proud of that, if I remember correctly. You were the one who was going to lead us out of here, as soon as you had Jennings all figured out, even though you already told us you had him all figured out. Well, it looks like you didn't. And it's a damn good thing you didn't convince us, either."

"He's dead," said Sam, in a dull voice.

"You think he's dead," said Mac, smiling at Willie. "You were told that he's dead. You think that you've seen him dead. He may not be dead."

"He's dead," said Sam. Tears began to slide down her cheeks.

"We're going to leave," said Willie.

"He's testing us," said Mac.

"He's dead," said Willie, "and we're going to leave. We're going to walk right out the front gate."

"I don't think that's a good idea," said Mac. "He knows that we've figured him out. He let us figure him out, just like I said before. He let us think we've figured him out. But he's planning on a different level. Only I'm still ahead. I've got to where I know that he knows, and Jennings isn't aware that I'm ahead of the rest of you."

"We're still leaving," said Willie.

"It's not a good idea," said Mac. "Even if he really is dead."

"It may not be a good idea to you," said Willie, his voice angry, "but, goddamn it, I'm leaving. And if you or Sam want to come with me—" Willie stalked from the room, raging, and slammed the cell door behind him. Sam looked at Mac helplessly. She got up.

"He may be right," she said. "Jennings is dead."

"I hope so," said Mac. He sighed. Sam hurried after Willie. Mac went to the window, then sat on the edge of his cot so that he could still look out and down to the yard, several dozen stories below. He watched for a long time. He saw many people from many dorms cross the plain-colored yard, toward the front gate. He thought he saw two people who might have been Willie and Sam. Then he saw two more people who looked like Willie and Sam, and then another couple. After a while, Mac gave up. He stretched out on the cot and tried to take a nap.

He was awakened from a light sleep by a knock on the door. "Who is it?" he asked.

"Jennings," came the answer from the hall. The door opened, and Jennings came into the cell. Mac sat up, startled and afraid. He said nothing. "Mind if I sit down?" asked Jennings. Mac couldn't answer. Jennings sat on the foot of the cot and began talking. "I want to make some things clear to you, Mac," he said. "It's best to rule people with their freely given devotion. But that's not necessary. If you can't have their devotion, you can govern them with their respect and a neutral manner. If you can't have that, then you can govern them with their fear and a strong executive branch. And if you can't even manage that, why, maybe you ought to get out of the government business altogether." Jennings paused and gave a little laugh. "I find that sometimes I don't even have the fear to work with. Like in your case. You're not afraid of me, are you? Or, I mean, you weren't. Before. You know."

Mac just stared.

"Anyway," said Jennings, not particularly noticing Mac's reaction, "in the case of a person like you, I have to rule by other methods. Bribes and threats are out. You wouldn't fall for either. You like to think that you like to think. That's your bait on my hook. So, what the hell. That kind of thing costs me less than a strong army would." Jennings laughed again. The warning bell on the wall rang. Mac looked up at it; he remembered that it was still Sevenday, that it was time for punishment and reinforcement. Jennings just smiled and shrugged.

"I used to think you were all power and affection," said Mac. "Like a father. Power and affection make a strange mixture, but you never lose either completely. I was wrong. You're a demon."

"You had me figured out," said Jennings. "You thought so, anyway. I let you think so. But you knew I let you. And I let you know that, too. You can't catch up. You can't really understand. That's why I give the lectures and you take the notes."

"You're a demon," said Mac.

Jennings laughed. "Everybody has what he wants. Except me. I'm dead."

"What about them?" Mac waved a hand toward the window.

"Sam and Willie? They have what they want. They're walking out the front gate, just about now. They have each other. They have what they want."

"You're not going to stop them?" asked Mac.

"Stop them from doing what? They don't mean anything. They could have gone any time."

"What about me?"

"What about you, Mac? Do you mean, are you worth anything? I won't answer that. You figure it out. You're good at that. You have what you want, don't you?"

"Do I?"

"Do you want to leave?"

"No," said Mac.

"And you're not. What do you feel like doing?"

"Sleeping," said Mac. He stretched out again, yawned, and closed his eyes. When he opened them again, Jennings was gone. Mac was sure that he had not dreamed the conversation. "It was another Sevenday illusion, like the movies," he thought. "I can figure it out. And I have all night to do it. Jennings' murder might have been a Sevenday illusion. This entire week might have been. . . ." Mac took a deep breath and smiled. Jennings was right. Everyone had received what he wanted.

Without getting undressed, Mac slid beneath the blankets on his cot. The gray winter light was failing, and the room was dim. Mac felt warm and comfortable. "Nama, Nama Sebesio," he murmured, not knowing what the words meant. He was soon asleep.

It was the second week in December; the weather was actually fairly mild, bright, clear, temperature in the high fifties. The yard was brown and grassless. Where rain had made mud a few days before, there were hard, dry ridges of a lighter buff color. The high gray walls around the yard were close and cold.

C